The Book of Drachma

# LAMINAR FLOW

## SECOND EDITION

## Timothy H. Cook

This work is dedicated to the
memory of Hale Henry Cook, MD.

# Acknowledgements

This work would not have been possible without the sincere diligence of Michelle Ogle and would never have taken off without the love and patience of my wife, Sara Cook.

# Prologue

The day had started out like any ordinary day. Dr. Robert Gilsen made his morning rounds, then started at the office one half hour late. By the time noon came, he had to go back over to the hospital to check on Mrs. Talliaferro and her repeating arrhythmias. That took up all the time he had for lunch, because now the office was calling about a couple of patients with concerns that couldn't wait, and had to be seen today. One of them just needed to see the doctor for reassurance, but the other patient needed admission, which added an extra hour to the afternoon's load. Then, in the midst of all that, Steve Reeser called to ask him if he could look at one of his post-op hip patients with chest pain.

"Sure," he told him, "but it'll have to be after I'm done at the office. For now, though, I'd get an EKG, draw some cardiac enzymes, and put the patient on telemetry."

The last patient in the office was poor Mr. Alexandros, who had been waiting for two hours to be seen, but whose daughter, Maria, came with him, and took notes, so she could tell the other daughters what was wrong with papa.

His evening, back at the hospital, just got rolling when he was paged, STAT, to the fourth floor ICU, because Mr. Pullen's temporary pacemaker was not capturing and, sure enough, it turned out that the lead had migrated, and he had to reposition the lead, urgently. Then, as Dr. Gilsen was checking Steve Reeser's patient, he found that the old guy was having a heart attack after all, and needed to be moved to the "unit," where he began to show some alarming rhythms, and to drop his blood pressure. After wrestling for forty five minutes with the resuscitation, the poor man's rhythm gradually stabilized, and his blood pressure came up, but, being just one day post op from major hip surgery, the options were limited. Next he called Steve back to fill him in, and to give him the bad news. This was all before he was able to check on his office patient who had needed admitting, and, it turned out, was suffering from pneumonia.

By the time Bob was able to get his head above the turbulent waters of the evening, he realized he was famished. There was nothing left in the doctors' lounge, so he decided to head to the ER, where he knew he could find something to eat.

Sitting down in the space usually taken up by residents, he ate his cheese and pink meat sandwich, followed with a diet Coke.

"Hey, Dr. Bob, you look like you just escaped from somewhere unpleasant."

"Oh, hi, Judy. Yeah, you could say that. It was a bit hellish up on the floor, with Steve's patient going south . . . But you don't really want to hear about that. Just stopped by to grab this fine repast, before heading home."

Judy Morrison just smiled at him, touching his shoulder. Funny how that touch sent a soothing balm through his body, which was aching, stiff, and sore by now. He wanted to linger, but he knew he had to keep going, so he just smiled back and mumbled something that sounded like a thank you.

He picked himself up, and trudged out to his car stopping on the way to get his coat and gloves. He did not remember his drive home. When he did get in the garage door, all was quiet. He looked at the clock—it was 9:35 p.m.

With a sigh, he sat down and thought about his life. *What am I doing? How did I get to this position?* Yes, his life was, at times fulfilling, but a bit too busy, too out of control. Medical school, residency, fellowship had all had their times of intense chaos, but there seemed to be some order, some sense that there was someone overseeing things. Now there was no one but himself. He thought about how, in training, he had envisioned things differently, and how his life had gradually become something other, something he had no control over. *Ha*, he thought, *the more I am in control, the less control I have over my circumstances.* He thought about the last time he and his wife had actually sat down and eaten a nice meal together; it was when he went out of town to a conference.

He went upstairs, and there he found her, reading in bed.

"Hi, dear. What's that you're reading?"

"Oh, hi. This is just something I'm reading for my book club. Actually, it's quite entertaining—it's about the business of medicine—you know, all the money you make, what you should be investing in and all."

Bob just groaned. He was not, in any way a businessman, and the thought of his vocation as a business just irritated him. "You know that aspect of my practice, I would just love to turn over to someone else, someone I could trust . . ."

He didn't say any more, he didn't have to.

"I know. That's what makes you so endearing. Come here and give me a kiss, and tell me about your day."

Bob did that. "You know it was just another of those days, when everything takes so much longer than it's supposed to. When every patient and every family seems to want more than I'm capable of giving, and yet I feel I've got to try . . ."

"Yeah, it's why you're so popular, because you do try. You can't help it, and word gets out, and then people start expecting it of you."

"But it's beginning to tear me up. All these expectations . . ."

"And what are you thinking?"

"I was thinking of the last time we sat down and ate a real meal together, one with no expectations, no beeper, no hospital waiting to interrupt . . ."

"When was that?"

"In San Francisco, last year, right after my conference, in that seafood restaurant, looking out at the bay, when I ordered the cioppino, and you had never heard of it, and you ate half of mine . . ."

"And that fabulous wine . . ."

"Ah, yes, that pinot noir, that we were told doesn't really go with seafood, but the waiter recommended, and we finished the bottle, before that incredible dessert, with bananas, ice cream and flaming brandy."

"And you were thinking . . ."

"It's just that we seem to be missing out on something very significant, something that may be irreplaceable."

"Well, if you figure it out, let me know."

Bob then got ready for bed, climbed in next to Marilyn, kissed her good night, and was asleep before she turned off her reading light. He slept the deep sleep of one exhausted.

During the night, he dreamed a truly unusual dream. He found himself sitting in a crowded inn. He looked around and saw there were rough oak tables and equally rough oak benches, mostly filled with noisy, burly peasant-types, all dressed in clothes from a bygone era, rough and stained. Everyone had a flagon of deep, rich brown ale, and there was bread at each table. It was cold outside, but inside the inn it was warm, the atmosphere was jovial, with a sense of belonging and conviviality.

At the table next to his, there was a striking older man talking, telling a tale that told of magic, nostalgia, and history. All around him seemed to be held in a trance, as if under his spell. Bob was just one of the multitude, caught up in his words and gestures, rapt and attentive. His tale was one of innocence, betrayal and death, and was a tale of a book, sought after by powerful men of means.

When he had told his tale, he turned to another at the table and asked him to play something fitting on his harp. The minstrel agreed, and, after another round was poured, he took up his harp and began to play.

What began as just chords and strumming soon developed a life of its own, with a melody appearing as a vision out of his fingers on the strings. Now Bob became transfixed, as he had never heard anything like this before, his head swimming with the tune from the harp. As the music played, he drifted back out of the tavern, back to the outside, but before leaving the tavern, he caught sight of a strange staircase, which led upwards. And on the stairs was a very unusual man, holding a violin, and as Bob was drifting away, said, "Now, Master Robert, you shall come back to this place, and to these people. You shall tell them of the waters, and by this you shall earn your own place in history. And there is also a book, one of power and purpose. It shall be for the later ages, but not for thee."

Then, to the strains of that ethereal music, he was carried in his dream to an even more distant place, to a deep forest, with running water, in springtime, with the smell of newly turned earth.

# Chapter One

January fourth, 3:00 a.m., one of those times when this chosen profession made its harshest demands. The call was from the emergency room, and Josh Crabtree was in trouble again. This pathetic soul was in need. His new heart valve, just put in five weeks ago, showed signs of trouble one week after implantation. Jeffery Reichert, the cardiac surgeon, had called in Dr. Gilsen mercifully early this time, and together they figured they could buy time with "medical management." Time seemed to have just run out. The ER doctor was not one to panic, but his voice this time had that special urgency which signaled a disaster in the works.

"Josh Crabtree's here. His parents brought him in saying he passed out at home. He's breathing about fifty per minute, gasping. His temp's thirty-eight point three, his heart rate's one-sixty and irregular with new atrial fib, he's got rales all the way up. Chest x-ray shows pretty clear-cut pulmonary edema, and his Po2 is only 48 with O2 running at 50 percent by mask. It really doesn't look good."

Robert Gilsen, MD, board certified cardiologist, university trained and hardened, fought back a lump in his throat. *It's not supposed to happen this way*, he thought, but shook his head clear enough to ask, "What have you done so far?" As Jerry Beasley, the ER doctor, filled him in on the initial treatment given, and provided more details about the circumstances of Josh's presentation to the hospital emergency room, Dr. Gilsen tried to clear the fog of sleep from his head. With enough information to know that the treatment was so far appropriate, and that the right diagnostic tests were done or underway, he could begin to plan some rudimentary strategy for tonight. "Have you notified Dr. Reichert yet? He'll need to know we've got trouble brewing."

"He's out of town, but I got a hold of his fellow. He said he'd be right down, but to go ahead and get a hold of you."

"Yeah, that's right. Jeff told me he was going to be in New Orleans this week. Who's the surgeon covering?"

"Hold on, I'll check . . . it's Greshin. You want me to get a hold of her?"

"Do that, but don't waste time. You keep the kid alive 'til I get there."

Dr. Beasley paused only a few seconds. "Okay, will do. But have you looked outside? You be careful driving down here."

"Right. See you shortly." He hung up the phone and reflexively turned over and kissed his wife, warm and soft, oblivious. "Hon, I've got to go in."

"Mmff, be careful," she said, without coming to consciousness.

As he dressed, Bob Gilsen had time to try keeping his mind awake, reacting and planning, and going over Joshua Crabtree's singular history. This "kid" of twenty-eight never seemed to have gotten a dose of good luck in his life. Somehow, though, there never seemed a trace of bitterness or envy in any of his encounters with this shy, sweet, feeble, and mentally retarded young man.

His origins were as mysterious as the medical problems that would plague him in later years. Twenty-eight years ago an infant of approximately four months of age was brought in to the office of a Dr. Yordy, general practitioner, in a small town near Berea, Kentucky. A very young, poor, sandy haired woman brought the baby in to the office, said his name was Josh, and that he was very sickly and wouldn't nurse. As the nurse took the child, the young woman turned and fled, unrecognized and never found. The infant, listless, febrile, and scarlet red was desperately ill, needing care that Dr. Yordy was ill equipped to provide. He was able to arrange transport to facilities in Lexington, where medication and supportive care were given and to the surprise of all, the baby recovered from his acute illness. As no parents or relatives of any kind could be located, Josh became a ward of the state. Normally, this would mean a life sentence of benevolent incarceration in state institutions, especially for an infant who was clearly not right. Even at that stage of life, though, Josh possessed an inexplicable ability to touch the lives of those caring for him.

So it happened that Janie Crabtree was touched by this infant's undeniable human need. She couldn't bear the thought of abandoning this child to the willful powers of the state, and it was with sheer determination that she rode over the obstacles in her way to adopt Joshua. Janie and her husband, Earl, had tried for ten years to have a child of their own, and following her last miscarriage, Janie had finally come to terms with what seemed a rather harsh reality. Then Josh appeared in her life, and she couldn't let go. As the LPN working on pediatrics on the night shift, she had more opportunity than the day or evening nurses to spend time getting to know her charges. Josh's unexpected recovery and lack of any family made him somehow more precious and harder to release.

She was not naïve, and knew full well that Josh's illness, combined with prior lack of nurturing, and likely absent prenatal and perinatal care had left the baby weak, slow and in near constant need of attention. Then there were the medical problems. From the beginning there were feeding difficulties and intolerance of formulas, projectile vomiting and diarrhea. Worse, though, were the seizures, and medication to control them, always incompletely successful.

At one point, a heart murmur was detected, but thought at that time to be merely a manifestation of fever and anemia. All told, Josh spent three months of his first year in the hospital before being released to Janie's and Earl's devoted care.

The first few years were marked by repeated bouts of infection, generally the common infant ailments of the respiratory and digestive tracts, but with an occasional infection serious enough to warrant hospitalization, including a rather prolonged case of pneumonia of undetermined cause. Again, during this hospitalization a heart murmur was noted, but was thought to be a result of the infection and accompanying anemia, but "should be followed."

By the time Joshua reached four years of age, it became more readily apparent that he was significantly impaired, both mentally and physically. His speech was minimal. He was uncoordinated, small, and weak; cheerful, but panicky when away from Janie and Earl. Janie had long since quit employment to care for Josh at home. Their visits to the clinic were frequent, and they became well acquainted with the pediatric staff and residents. An odd sense of family developed, and Josh's illnesses became everybody's business.

The seizures continued to occur, with variable severity, and they became a common topic of debate among the medical staff caring for Josh. Should he be given Dilantin instead of Phenobarbital, and was the Phenobarbital interfering with his already impeded development? What about the facial anomalies likely to develop with long term use of Dilantin? Repeated respiratory infections also developed, including ear infections, which led to his first surgical procedure, a tonsillectomy. At that time tonsillectomies were considered routine and recommended for nearly all children at some point in their development. Joshua's surgery, however, was anything but routine. First there were the repeated seizures as the anesthesia was administered, then the uncontrolled hemorrhage. Again, Josh seemed near dying, and again the murmur was noted. This time debate arose as to whether the heart seemed to have enlarged on the chest x-ray. Again it was thought that the murmur should be "followed closely." It wasn't until Josh was six years old that his heart murmur was regarded as definitely abnormal, and likely representing a congenital abnormality of the aortic valve. Dr. George

Wentz, a pediatric cardiologist of some renown had been asked to render an opinion as to the nature of Joshua's murmur. Dr. Wentz was a visiting lecturer at the time, and had suggested that some "interesting cases" might provide him and opportunity to demonstrate the finer points of physical examination of the heart in children. To a rapt audience of six white-coated doctors and Janie, Dr. Wentz demonstrated that, in addition to the more obvious systolic murmur which a number of physicians had noted, a softer, fading diastolic murmur was evident if one placed the stethoscope just there and listened at the end of expiration. To Janie, Dr. Wentz carefully and graciously explained that, based on his examination, it appeared that Josh had a defective aortic valve, likely that he was born with this abnormality, but it had not yet caused significant trouble. He further commented that heart murmurs, even in children, are so often overlooked, and often innocent, but that this particular case represented someone who would eventually need treatment. It was his sincere hope that the surgical treatment of congenital heart disease would improve and progress enough within Josh's lifetime that he could be safely and effectively treated with an operation to replace or repair the defective valve, as medical therapy had severe limitations.

Despite the grim news, Janie's recollection of this encounter was not a bitter one. Rather, she remembered the incident with a feeling of awe and humility, as if she had been visited by an important messenger from a higher power or authority.

The ensuing years brought further difficulties, but also occasions for hope. With changes in medication, Josh's seizure disorder was better controlled, and consequently his physical and mental development accelerated, never quite up to normal, but gratifying to his parents. As developments in cardiac surgery were announced in the medical and lay press, Janie would regularly read all she could find on the subject, and bring along any journals or clippings to share with the physician at Josh's clinic visits. This became much more than idle speculation or wishful dreaming as Josh began to show signs and symptoms of cardiac stress, or decompensation, during his preteen and early teenage years.

As his cardiac status became more clearly defined in time, largely due to major advances in diagnostic testing, some of Joshua's ailments remained a puzzle. Unexplained fevers, spells of lethargy, a persistent anemia and bleeding tendency all remained annoyingly mysterious. With each acute illness severe enough to require hospitalization the toll on Josh's heart was more obvious. A simple cold would make him short of breath, but influenza or pneumonia would bring him to the brink of respiratory failure.

Dr. Gilsen's first encounter with Joshua was shortly after the Crabtrees' move to Ohio. Earl's engineering work had fortuitously led him to an interest in the newly developing and expanding field of computer science. This, in turn, provided Earl steady employment opportunity, and measure of security for his small family. The move to Ohio was an unbeatable opportunity for Earl, but was a major crisis for Janie. Leaving her relatives in Kentucky was not a big deal, but to leave her medical family, Josh's family, was heart-rending. Janie realized that again her considerable determination was going to be needed to assure that her precious son would receive the best possible medical care. She would leave as little to chance as humanly possible. This was the setting that Bob Gilsen, unwittingly stepped into on a Friday afternoon nine years before. It had already been a long day in the middle of his first year of cardiology fellowship. Cardiology clinic today seemed like just one more thing to get through before he could get back to work on more important matters on the inpatient wards. The day had been an endless stream of old men with complaints of chest pain, difficulty breathing, weakness and swollen feet. Coronary heart disease, with or without heart failure, seemed to be the order of the day. So, when he picked up the next chart, and noticed with a start that this patient was only nineteen years old, Bob's face cracked a relieved smile. This, he thought, was going to work out after all, and might even be interesting. A young kid, probably healthy, with a heart murmur. It shouldn't take more than twenty minutes to see the patient, review the chest x-ray and EKG, lay down a load of reassurance and get out of there. A nice change from the sick old men.

"Good afternoon, I'm Dr. Gilsen," he said cheerfully as he entered the cluttered little exam room. Then his face and body froze. Across the room, in the dingy wooden chair, sat a demure middle-aged woman, composed and neatly dressed, but with an expression of such intense challenge that all Bob's intellectual defenses were put on instant alert. But what really caught his attention was on her lap. There was no doubt what that two-inch stack of papers represented—copies of outside records, apparently several hundred pages worth. Dr. Gilsen groaned inwardly, and turned his attention to the patient. There on the padded metal examination table sat a tiny figure, pale, slender, visibly apprehensive, short of breath, slightly dusky about the lips, and with swollen feet.

With his head suddenly reeling at the formidable task ahead of him, Dr. Gilsen paused to try to gather his thoughts together and, most especially, to figure out where to start. Fortunately for him, Janie took over at this point. "Josh is nineteen years old," she began. "He has congenital aortic valve disease. He also has a seizure disorder, and he's prone to getting infections. He's always been anemic and he bleeds easy too. Josh is mentally slow, but he's been making a lot of progress since his seizures have been better controlled.

"We've moved here from Lexington, and they told us there to try to get an appointment at the University Hospital as soon as possible with Dr. Levine. We got an appointment with him for June, but he's taken sick, and can't wait that long. I do hope you know something about congenital heart disease." Janie's pressured speech and intense tone hit their mark. Bob Gilsen could see his work was cut out for him, and his evening was shot. This was, however, going to be interesting, and most definitely a change from the sick old men.

Bob again turned his attention toward his patient. "Joshua," he said, "your mother said you've taken sick. Can you tell me how you're feeling?" Josh turned toward his mother, shivered, and made a faint, unintelligible sound.

"He started coughing last Friday," Janie answered for him. "At first it wasn't much, but two days ago he started chilling and running a temperature. Today he's just gotten steadily worse. His feet have been swelling up, he's getting more and more short of breath, and now he's started coughing up some thick phlegm with blood in it. I'm just sure he's got pneumonia again. He gets pneumonia so easy. Maybe I should have brought him in sooner. I do hope you can help him. His case is very complicated, and we're new here, and his doctors are all back in Lexington ..." Janie's speech remained pressured, but her manner was controlled. There was intensity but little emotion in her voice, as if she had been through battles tougher than this, with scars to prove it.

With some deliberation, Bob was able to piece together enough of Josh's variegated history to get a sense of where his current symptoms fit into the scheme of things. His physical exam, however, was limited. It was clear that Josh was in at least moderate respiratory failure. There was the cyanosis about the lips and nail beds, there were crackles indicative of fluid in both lungs, a loud murmur in the aortic area, radiating to the neck, there was swelling of both feet, and his temperature and pulse were elevated. Three things were clear at this point: first that Josh needed to be in the hospital, second, that Janie was almost certainly right about Josh having pneumonia, and third, that there now appeared to be a component of a more ominous problem—congestive heart failure. Bob Gilsen carefully explained to Janie, that while Josh was getting some oxygen, and getting the necessary tests done, that he would be presenting his case to Dr. Sheila DeJong, the attending cardiologist. And further, that he himself would see to it that Josh would be receiving the most expeditious care possible.

Janie sensed both caring and competence in this tired-looking young doctor, and visibly relaxed. "I'm most obligated to you, Dr. Gilsen," she said, betraying her stern and correct Kentucky upbringing, "you will be looking after Josh in the hospital, won't you?"

"Well, I'll be part of the team caring for him, but I won't be the only doctor looking after Josh. You see, he'll be on the cardiology service of either Dr. DeJong or Dr. Clancy, and there will be residents, interns, and students all participating in his care."

The look of intensity returned to Janie's face. "But can I get a hold of you if I have questions or concerns? You see, it's hard to completely trust anyone in a scary new situation."

Bob Gilsen understood this very well. "Sure," he said, "here's the number to call anytime, day or night, just ask for beeper 336. Also, here's my home number." He wrote the numbers down on a prescription blank and handed it to Janie, not even realizing that this was the first time he had ever given a patient his unlisted home phone number.

"Thank you," Janie said, carefully folding the paper and putting it away in her purse.

"Thank you, Dr. Gilsen." said Joshua, quietly but distinctly.

Bob felt a lump in his throat, and fought back a tear. This young patient in need had touched him in a way he could not define or explain.

Throughout the intervening years, Bob had become Josh's advocate as well as personal physician, and when it came time to do battle with the powers that resisted his medical and personal needs Janie and Bob were a seemingly unbeatable team. The biggest and longest battle they fought on Josh's behalf was getting a surgeon to agree to do an aortic valve replacement. As the years went by it became more obvious that a valve replacement would be the only thing that would keep Josh out of constant difficulty with congestive heart failure. The cardiac surgeons, however, saw Josh's situation as excessively risky. Further, they argued, his mental retardation, seizure disorder, repeated infections and bleeding tendency all probably limited his life expectancy as much as his aortic valve disorder. Janie's and Bob's arguments all centered around Josh's undeniable need and his unique persona—not very persuasive arguments to most hard-bitten cardiac surgeons.

So, when Dr. Jeffery Reichert joined the faculty, full of enthusiasm, new ideas and the latest technical advances picked up in his training in Pittsburgh, Janie and Dr. Gilsen struck again. This time they were successful. Preoperately, all the best possible experts were consulted, including specialists in hematology, infectious diseases and neurology, all providing their most carefully considered recommendations for pre and post operative management. It was not completely clear how much of all this Joshua understood, but his trust in Janie and Dr. Gilsen was simple, complete and wholehearted.

The surgery itself went off without any difficulty. Joshua's small, deformed aortic valve was replaced by a gleaming stainless steel and plastic prosthesis consisting of a ring within which a flat disc tilted on two eccentrically placed hinges. Even the early postoperative period seemed incredibly smooth. There was no difficulty weaning Josh off the bypass pump or even the ventilator. The first hint of trouble came five days later, when, as part of Dr. Reichert's research protocol, Joshua underwent a trans-esophageal echocardiogram. An echocardiogram, or ultrasound study of the anatomy and function of the heart, is routinely an excellent means of determining valve function. However, because the metal in a valve prosthesis will not allow normal transmission of ultrasound waves, the usual echocardiogram is often unsatisfactory in visualizing the anatomy and function of a prosthetic aortic valve. The recent development of trans-esophageal echocardiography, though, provided a relatively "noninvasive" means to accurately evaluate the function of metallic aortic valves. Five to six days after aortic valve replacement Dr. Reichert would obtain a trans-esophageal echo routinely to evaluate the success of surgery, and to learn early if any problems were likely to occur.

Bob recalled that moment vividly when Dr. Reichert and Dr. Phil Andrews, the resident expert in trans-esophageal echo, called him up to the lab. "Bob, you got a minute? You should see his echo." That alert, electrified quality in the voice of a referring physician usually meant an interesting case, and Bob Gilsen's reflex response was usually one of similar enthusiasm. This time, however, he felt a very different sensation in the pit of his belly—one of dread, close to panic.

"Sure, I'll be right up," he managed to say, then quickly excused himself from rounds and dashed up the two flights of stairs to the echo lab. There, in the dimmed room two physicians were seated, intently staring at a small TV screen. The image was black and white, moving, but there were bursts of unreal, bright yellow, red, blue and mottled color showing up between parts of the displayed images.

"Look at this, Bob. Here, let me rewind this tape a bit to show you. Okay, here's the important part." Bob did not share Dr. Andrews's enthusiasm, but pulled up a chair hurriedly and stared at the small screen. The picture clearly showed Josh's new aortic valve, seated in its anatomically correct location. A smooth flood of red color could be seen going across the valve with the disc in its tilted open position, indicating normal forward flow. But with the disc in its closed position, a garish jet of mottled blue/white/yellow/red flame could be seen shooting back into the left ventricle from a point of origin next to the new valve. "See, there's no question about it," Phil Andrews continued. "You guys have got you a major paravalvular leak."

Bob's insides churned with anxiety. He had listened to Josh's heart just yesterday morning, hearing only the reassuring clicking sounds of the tilting disc, and no diastolic murmur to suggest any valve incompetence. "Listen, Bob, why don't you go down and take a look at Josh, see what you think clinically. You know, we find these paravalvular leaks pretty commonly on echo. Some of them are a lot more impressive on the screen than they end up being in real life, and some of them seem to seal themselves without intervention." Bob couldn't decide if Jeff Reichert was being glib or trying to be reassuring. His anxiety must have been apparent in his expression.

"Yeah, I know that, Jeff, but with Josh . . . Jeez, it's the last thing he needs." He paused a moment to get himself back "in gear," to start thinking clinically and clearly. "Anyway, how's his ventricle look on the echo? That's really got to be our biggest concern right now."

"His LV function looks pretty decent, some hypertrophy of course. Here, let me show you." Phil fast-forwarded the videotape to show clearly the functioning of Josh's left ventricle, the heart's major pumping chamber. They could see with some reassurance the vigorous contractions of Josh's left ventricle. Something wasn't quite right, through, perhaps a little bigger in size than before surgery.

"Look, do me a favor, Phil. Would you get out his pre-op echo report and check the LV measurements to compare with these, and then give me a call when you got it? Thanks. And Jeff, did you order a chest x-ray on him today? Okay, I'll take care of it, and I'll call you after I've seen him. Thanks loads, guys, you've really made my day."

Actually, Josh didn't look bad at all. There was no clinical evidence of heart failure. He was eating, his color looked good and his chest x-ray was reassuring as well. All his lab tests were in order. *Maybe we'll get by this time*, Bob thought, and, in fact, Josh's course over the next few weeks seemed to confirm his cautious optimism.

But now, all his optimism seemed a rosy fantasy. Bob slipped his shoes on, walked down the carpeted stairs to the front hallway and got his coat out of the closet. *Better get a couple swallows of coffee in me if I'm going to drive,* he thought, and slipped over to the kitchen, found some cold brew in the bottom of the pot, heated it briefly in the microwave, then swallowed the half cup of bitter dregs. He then stepped into the garage as he put his coat on, slipped into the driver's seat of the Toyota, pushed the button to open the garage door and eased out into the night.

# Chapter Two

The night of January third was overcast and bitterly cold. Craycroft had had more than his usual difficulty falling asleep that night. Even the wine hadn't done anything to ease the general anxiety of the council, or his own internal rumblings. It had certainly been difficult that evening to determine whether he was becoming ill or just sick at heart. It had taken a second draught of the medicinal brandy to quiet the insistent voices of memory and dread, and allow him a measure of uneasy sleep. And now these bells, in the middle of the night. "Curses, not now! Not so soon," he thought as he fought against his own inertia, and struggled to get out from under the twisted covers.

He was not summoned often in the middle of the night, and on the few recent occasions that he had been, he had arrived too late to do any more than comfort those in attendance, and make note of the situation for his report the next morning. Considering the foreboding surrounding him, and apparently all the council that night, this call was not likely to signify anything easy or trivial.

Sitting on the side of the bed, he felt blindly for his slippers, found them, then stood up to reach the lamp and adjust the flame enough to find his robe. A chill draft reached him from across the stone room, and he shook miserably for several seconds before he was able to slip on his threadbare, but warm robe. The right side of his head was throbbing painfully, his chest ached, and his mouth felt like wool, but he was walking. He was almost ready when he heard the summoning knock at his door.

"Master Craycroft, Master Craycroft, you are needed at once. Are you within?"

"Yes, Page, I heard the bells. You may enter."

The heavy door opened soundlessly, and the young messenger swept in, bringing another stinging draft of night air. "It's the Lady Vincente, Master Craycroft." The page spoke quickly and in gasps, his breath heaving and condensing in the cold. "Councilor Rust bade me bring you at once. He said it was most urgent and delicate."

"Say no more. Let us be on our way."

Craycroft stooped to pick up his leather satchel and his scarf, then he and the youth stepped out into the arched hallway, dimly lit with sputtering torches, and found their way down the long, dark curving stairway toward the courtyard.

The Lady Vincente, Felicia in her younger years, had been a striking woman. Craycroft remembered that in his own youth he had been quite smitten with this raven-haired daughter of the powerful foreign ambassador. The graceful walk, slender arms, dark eyes, and devastating smile had turned many a head, including his own. At that time, he was a shy, freckled, gangly child of working parents, and their last remaining hope of rising above eternal poverty. He remembered with a twinge of pain that first encounter.

Craycroft, known then as Will, had been a mixed blessing for his parents. A stubborn, serious, quiet, but incredibly curious child, born to a metal smith and kitchen maid, fairly late in years. The two older children had both died in that terrible winter ague, five years before Will's birth. Early on, two things became obvious. The first was that this child somehow seemed marked for a fate greater than his parents—something in those searching eyes, constantly questioning intellect, and unyielding temperament suggested both hope and anxiety. The second was that

Will was not physically cut out to follow in his father's occupation of metal smith. He was not sickly, merely thin, painfully clumsy and sensitive.

He was nine years of age at the time. Living within the confines of the court had provided Will occasional opportunities for limited education, obtained mostly on the sly, as well as opportunities to earn a very meager income as an errand runner. On one of his errand runs, he was told to deliver a bouquet to the wife of the newly arrived ambassador. Upon arrival at their door, he was met by a slender girl of twelve or thirteen years, wearing a velvet gown of deep burgundy. Without looking up, he pointed the bouquet of flowers toward the middle of her gown and said the flowers were for the Mistress, a token from the house of the earl. Instead of the expected swift grab of the contents of his hand and slamming of the door, the girl reached out her slender arm, gently lifted his chin, and, looking directly at him, smiled. A blow to the head would not have been more shattering that than smile. The utter beauty of that vision, coupled with the instant reminder of his station in life, was almost more than Will could bear.

He thought about that moment again, that and the many changes the years had brought to his life and the life of that beauty. The need must be grave indeed. His head cleared somewhat as he and the page shuffled out into the courtyard. An icy blast tore at their robes, and they instinctively huddled together, facing into the wind, walking as quickly as they could in step. As they crossed the dark courtyard, Craycroft could see that lamps were lit and there was smoke billowing from the chimney at the Lady's chambers. He took some measure of encouragement from thinking that perhaps his feet might at least thaw out. Even in times of great crisis, he often found himself considering mundane things like cold feet and simple hunger, perhaps as a means of maintaining perspective, or perhaps as a way of reducing his own fear and sense of helplessness.

They reached the opposite end of the courtyard and gratefully turned in to the entranceway of the east tower, out of the raging wind. With their eyes still smarting from the blast, they took just a moment to catch their breath before finding the door to the upward stairway. "I know full well that my meager lamp would not have remained lit through that gale in the courtyard. Page, can you see the door?"

"Nay, but here it is by touch. Can you take my hand?"

Master Craycroft took hold of the youth's cold hand, and together they ascended the stairs cautiously, keeping their eyes upward toward a faint light at the turn of the stairway.

"Tell me, Page, do you have any knowledge of the Lady's distress this night?"

"Master, I have none."

Craycroft could not be sure if the youth was being honest or merely correct. He had learned long ago that the information available from the "little people" was frequently more useful and accurate than that provided by the more cautious lords and ladies, and he instinctively took every opportunity he could to get what he called the gritty facts. So far, he knew little about Lady Vincente's recent illness, but enough to make him suspect that it had something to do with the council's restlessness of the previous evening. He would not have been expected to attend if their concerns had been merely political or economical.

Craycroft and the page were met at the top of the stairway by Councilor Rust. Rust always appeared distracted and poorly organized (though his actions spoke otherwise), and were it not for the obvious gravity of the situation, his appearance this night would have been comical. Tall and gaunt, with a large, narrow face, framed by a chaotic mat of reddish hair and beard, streaked with gray, he stood, gesticulating awkwardly to a servant in the hallway at the top of the stairs.

"Ah, Master Craycroft, thank God you have come! But, please, a word with you in private before you attend to the Lady."

"I am sure, Councilor, that your concerns are of importance. But I am summoned in the middle of the night to see someone presumably quite ill. I suggest you hold your story until I have, at the very least, been able to discern whether our Lady might be dying or in need of respite from pain." He spoke in an even, unhurried voice, and with such authority that even Councilor Rust was taken aback. This was clearly Master Craycroft's private domain. His authority in the face of illness or pain had been won slowly, not bequeathed as birthright, and represented earned power that was no longer challenged.

"Of course, you are right," said the Councilor. "I will await your word."

The page suppressed a slight smile, then he and Craycroft shuffled on down the hall to the Lady's chambers. At the doorway, they paused, and, turning to the youth, the master said, "Listen, lad, and make haste with your task. I have need of a basin of water, warmed mildly, to which has been added four drops of aromatic oil and a pinch of salt. Bring me this and something hot to drink. Again, make haste, but take care."

Craycroft knocked firmly on Lady Vincente's outer door and was admitted promptly by one of the maids, who closed the heavy door quickly behind them to minimize any cold air reaching inside. "Please enter, Master Craycroft. It is good you have come in haste. My lady does need your urgent attention. Please, this way." She led him through the arched hallway with its portraits, throne-like chairs, tapestries and coat-of-arms, and turned left into an anteroom, which, as he knew, led to the Lady's sleeping chamber. The maid knocked softly twice at the door, peered in quickly, and then led Craycroft into the room.

The bedroom was strikingly warm. A fire roared in the large fireplace, and the heavy drapes were carefully drawn to keep out any drafts. The master paused briefly to survey the surroundings, then turned his full attention to the lady in the bed. "I have not come too late this time," he thought, "but damnably close."

Felicia, Lady Vincente, hardly seemed the same beauty he had known in youth, and, in fact, hardly even seemed the same graceful woman he had seen just a few months ago attending to her father's details of travel. There she lay, flushed and febrile, breathing rapidly, and with some effort. She was not asleep, but seemed only dimly aware of the intrusion into her chambers. A fine rash on her face and arms, and perhaps a suggestion of jaundice, was apparent, even in the relatively poor light from the fire and burning lamps set about the room. He approached the bed, and heard a distinct rattling in the Lady's breathing. Her eyes were sunken, and not quite closed. She turned, ever so slightly, in his direction as he reached to touch her hand.

"Lady, I am here," he said, noting the coldness of her hand in contrast to the burning heat radiating from her body. "Have you any pain?"

"Good of you to come, dear Craycroft. No, I am free of pain at this moment." Her speech was faint, but clear, coming in segments between gasping breaths. "Jeanne has been attending to my needs faithfully these hours. I only . . ."

Her speech was cut off abruptly by a racking paroxysm of coughing. She was brought to a sudden sitting position, bent forward, as her weakened body was shaken by spasm after spasm. Jeanne had immediately brought out a towel into which her lady coughed up a considerable quantity of vile-looking matter, part blood, part foam, and part pus. After perhaps a minute of sustained coughing, which seemed considerably longer, the fit subsided, and she was able to lie gratefully, back on the pillows and sink into relative oblivion.

Craycroft had observed this with what seemed a dispassionate calm, and then turned his attention toward Jeanne. The girl was trembling uncontrollably, and fighting back bitter tears. He strode over to the other side of the bed, and touched her shoulder firmly, but gently. "Come, child, you can be of some help. But first, tell me of the circumstances leading up to our present state as regards your lady. Hold nothing back. Tell me all you can remember. None of this is your fault."

Jeanne swallowed hard, tried to talk, found she could not, then swallowed again. Her words came slowly at first, then more normally as she gained control. "As you know, sir," she began, "Lady was abroad, on travels, when we first knew of any troubles with her health. When her father heard of this, he had them bring her home at once. As you also know, his health had been poor, and he was failing by the time M'lady returned. This was perhaps a month ago. The lady's never been one to complain, especially when there is duty to be done, and it seemed only in character that she would attend to her father's needs, forsaking her own. The spells would happen, mostly at night, but I believe I may have been the only one who knew of them. She would tell folks she was fine and recovered from her travels, and go on attending to her master."

"Tell me, Jeanne, what did you observe about these "spells" and with what regularity did they occur?" Despite the usual hopelessness of attending the terminal stages of disease, Craycroft remained passionately fond of details, convinced that it was in the details, the "gritty facts" that truth and possibly hope resided.

"Well, sir, there was no regularity to the spells as I was able to notice, but I will tell you they were much less frequent and less severe when the lady first returned. At that time she would call me aside, and tell me to bring her some bitters, as she felt her digestion might be unsettled. But I could tell, even then there was something more. She seemed somehow restless, and her breath was heavy, as with effort. On some of these occasions, when I would come back with the bitters, it would appear as if she had exerted herself unnaturally."

"How do you mean, child?"

"Just that she reminded me of the times I have been most frightened, having fled from something of terror."

"Very well, that is quite clear. Please continue, and do tell how her manner and her spells may have changed."

Jeanne continued, somewhat warily, "At the first, M'lady would recover and seem whole and normal within the hour, and she would be back to her usual activity, with hearty appetite and spring in her stride. But as time went on, the spells would come, closer together and would last longer. Also, if I may be so bold, there appeared a slight change in M'lady herself. Mind you this may have been no more than concern over her ill father, but she became somehow less vigorous—her smile less bright and her appetite less hearty. As well, I noticed other things. She would begin to cough, most especially when reclining or in sleep, and then I noticed, when assisting in her toilet, the appearance of spots on her skin. They would appear in groups or clusters, small and red or purple in hue, generally after one of her more prolonged spells, and then would fade over the week. I believe that early on there was no ague in these spells, but most certainly there has been feverishness of late, and I would say that over the past two weeks she has been most warm to touch at all times I have attended her, even when she was most nearly her usual self."

Craycroft stood silent, closed his eyes as if in deepest concentration, his mind racing. When he spoke, it was with eloquence and reverence. "My child, your powers of observation astound me. Lady Vincente has chosen you well. But pray tell me two things more. First, has your lady had any occasions to swoon or faint, and secondly, have you perceived any change in the urine?"

Jeanne blushed slightly, and then answered, "aye, she has fainted twice, both times yesterday, and each time following a fit of coughing. As you mentioned it, I did notice a change of some redness to the urine, always at times when her spots would first appear."

Felicia stirred slightly in bed, turning her head toward Jeanne and Craycroft. She attempted to smile, but lapsed back to stupor before it formed. Craycroft took the towel from Jeanne and, in the light of the nearby lamp, examined its foul contents. Muttering inaudibly, he noticed that the peculiar odor of rank sweetness seemed very strong as he inspected the cloth.

"I have seen this malady twice before, and it is not good. We have no name as yet to give it, but I recognized its sinister visage. I will do what I am able for the lady, but I fear the worst. Have you summoned Father Henri?"

Jeanne inhaled sharply, closing her eyes tightly, fighting back a flood of tears. "Not yet, sir. You see, Councilor Rust . . ."

"Say no more, I will attend to it."

There was a knock at the bedroom door, and the page was let

in, bearing a basin in one arm and a steaming flagon in the other hand.

"Ah, good page, you do well. Place the basin there on the table, and hand me the flagon if you will. Come, Jeanne, I will need your assistance in this matter.

"Page, I have one more task for you tonight. Get you to the chapel and find Father Henri. Lead him here if he will come. Let him know the matter may not wait 'till morning."

Jeanne's eyes flashed with alarm. "But the councilor . . ."

He cut her short. "Jeanne, do not worry, I will take care of Rust. I already know more than he realizes. He will not do or say anything tonight. Now, Page, if you would be so kind . . ."

The page smiled slightly, saying nothing, then turned and left the room.

"Come, Jeanne, we must minister to our lady." They walked to her side by the bed, and then Craycroft reached into his satchel, rummaged about, and pulled out a ceramic object, vaguely globular in shape, with a spout protruding near the top to one side and a stoppered hole at the very top. He put his drink down on the table, handed Jeanne the ceramic object, then dug about in his satchel for two more items, one a long handled ladle, the other a sort of bowl with a flat candle inside it and holes around its rim. With the flame of a nearby lamp, he lit the candle inside the bowl, and then set it down. Then, with Jeanne still holding it, he unstopped the odd flask and, using his ladle, measured into it four scoops of the aromatic liquid in the basin. He then set the flask down into the bowl to which it fit precisely. Finally, he took from his satchel a small bottle of brandy and poured a small amount into the flask and returned the stopper.

"Now we must wait as the potion heats, then I will show you what you may do to provide your lady with some ease for her distress." Saying this, the master, now showing some sign of weariness, took his flagon, still steaming, and sat down on a stool near the bed. He inhaled the aroma from the glass, noticing the distinct soothing piquancy of Carlisle's Brew, and then sipped his drink noisily. "I must remember to reward this good page handsomely," he thought. The room was still except for the crackling fire, Craycroft's slurping and the rapid, rattling respirations of Lady Vincente.

Jeanne hovered uneasily about her lady's bed, watching intently as Felicia lay, not awake, but not soundly asleep, struggling to breathe. Nervously, she walked over to the maid who had been waiting by the door, whispered to her, then returned to her lady's side. Master Craycroft sat with eyes closed, deep in thought, sipping his brew. Only the irregular tapping of his foot gave hint to the emotional turmoil within his soul.

He thought back to the last time he had seen an illness to match this vivid description given by Jeanne. It must have been twenty years ago, when Master Cartho was still alive and, though not actively attending the sick, still available to dispense bits of wisdom to the younger masters and apprentices. He remembered reciting the tale to Cartho of the youthful merchant, come over from Italy, stricken with a gradually debilitating malady incredibly similar to Lady Vincente's. Cartho had told him to watch for further cases, as he himself had seen only five in his long years, each progressing similarly to a premature demise, and to make very careful and precise observations. "We may have nothing of substance to offer the victims of this mysterious disease," he said, "but we have a right and obligation to generations yet to come to make our observations clear and true, so that in due time the veil of mystery might be lifted, the illness better understood, and good treatment be given."

*Small comfort to us here and now,* thought Craycroft, *but you are right, as always, Master Cartho. I will dutifully observe and record.* A small tear escaped the corner of his eye, unexpectedly running down his rough, bristled cheek. He turned his attention back the apparatus by the bed. A wisp of steam was beginning to drift from its spout. He stood again, picked up the flask with a rolled cloth, and stepped over to the bed.

"Come, Jeanne, I will show you what to do with this." He gently roused Lady Vincente, and with Jeanne's help held her in sitting up. He turned the flask and held it so that the vapors coming from the spout were drifting toward the lady's nose and mouth. "Now, my Lady, breathe in this mist as you are able, taking its moisture deep within. It should ease your respiration and provide some comfort. You may yet cough, but that is no matter."

As the mist escaped the flask, Felicia breathed in the aromatic fumes, and did, in fact, seem, after several minutes, to breathe somewhat more easily. Another fit of coughing then interrupted the efforts of Craycroft and Jeanne. Again, she coughed up a copious amount of vile matter, and again sank back exhausted on the pillows. Craycroft replaced the flask in its lighted bowl and instructed Jeanne in its care and replenishment. "As often and as long as she is able, try to repeat this mist treatment through the night. I will leave the materials here. I do believe our lady is in good hands, and is as comfortable as conditions will allow."

As he was speaking, Father Henri and the page were let into the room. The brown robed father was panting slightly as he shuffled toward the bed. "Master Craycroft, I am glad you summoned, I was aware the lady had been ill, but not to this extent."

"Good Father, you come in time. I have instructed Jeanne in the treatment I can offer, but I fear our lady needs your care more than mine at this moment. I will return here by morning. I commend her to your care for now."

Craycroft picked up his satchel and headed for the door. "Page, come with me. We must find Councilor Rust. He and I have matters of some urgency to discuss before morning."

"Craycroft, I thank you" Lady Vincente said, softly, but distinctly. "Do not let Rust mislead you."

"Rest assured, dear Lady, I will beware."

"Come, Page, let us make haste." With that, the two walked out into the cool hallway, then out into the frigid night. "What is your name, son?"

"Drachma, Sir, but I am called Tom."

"Very well, Tom, I will see to it that you are properly rewarded. We are certain to find Councilor Rust in his quarters. Let us look there."

# Chapter Three

It was worse than he expected outside. There was stuff falling from the sky that should have been snow, as cold as it was, but this wasn't snow. It made noise as it hit the windshield, and then turned into frozen mush. Bob turned on the wipers, but that only made matters worse, because now he couldn't even see out at all. He skidded to a stop and turned on the defroster full blast, hoping to clear a big enough area to drive. Impatiently, he turned on the radio, but the NPR station was playing some painfully modern jazz. He fumbled in the dark for a cassette tape and slipped it into the player. Somehow the renaissance lute music on the tape seemed altogether too soothing, but it would have to do. The windshield remained opaque. There was no choice—he would have to get out and scrape. The small ice scraper was usually in the glove compartment, but he found it after a brief search under the front passenger seat. Getting out of the car quickly, he slammed the door a little harder than he planned, just hard enough to lose his footing on the icy pavement. Bob hit the ground hard, landing painfully on his right elbow and thigh, and found, as he looked up, that he had scratched the door of his new car with the scraper on his way down.

*Oh, damn* he thought, a moan escaping his lips, *what else could possibly go foul now?*

A bit more cautiously, he eased himself back up and began scraping at the frozen matter on the windshield, muttering curses at himself for not putting on gloves. The sleet and snow mix that was failing stung his neck, ears and bare hands. Eventually, the defroster began working, and he was able to fairly quickly clear a sizeable area of windshield, enough at least to see to drive. Sliding gratefully back into his seat, he rubbed and blew the numbness from his hands, then put the car back in gear, and eased back out onto the road. Mercifully, at this hour there would not be any traffic to deal with.

The drive to the hospital could take anywhere from fifteen to forty minutes. At three or four in the morning it would not usually take more than fifteen, but he had already wasted ten minutes with his antics on the ice. He was at least wide awake now, but sore and shaky, and still fuming. He tried to focus again on his reason for getting out in this weather in the middle of the night, and the poor soul in need of his services.

It took another twenty-five minutes of very careful driving to finally get to the hospital. With relief, he slid into the doctors' parking lot and found his space, fortunately unoccupied. The effort of the drive, with its necessary vigilance, left him shaking even more as he, cautiously this time, got out of the car and headed into the cavernous entrance of Memorial Hospital. Inside, he hurried toward the Emergency Room, pausing only briefly at the panel of switches near the operator's desk, where he found the one next to his name, and flipped it, indicating to the hospital operator that he was now "in house." The ER was on the ground floor of the oldest building in the chaotic sprawl that represented Memorial Hospital. Dr. Gilsen headed there quickly through the maze of green and beige corridors, feeling both the relief of being indoors and the intense urgency of his call this night.

The ER was buzzing. The noise, the smell, and the sights were an assault on the senses. Were it not for his own sense of purpose, Bob might have noticed the rancor. Instead, he headed straight for the "Cardiac Room" where Josh was certain to be.

The Emergency Department was divided into a medical and a surgical half, with the nurses' station, small lab, a tiny lounge, and storage closet separating the two sides. Bob pulled his stethoscope out of his pocket, and then tossed his coat on an unoccupied chair in the lounge as he hurried across to the medicine side. As expected, Josh was in the "Cardiac Room." Dr. Gilsen took just a few moments to absorb the scene and begin to make sense of the seeming chaos in that overcrowded room. Surrounding Josh on the table in the middle of the room was a mixture of people, equipment, sights, sounds and smells, all indicating extreme urgency and mobilization of the immense technological resources that went with an emergency.

A respiratory therapist was adjusting the oxygen flow to a mask held by elastic to Joshua's face. An ER nurse, in a gray-green scrub suit, was setting the numbers on a complex box attached to an IV pole which precisely controlled the rate of infusion of the fluid mixture running into a vein on Josh's left forearm. A similar apparatus was connected in turn to similar IV tubing, but, in this case, attached to a manometer which constantly monitored, with extreme precision, the blood pressure in his radial artery. This information was being displayed in graphic and numerical fashion at the bottom of a TV type screen near the head of the table. Immediately above this display was a graphic representation of the rise and fall of Josh's respiratory efforts. At the top of the screen was the traditional electrocardiographic display of his heart rate. Stuck to Josh's bare chest were three foam and plastic patches to which were connected the lead wires carrying electrical signals up to the electrocardiographic monitor. A plastic bag was hung at the side of the table, directly connected to more tubing which carried the scant amount of urine emanating from Joshua's catheterized bladder.

Accompanying this was the familiar beep-beep-beep of the audio signal of heartbeats, the gurgling of oxygen bubbling through a plastic canister on the wall behind the bed, the hissing sound of a suction apparatus left on, and the droning of multiple electromechanical machines throughout the room. The mixture of smells was subtler, but also more insinuating. The usual hospital disinfectant smell was there, as well as the adrenaline sweat smell of the desperately ill, mingled with musty odors of clothes worn long hours, and a unique smell that was a much a part of the old building as the stonework and foundation.

Despite the urgency and distress of the situation, Dr. Gilsen found that he was in his element, suddenly calm, alert, and thinking clearly. He absorbed the enormous amount of information available from within the room as if breathing it in. Almost unconsciously, he added the data to what he already had known of the situation, and then readied himself for the work ahead of him.

"Hi, Judy" he said, addressing the RN, "I'm glad to see you're on tonight. Looks like we've got our work cut out for us. Do me a favor. I'm going to start here with Josh, while I'm examining him, would you get me his chest film, his latest blood gases, any new labs or information you've got. Then find the cardiac surgery fellow and Dr. Beasley, and tell them I need them here right away. Oh, and find out where his parents are waiting—we're gonna need to do some serious talking."

"Okay, Dr. Bob, you got it. His chart's back there on the desk with most of his labs and vitals. They're just running a new set of gases, and I'll track them down for you. Dr. Hurwitz just left here to check on unit beds, said he'd be right back. I'll get Beasley for you." She turned to Josh, touching him gently on the forehead. "Josh, Dr. Gilsen's here. He'll take care of you." Judy smiled quickly, then turned and started out the door. Bob, before you leave, let me see you briefly, okay?"

"Sure, Judy, I'll try to remember."

He walked over to Josh, automatically hanging his stethoscope on his neck. "Josh" he said, "I know you're having trouble. We've had trouble before, and we'll do whatever we can to help you. Tell me, are you having any pain?"

"No . . . Dr. Gilsen . . . I'm not . . ." he spoke in short bursts, between gasping breaths. "I just . . . can't . . . breathe. Thank you . . . for . . . seeing me."

Dr. Gilsen began his examination. He noted the cold, clammy sweat on the face and trunk, the slightly dusky color of the lips and nails, the extreme coldness of the hands and feet. The veins in Josh's neck stood out like ropes, and the pulsations in the neck were irregular, rapid, and almost chaotic. He listened with his stethoscope to Josh's chest and could hear loud, moist crackles everywhere. Except for the mechanical clicking of the artificial valve, Josh's heart sounds were almost drowned out by the noisy respirations. His new scar stood out like a red snake, running the vertical length of his slender chest, but there was no worrisome swelling or pus, and no inappropriate tenderness to touch. His abdomen was mildly protuberant, and the edge of the liver could be felt several finger breadths below the ribs. There was swelling in the feet and lower legs, and when Dr. Gilsen pressed the flesh of Josh's shins, it left indentations. Mentally, Josh seemed to be pretty much his usual self, though the effort of breathing seemed to be taking most of his concentration.

Something didn't quite fit the picture, some piece missing. Dr. Gilsen turned and walked over to the desk and quickly thumbed through the chart put together on Josh. He looked at Dr. Beasley's scrawled notes, and what he could decipher seemed to confirm what had been told him over the phone and what he had just found on examination. The lab reports showed nothing either startling or very illuminating, only reconfirming the general sense that his was a patient in distress. He noted that the blood cultures he had suggested had, in fact, been drawn, and that the intravenous therapy, including antibiotics had been started. He put the chart back down, closed his eyes briefly, and just concentrated. No, there was still something. He walked back over to Josh's bed and listened again to his heart sounds, concentrating totally. Yes, the heart sounds were muffled, rapid, irregular, as before, but there was something more. Between the first and second sounds, listening at a point just left of the sternum, he could hear, not quite drowned out by the loud respiratory noises, a new murmur. The significance of this was just dawning on him when something in Josh's expression caught his eye. He looked up to see Josh's face turn steely gray, rigid, with jaw clenched and eyes staring straight ahead, not seeing. The alarm on the cardiac monitor squealed as it's signaled the sudden change in rhythm, no longer the neat and narrow complexes of an orderly rhythm, but the wide, rapid undulations of ventricular tachycardia.

Dr. Gilsen responded immediately. He turned quickly to the respiratory therapist. "Sheila, get an Ambu bag and mask, and get ready to ventilate him." He felt Josh's neck along the right carotid artery. He could barely feel a rapid, thready pulse beneath the tips of his fingers. Looking at the monitor screen, he could see that Josh's blood pressure had bottomed out, reading only 42 over 15. Turning immediately to the defibrillator behind him on the "Crash Cart" he turned the power on. He then found the package containing two electrode gel pads and tore it open, placed the two pads on Josh's chest, and got ready to cardiovert, setting an energy level of 100 joules. Judy Morrison and Dr. Beasley came rushing in at that moment, having heard the alarm of the cardiac monitor.

"He just went into v-tach and started seizing" Dr. Gilsen explained. "He's barely got a pulse, and I'm going to cardiovert at a hundred. Judy, could you get some lidocaine ready to push?"

"Sure, doc, you go ahead and shock him."

Dr. Gilsen placed one paddle on the gel pad on the upper chest, right of the breastbone, and the other on the lower left chest. He took another look at the monitor, noting that the malignant arrhythmia persisted, unchanged. "All clear! I'll cardiovert on three!" He looked around to make sure no one was carelessly touching the patient or table. "One . . . two . . . three!" He pressed the two red buttons on the defibrillator paddles. There was a very brief pause, less than a quarter of a second, then a soft sound like a kiss. Josh's body instantly jerked, and his arms flexed toward his chest, and he moaned. All eyes turned toward the monitor screen. The green electric line had shot off the edge of the screen with the shock, then returned to baseline, recording a flat line for one very long second. The reassuring squiggles of a rapid sinus rhythm then appeared on the screen. All in the room exhaled at once, a collective sigh of relief.

Dr. Gilsen turned to Sheila, at the head of the table. "You got the Ambu bag? You may need to assist his respirations." The respiratory therapist fitted a thick plastic mask, which was attached to a self-inflating bag like a small football, tightly over Josh's face. With each of Josh's respiratory efforts, she squeezed the bag, sending the oxygen rich flow into his airways. Dr. Gilsen then felt Josh's neck again, noting that his carotid artery pulsations were much stronger, and now regular. "He's got a pretty good carotid pulse now. So, let's have someone call for a twelve lead EKG, and Judy, let's give him 75 milligrams of lidocaine IV push, then start a drip at 45 cc an hour." He looked back at the monitor screen, at the arterial line tracing, noticed that the blood pressure was now reading 96 over 45. "His pressure looks better. I sure hope his rhythm holds. He'll do a lot better in sinus rhythm than in atrial fib. Has anyone seen the surgeons? We need them down here real soon. If someone can get me a five cc syringe and a blood gas kit I'll go ahead and get another set of gases from the art line."

The ER staff had come to learn over time that, under circumstances like this, Dr. Gilsen's questions, directions and orders, delivered in his quiet monotone, were to be acted on as quickly and carefully as humanly possible. This was not time to debate and ponder. Judy Morrison took the cue, and secondarily shot directions at Dr. Beasley, the other nurses, doctors and attendants who happened in at the sight of the sudden increased activity in "Cardiac."

Bob slipped the defibrillator paddles back into their places on the "Crash Cart", and turned his attention back to Joshua. Judy had delegated the task of drawing the blood gases to the medicine intern, and had sent Dr. Beasley to get hold of the surgeons and to bring back the chest x-ray taken away by the cardiac surgery fellow, Dr. Hurwitz. Marty Perez was sent off to get the EKG machine, while Judy herself attended to the task of mixing and administering the IV medications.

Bob looked up again at the monitor. BP 102 over 65, heart rate 116 and regular, respiratory efforts again strong and regular.

So far, so good. He looked at Josh's face. The eyes were closed. His color wasn't great, but it was better. The therapist seemed to have no trouble "bagging" him. His neck veins remained distended. Listening to his lungs, he could still hear the moist rales of fluid that had leaked from the tiny pulmonary capillaries into the air spaces. He placed the diaphragm of his stethoscope again left of the sternum, and listened with renewed intensity. Again, between noisy breaths, he could hear the crisp clicking of the mechanical valve. Yes, it was still there. Between clicks he could still make out the faint, blowing murmur he had heard earlier. There was no time to sort things out noninvasively this time, though. The surgeons were going to have to go in there, find out what had blown open, replace or repair what they could, then get the heck out of there, and hope everything held this time. The most he might be able to provide the surgeons in the way of a preoperative evaluation would be to get a quick surface echocardiogram with color Doppler. He was not looking forward to dealing with Dr. Greshin, or trying to explain to Janie and Earl why a cardiac surgeon they had never met, and one who had never been in favor or operating on Josh in the first place, would be taking him to the OR in the middle of the night to do a procedure with a very high likelihood of killing him.

"Judy, I'm going to need one more big favor quickly, if you can swing it. While I go talk to Josh's parents, see if you can find one of the cardiology fellows or techs, anyone who knows how to run an echo machine, have them bring it down here, and we'll try to get a quick look by echo before the surgeons have to haul him off. And have them make sure it's one with color."

"That's a tall order at four in the morning, Bob. I'll do my best." She smiled briefly, then turned her attention back to the increasingly complex IV apparatus. The smile caught Bob just slightly off balance, reminding him of something or someone he couldn't quite define or exactly remember; something vague, distant, but compelling. He tried to shake off the feeling, to concentrate on matters more immediate.

"Where are Janie and Earl, are they out in the main waiting area?"

"No, last I saw they were in that small lounge by the cafeteria."

"Okay, I'll go find them. Call me right away if the surgeons get here."

Bob turned his attention one more time to Josh. He went up to his head, and touched his face. Sheila pulled the mask away at Dr. Gilsen's request. "Josh, can you hear me?"

There was no immediate response, and his eyes remained closed. He reached again toward Josh's face to open his eyes, but Joshua's eyes sprang open on their own. Josh turned his head toward Dr. Gilsen, but the look on his face was unlike anything Bob had ever seen, on Josh or anyone else. His eyes stared straight through Bob to something seemingly in the distance. He seemed somehow knowing and powerful, ageless. A chill went down Dr. Gilsen's back. Then, without help or warning, Josh sat straight up. Before anyone could move to restrain him he spoke, but his voice was as unlike him as his expression. In a voice as loud, clear and reverberant as a shot in an empty cathedral, he filled the little room with the words, "*Drachma, beware Drachma!*"

For several seconds there was silence. Then, as awareness returned to the people in the room, it was Josh again, lying back on the table, in a full-blown seizure. As the medical team sprang back into action, Bob couldn't escape the scary feeling that somehow that bizarre incident had been directed at him. The logical, rational part of him remained attuned to the business at hand, methodically handling Joshua's urgent medical needs, while another; less clearly realized part of himself shook with ill-defined fear.

Fortunately, this time Josh's heart rhythm remained stable and the seizure quickly subsided. As everyone in the room began to breathe more normally again, the surgeons, Dr. Hurwitz and with him Dr. Barbara Greshin, made their entrance. Dr. Mark

Hurwitz, second year cardiac surgery fellow, was a short, taciturn, pale young man with permanently tousled black hair. He was dressed in the traditional garb of surgeon-on-call, namely an incredibly rumpled scrub suit with nameless stains covered by an equally disreputable, formerly white lab coat. Dr. Greshin, a small, slender woman with colored dress, covered by an immaculate white lab coat, with her name tag pinned just right, only one pen in the top pocket, and stethoscope folded carefully in the lower pocket.

As Dr. Hurwitz put the chest x-ray he brought up on the view box for Dr. Gilsen to look at, it was Dr. Greshin who spoke. "Well, Bob, this is quite some mess you and Jeff have handed me." Bob groaned silently, suddenly noticing the aching in his arm and leg where he had fallen earlier. This was not going to be easy. "What can you tell me that Mark doesn't know about the case that might be helpful and please keep it brief. It looks like we're going to have us a long, messy operation that needs to get started soon if you want a live patient at the end of it."

Fighting back some bitter resentment, and quickly swallowing a lot of pride, Dr. Gilsen explained, as succinctly as he could, the course of events that followed Josh's surgery, leading up to the events of the past forty-five minutes. He then told Dr. Greshin of his tentative plan to try to get a quick echocardiogram in the ER before taking Josh to surgery.

"You know, Bob, that sounds like a great little idea if you can get it done in the half hour or so it's going to take to get the OR ready. Now, let me take a look at this fine young fella a minute."

While Dr. Greshin quickly examined Joshua, Bob went over to the view box and pondered the information available on the x-ray film. Clearly, there was the pulmonary edema Dr. Beasley had described. But there was more. Some of the pulmonary densities looked more suspicious for pneumonia. Dr. Greshin was right. This was a mess.

He turned to Judy once more. "Look, Dr. Greshin and I better go talk with Josh's parents. See what you can do about getting someone down here with an echo machine. And say a prayer, cross your fingers, do whatever you can to keep him going. We haven't lost this yet."

Judy looked at him and nodded. There was concern in her expression, but something more, as if she had sensed that same inexpressible fear. For the third time, Bob felt a chill run down his back.

Dr. Greshin completed her brief examination of Joshua, who was unresponsive following his most recent seizure. She shook her head as if resigning herself to carry out a most dubious task, then looked again at Dr. Gilsen. "Okay Bob, let's go have a little chat with Joshua's parent's"

Bob noticed that Dr. Beasley had returned. "Jerry, would you check on those latest gases for me and adjust his oxygen? If you've got to intubate him, go ahead. He's going to surgery anyway."

With that, the cardiologist and the cardiac surgeon headed out to find Janie and Earl. Mark Hurwitz shuffled behind the two, saying nothing, and thinking his own private thoughts.

Bob really dreaded moments like these. *There is no amount of training that could have prepared me*, he thought. *Maybe I shouldn't care this much.* Suddenly he felt slightly dizzy, a little nauseated, and very tired. The surgeons did not seem to notice, and in a few moments the feeling passed. They walked on down the corridor toward the cafeteria.

# Chapter Four

Councilor Rust was, in fact, waiting in his chambers for Craycroft when he and the page knocked at the door. The councilor himself let them in with what seemed an oddly warm welcome, considering the time and the circumstances. "Please, enter" he told them. "I have a warm fire inside, and whatever you might need for comfort I will obtain." There did not appear to be any animosity or agitation in his manner, in great contrast to their recent meeting at the top of the stairs.

"Thank you, good Councilor," said Craycroft warily, "your welcome is appreciated on a night such as this." His words were gracious, but his voice and bearing tense as he and Tom entered. They were led in through a cluttered hallway to a modest sitting room. Tom waited at the entryway, casually leaning against the open door, as Rust and Craycroft went on in.

"Do let me know if there is anything I may get for you," said Rust, his attitude seemingly genuine. "Please, take a seat by the fire. We have much to discuss, and I wish you to be comfortable." Despite his misgivings, Craycroft visibly relaxed and sat down heavily in a worn, comfortable chair near the crackling fire. Rust moved over to a heavy, padded chair and sat down, facing the master.

Craycroft pondered the change in attitude. There at the stairway, Rust had seemed tense, distracted, and hardly able to restrain his sense of urgency. But now, here in his own quarters, sitting in the warmth of his fireplace, was a very different man. Here was the benevolent councilor, the wise leader, ready to sit down and discuss matters in depth, as if time was of no concern. Craycroft felt suddenly off balance. *I must be very careful*, he thought, *he has regained control, and I am now in his domain.* Rust had the reputation of being an eccentric, an amusing caricature on the council. Those with any experience in council business, though, knew otherwise. There was no one with greater knowledge. Craycroft himself had been witness to more than one occasion in which unwitting souls had fallen victim to their misperception of Rust's abilities.

"Councilor, what has happened during the time I have been attending Lady Vincente? The matter seemed most pressing when we spoke earlier, but now, it would seem, we have as much time as we need." He decided to play his own gambit, "For if that is the case, I would prefer to retire to my own rooms, and discuss these matters after obtaining some needed sleep."

The councilor's eyes flashed for a mere instant, then the calm returned. He did not speak for several seconds, and seemed lost in thought. "Ah, Master Craycroft, I fear we misjudge each other," he said at last. "You know as well as I that there are issues before the council, and that Lady Vincente's condition has great bearing on what will be decided. I have hoped that with your knowledge, both of the Lady's state and of Council matters that you could be of the greatest help."

"To whom?" Craycroft couldn't help asking.

The councilor sighed. This was not going to be easy. Clearly he would need to reveal more than he intended. "Perhaps we should start at the beginning."

*Splendid*, thought Craycroft, *which beginning?*

Neither man spoke for a period of time, creating an awkward silence. Rust shifted in his seat, but Craycroft remained still and unreadable. Finally, Rust broke the stillness. "Tell me, Master

Craycroft, what do you know of Lord Vincente's business, and whether his most untimely death had anything to do with his business or travels?"

"You do not ask a simple question, and my answer, I fear, will not be simple either. As you are well aware, my life's devotion has been to the study of illnesses, their causes and cures. You are also understanding of the fact that I do not accept the traditional explanations of the causes of disease, espoused by generations of physicians since Galen. Further, you know that if my theories and practice were to be openly written and disseminated, the king's advisors would find cause to have me removed from the service of my people, and likely killed or imprisoned. That I am allowed to continue my work here is testimony to two facts, the first being my successes in the treatment of the scorbutus, as well as some cases of dropsy. The second is the mutual fondness between the earl, his family and me. The council has been most indulgent and understanding of this, but, as you know, some members have found this a source of irritation and jealousy. To answer, then the second part of your question first, I would say that, yes, Lord Vincente's illness and death were a direct result of his businesses and travels, but you hear this told you by something of a heretic."

He now had Rust's complete attention, and, in spite of nagging voices in the back of his mind advising caution, he continued. "You must understand that I have been taught, and also have observed over years, that diseases form patterns which allow us to name them and recognize their appearance in diverse persons. Some illnesses, however, seem to strike only at certain times, or strike only certain kinds of persons. It is with this knowledge that I am able to tell you that Lord Vincente's demise was attributable to his businesses in foreign parts. To answer the first part of your question, then, I must tell you that I have little direct knowledge of his businesses, as these were neither any concern nor any interest of mine, but I have strong suspicions as to the nature of some of them."

The councilor pressed for details. "Please continue, Master

Craycroft. I am most interested in your suspicions, and also your conclusions as to the nature of Lord Vincente's malady."

"Ah, good councilor, there is more than curiosity that motivates you in this matter, I fear. Before I divulge more, I should know something of what you intend to do with the information I am able to provide. You are not alone in the pursuit of the knowledge and conclusions I hold in this regard."

Rust realized with a start that Craycroft had just regained the upper hand. He had provided just enough information to tantalize, but not enough to make gains. Further, it now appeared that there was likely someone else, most certainly another councilor, after the same knowledge. He began to understand that Craycroft's power resided in more than just his abilities as a healer, and that this was no pawn, easily manipulated. He would have to bargain, something he did not, by nature, enjoy doing.

"Very well, Craycroft, you have made your point. As you well know, the council has been debating this past month the problem of the painters and potters that have taken ill or died. You have reported to us your conclusions that there was enough similarity in their illnesses and deaths to suspect that there must be a common thread of occurrence, and that some substance common to both trades must surely be at the root of the illness; as others, including their wives and children have not suffered from the malady, nor have other professions." He paused a moment, buying time to think. "Further, and this I do not think you knew, I was assigned the task by the earl of investigating what the common threads might be, and reporting back to the earl and also the council."

"Please, Councilor, continue. This I did, in truth, learn of quite recently. As well, I learned that your report to the Council was not received with any confidence, and instead raised more debate, which carried into the session this past evening."

"Quite correct. I still shudder at the remembrance of some caustic remarks directed toward me by Silvo. How unlike him!"

"Ah, and somehow you feel that Lord Vincente's death may have been part of this riddle, and perhaps even the Lady's illness, and that I might be of some use to you in settling this matter, possibly before the king's messengers take word of our troubles back to the mainland. Is this not so?"

"Master Craycroft, I have woefully misjudged you."

"But Councilor, you and I know there is more. I have, after all, had opportunity to talk with Lady Felicia."

Rust's face became chalky white, and for an instant a look of panic flashed in his eyes. "What can you possibly mean by that?"

"Simply this, Councilor: you have been assigned that task of investigating the deaths of some of our most valued craftsmen. It appears to many that the death of our esteemed nobleman of late may have a clear bearing on the matter. Further, that his beloved daughter is also near to death herself," Craycroft's voice barely held steady, through intense force of will, "and may take with her to the grave some vital information that could help us all. In light of this, I know that there is much that you and Lady Felicia would rather not have brought to public knowledge, and, insofar as she has been a true friend to me since my youth, I do and will respect this. But bear this in mind: I am the only one who is able to provide you with the help you will truly need for your work. You will need to trust someone with the ungilded truth, else risk providing the earl a sham report, and I do believe you understand what consequence that could bring."

"I do," Rust answered quietly. He sat, deep in thought, for several minutes. The room remained silent except for the occasional popping from the fire. Craycroft was profoundly tired, and had nearly fallen asleep before Rust spoke again. "Master Craycroft, I feel smitten by the truth of your words. You are, by reputation, an honorable man, and my experience would lead me to believe that you are. As you have said, though, I have much at risk; more, I think, than even your keen understanding would have led you to know. I do desire to trust you. I have no real choice."

"That is good, Councilor. Now, however, I am too weary to continue this discussion. May I suggest we meet again in the morning hours, before business commences in the market, and may I also suggest that we meet in my study, as there is much that I have compiled there of pertinence to your inquiry."

"I shall be there," Rust said, showing signs of fatigue himself. Craycroft moved to get up, and found that he had become rather stiff, sitting as he had all this time in the comfortable chair. The thought of facing the bitter cold wind of the courtyard was even more of a dread than before, when duty had impelled him. "I must see to our Lady's condition once more before returning to my chambers," he said, almost to himself. "Good rest to you, Councilor."

"And you, Master Craycroft. I will see you to the door."

He moved toward the hall, with Rust joining him. They found the page asleep in the floor of the hallway. "I do wonder how much of this he heard," thought Craycroft. As a page himself in younger years, Craycroft had learned much about the art of human relationships, listening in on conversations thought to be beyond his care or understanding. He bent down and gently shook Tom's shoulder. "Come, Tom," we must be off again. Our Lady remains my prime concern this night. I must be sure of her comfort before retiring once again."

Tom roused himself quickly, somewhat embarrassed at his slumber. Together, the three walked slowly to Rust's outside door. A draft was palpable, blowing beneath the heavy oak door. The two men bid each other farewell, then Tom and Craycroft set out into the cold again, on their way to Lady Vincente's chambers.

The breeze was only slight, but bit through their clothing and stung their faces. As much as they could, Tom and the master walked close to the massive stone wall, under the covered walkway, their pace quickening with each step, until they were almost running as they turned the corridor to the lady's rooms. The predawn hours were still and very dark, and their knocking seemed to echo loudly through the corridors and great courtyard. A dog barked in response; others joined in briefly, then the stillness returned. Craycroft was about to knock again, when a maid answered the door.

"Do come in, Master Craycroft," she said, "Jeanne told me you might yet return this night. I believe the lady has been at greater ease this past hour."

"Thank you, Frieda." He recognized the woman as one of Felicia's long-time devoted servants. She shut the massive door behind them as they entered, then ushered the master and page toward the lady's bedchamber. They paused at the bedroom entrance while Frieda went in to announce Craycroft's presence, then returned to let the master in.

The light was dimmer, but the room remained hospitably warm. Craycroft found Jeanne's presence at her lady's bedside deeply comforting. He also made a mental note to remember how observant and precise Jeanne's answers to his probing questions had been, in spite of the obvious gravity of the circumstances. "She could prove an invaluable ally some day," he thought.

He walked over to the right side of the bed, next to Jeanne, and for some time stood quietly, observing Felicia and her surroundings. He noticed that the lady was sleeping, peacefully it seemed. Her breathing remained rapid, somewhat irregular, but less labored. Despite her overall pallor, her cheeks were flushed and lips still dusky. He knew without touching her that the fever still burned within. Beside the bed, his mist-making apparatus stood in its holder, gently steaming. He nodded to Jeanne, saying nothing, but indicating his sense that appropriate care was being rendered. In spite of his initial misgivings, he now felt that Felicia was at least likely to survive the night. He turned as if to go, but Felicia's hand touched his. When he turned back he saw that she was awake.

"Please," she said, "stay but a few minutes, and tell me of your talk with Rust." Her words were spoken softly, slowly, between breaths. "It is right that Jeanne should hear."

"Ah, my Lady, I did not wish to disturb your slumber." The master bent down on one knee at the bedside, a gesture both of respect and friendship, their hands still touching. "I did, in truth, speak with the councilor in his chambers. His task is great, as you are aware, and his first intentions were, if truth be known, an attempt to make use of my knowledge without giving up anything of his own."

Despite her state, Felicia smiled, almost chuckled. The years had taught her much about her odd, but wonderful, friend. "Will," she said, reverting naturally to his first name, "maybe I should have warned Rust about you."

Craycroft savored the awkward intimacy of the moment. When he spoke again, there was a touch of chagrin in his voice. "My lady, you know me all too well, I fear. Rest assured, though, I was restrained, and I do believe that I have won his confidence. He has most certainly come to realize that his investigation will come to naught without my aid and his candor. I hope in time he will also come to understand that he has nothing to fear from me if he speaks the truth as he knows it."

A sudden seriousness in Felicia's expression caught his attention. She turned her gaze directly at Craycroft. "Friend," she said, "I know my time is near. Father Henri has been here, and I am prepared, though still afraid of the coming darkness."

Craycroft tried to speak, but no words came. He swallowed, fighting back a harsh impulse to weep openly. With a great effort he gradually regained his steady composure. Felicia sensed his turmoil, and waited. When he was able to look at her again, she continued.

"Listen, there is much you need to know that duty has thus far prevented my telling you. But when I am gone you are the only one who can be trusted. I have faithfully written down all that could be of value and kept a secret record in my possession. Jeanne alone knows the location of this record. I have asked that she give you this record when the time comes."

The strain of telling this was severe, and Craycroft immediately sensed her exhaustion. He reached out to touch her face when she was seized again with a powerful fit of coughing. Jeanne was ready instantly to assist her. The paroxysm was as severe as the first one Craycroft had seen, but not as prolonged. Her lips, fearfully blue, quivered as she lay back, spent. Perspiration covered her face, neck and torso. Her arms hung limply at her side as she drifted back to sleep. Craycroft stood again, as Jeanne carefully and gently mopped her lady's perspiration with a soft cloth.

He stood by, saying nothing for several minutes—simply reassuring himself that Felicia remained at rest. Finally, he spoke to Jeanne. "I fear I must return to my quarters. I do believe our Lady will live the night, but please send word at once if her condition alarms you. I will ask that Tom, the page, stay here until morning as a messenger available to you. I believe him to be swift and trustworthy. I ask only that you provide him sustenance in the morning. I shall see to his wages. You already know what to do for the mist treatments, and I would have you continue them as conditions allow." He turned to leave, then as an afterthought, said "do remember, Jeanne, there are persons hereabouts of questionable scruples. Be careful whom you trust."

"Of course, Master Craycroft. Do try to get some rest. I will attend to M'lady."

Master Craycroft thanked her, then turned again to leave. He stepped out into the hallway, where he found Tom, and gave him instructions. Frieda had apparently gone back into the chambers, so he let himself out, back to the now still coldness of predawn winter. The walk back to his quarters provided him another opportunity to think and remember. For reasons he could not then explain, what he remembered again was Master Cartho and his oft-repeated admonition. "We are nearly powerless," he would say, "in our own time, and with our own skills, but power will come to future generations, power to harm and to heal. Our task is to observe and record with absolute honesty, to provide fertile soil for the healing power to grow uncorrupted."

*Ah, Master Cartho*, thought Craycroft, *tonight I have need of that power. That, and a good night's sleep.*

# Chapter Five

At 6:00 a.m. Dr. Gilsen was the sole occupant of the doctor's lounge. It was now early Saturday morning, but still looked and felt like the middle of the night. He hung up the dictating phone after verbally rendering Joshua's history and physical exam over the wires to a cassette tape somewhere in Medical Records. The task of dictating histories and physicals, discharge summaries, operative records, consultations and the like fell within the general category of "paperwork" a burden universally detested by practicing physicians, and relegated to time slots not taken up by the much more important business of "patient care". Having gotten that out of the way, Dr. Gilsen realized the sudden tranquility about him. There were events that had taken place in the past few hours that had left him feeling frustrated, puzzled, angry and bewildered, but until now he had not had the time to acknowledge or consider either the events or his own feelings.

He thought back to the encounter with Janie and Earl and the surgeons. He had gotten used to Janie's cautious questioning of everything in regard to Josh's care, and walked into that expected confrontation with the certain knowledge that he would have to play liaison between the willful, arrogant surgeons and the ever suspicious Janie. What did occur threw him off balance (and feeling the sore spots on his arm and leg, realized that it wasn't the first time that night).

The three doctors had entered the small lounge by the cafeteria to find it deserted except for Josh's parents. As frequent visitors to the emergency room, they had come to realize that this little alcove was one of the few places they could wait close enough to the ER to stay in touch, but still get away from the drunks, the blood, the vomit and the general distress of the regular waiting room. Janie and Earl rose at once as the physicians walked in, their faces tense and alert with anticipation.

"Janie, this is Dr. Greshin. She is the cardiac surgeon covering for Dr. Reichert while he's out of town," Bob explained, searching Janie's face for some expression to indicate how she might react. "Dr. Greshin, these are Josh's parents, Janie and Earl Crabtree."

Dr. Greshin made no move to shake hands. Instead, she nodded toward the chairs they had been occupying, then, pulling up a chair quickly herself, sat down. "Listen, you all had best sit down for a bit. We've got some hours of work ahead of us, and I'd like to try and explain what we're up against and what we're gonna need to do."

Bob braced himself for the expected flood of questions and challenges from Janie. Instead, she and Earl sat down quietly and turned their attention to Dr. Greshin, who explained tersely what seemed to be the pertinent facts of the case. Dr. Gilsen could not have known, of course, but Janie's expression and rapt attention were a replay of the encounter, years before, when Dr. Wentz had pronounced his medical benediction on Joshua. What Dr. Gilsen did feel (but at the time did not recognize it as such) was resentment that this surgeon, whom Janie and Earl had never before met, had come into an emotionally charged situation involving his patient, had taken over center stage like a hero, unchallenged, and laid out a plan for salvaging this mess. The mess, by implication, was largely Dr. Gilsen's doing. Further he was confounded by Janie's uncharacteristic and unexpected passive acceptance of the situation as spelled out by the charismatic

Dr. Greshin. Bob glanced over at Dr. Hurwitz, who, as usual, seemed completely self-absorbed, almost bored.

"So, I hope you all can see what we've got to do here in the next few hours," Dr. Greshin continued. "If you've got any questions, please ask them now, 'cause time is not on our side tonight."

"No, Dr. Greshin," Janie answered, "I believe you've made the situation quite clear. I just know you'll do your very best for Josh. We'll leave things up to you at this point. Only, please let us know how things are going when you can."

"Certainly, Mrs. Crabtree, we'll keep you informed. Now, if you'll kindly excuse me, I'll have the nurses get together the necessary forms for you to sign. My fellow, Dr. Hurwitz here, can help explain anything that might still be unclear." With that, she rose to leave, but before stepping out, turned to Hurwitz and said, "Mark, you try and make sure we've got this rolling within the hour, okay?"

As Dr. Greshin's presence faded gradually, Bob realized there were still many things that needed to be done before Josh would be going to surgery, including the business with the echocardiogram. *Lord, I hope Judy's kept things under control,* he thought, remembering the seizure and the cardioversion, and the fact that no one had told Janie and Earl about either.

"Janie," he said, remembering once again the peculiar events, "I've got to ask what may seem the strangest question, but do you have any idea who or what Drachma is, and why Josh might have used that name?"

It must indeed have seemed the strangest question, because in the next instant everyone in the room started at Dr. Gilsen as if he had just made a smelly mess on the carpet. After a most awkward silence, Janie finally ventured to ask, "Whatever do you mean, Dr. Gilsen? I don't believe I've ever heard that name before, and I sure don't recall ever hearing Josh mention any name like that."

"Well," he hesitated to even bring it up, "Josh had a seizure while I was with him in the ER a little bit ago, but before the seizure he sat bolt upright and mentioned something about

Drachma. I don't know, maybe it was a dream he was waking up from or something. There was just something odd about it, like it might be something or someone special . . ."

Unexpectedly, Dr. Hurwitz spoke. "If it means anything, a drachma is some form of Greek currency. That's weird, Bob. I sure wouldn't expect Josh to have known anything like that."

Dr. Gilsen could feel the conversation taking an unwanted turn at that point, subconsciously noting Hurwitz's use of the past tense, and was relieved when Judy interrupted to inform him that one of the cardiology fellows had been found "in house" and had been persuaded to bring down an echo machine, and would be setting that up within the next few minutes.

Thinking back on that moment, Dr. Gilsen remembered that he had promised to try to see Judy before she left after her shift. He looked at this watch and realized there was still almost an hour to go before her shift ended at seven. He still had some time to check back with the OR and see how surgery was proceeding with Josh.

Before heading off toward the operating rooms, he acted on a sudden whim and went into the small medical library adjacent to the doctors' lounge. The library was a cluttered little room with a number of mostly outdated medical texts on the busy shelves. In addition, there were fairly current copies of a handful of medical journals filed and unfiled about the room on the shelves and tables. An abandoned sandwich and a half empty cup of cold coffee sat under the reading lamp on the table by the general encyclopedia as well on the bottom shelf. Indeed, on the shelf, in the far right corner was an old Britannica. Finding the volume labeled Daisy—Educational, he opened it and found Drachma: The silver coin of ancient Greece, and the monetary unit of modern Greece, derived from the verb "to grasp". Bob was no less puzzled than before, but as he put the volume back in its place on the shelf, he felt again the chill down his back and the overpowering sensation that this was all part of something larger and scarier than anything he had ever experienced.

*This is stupid*, he thought, trying to suppress what seemed so outlandish, *I probably just need some sleep.* The idea of a desperately ill, retarded young man, about to undergo emergency cardiac surgery, spouting off about Greek money just before having a generalized seizure was more than he cared to ponder at that moment.

Bringing himself back to consider the present circumstances, he realized just how lucky Josh was to make it the OR this time. The echocardiogram had been a scary sight. As he and Judy had been walking back to the ER, Ginny Nash, the cardiology fellow doing the echo, burst out of the Cardiac room looking for him. "Dr. Gilsen, you've got to see this, quick," she spouted, "looks like that aortic seal has blown wide open, probably a rim abscess." Residents and fellows in academic medical training lived for moments like this, discovering what they called "great cases". These were the patients with vivid and extraordinary medical problems, the subject of animated discussions months and years later at dinners or conferences with other doctors.

Bob Gilsen's reaction had been quite different—a mixture of urgency, dread and genuine concern. Still, he was able to appreciate his younger colleague's unbridled enthusiasm, and swallowed his own misgivings. "Okay, Ginny," he said, "let's get in there, look at the pictures, get something quickly on tape, and get him on up to the surgeons with some helpful info. We can review the tape later. You'll probably want a copy made for yourself as well."

Inside the Cardiac room the lights had been dimmed for better viewing of the screen. Josh had been turned on his left side, was still breathing rapidly, but seemed in no worse shape than when Dr. Gilsen had last left the room. A quick check of the monitors showed blood pressure, heart rate and rhythm and respiratory pattern stressed, but stable. Dr. Nash walked over to Josh's bed, picked up the transducer attached by a thick cord to the echo machine and placed the gel-covered tip on Josh's bare chest.

"All right, Ginny," Dr. Gilsen began, "let's get a quick parasternal long axis shot, then some apical views with color Doppler, then get out of here with our machine. We can forego the short axis views to save time."

"Okay, here's our parasternal long," Dr. Nash said, adjusting the calibration. "There, look at the motion of that valve . . ."

Bob stared at the screen, fascinated, but sick at heart. There he could see the artificial valve in its location in the aortic annulus, but with each contraction of the heart he noticed that it wasn't just the tilting disk that moved, but rather the whole valve apparatus swung out into the aorta and slapped back in place as the ventricle opened back up.

"You got that on tape, Ginny? Okay, now let's get a coned down view of the valve and turn on the color."

A magnified image of the aortic valve appeared on the screen, then, with the push of a button a flood of color showed on the image, representing blood flow across the valve area. It was apparent that blood was flowing not just through, but also *around* the prosthetic valve, indicating that the sewn seal of the artificial valve had broken open. This was almost certainly due to breakdown of tissue around the valve from infection, specifically an abscess of the aortic ring.

"This is bad, Ginny. The surgeons are really going to have their work cut out for them, trying to put sutures into that infected, tenderized heart muscle.

Under Dr. Gilsen's direction, Ginny Nash quickly recorded the necessary images on videotape for later review, and then shut down the machine, preparing to take it back up to the seventh floor. Dr. Gilsen took the videotape with a promise to return it to Ginny first thing Monday morning.

"Now, we've got to find the surgeons. They're not going to be pleased with what I've got to tell them. I doubt whether they'll even want to look at the tape, but I'll have it just in case. Judy, you think you can find Hurwitz for me? He needs to know we're ready."

Dr. Gilsen was right. The surgeons were not pleased. When he described the echo findings to Dr. Greshin, he could see the dismay cloud her face for an instant, then saw the dismay turn into action. She quickly picked up the nearest phone, got hold of the nurse in charge of the OR, and set the machinery in motion to get Josh up to the OR as quickly as possible, with anesthesia and necessary support staff ready and waiting.

"Look, Bob, we've got maybe ten, fifteen minutes before I'll need to go scrub, why don't you show me what you've got on tape. It sure wouldn't hurt to see what we're getting into. There should be a VCR somewhere on this floor. If not, I know there's one up by OR."

Dr. Gilsen showed her the tape, pointing out the pertinent features of the limited examination.

"You know what my concerns are, I imagine," she said. "When we get in to replace that valve, not only are we likely to find mushy tissue to try to sew into, but we're getting damn close to the coronary ostia. It wouldn't take much of a slip to tie off a coronary. I do seem to remember some of us were less than enthusiastic about taking on this case in the first place."

Bob winced as the barb hit home. "Yeah," he said, "thanks for reminding me."

He wondered just how much Janie and Earl understood of the precarious precipice Josh was sitting on. He had survived so much in his short life, but this was a point of real desperation. Even if he survived the operation, his chances of returning to some form of functional status seemed poor. Janie and Earl needed to hear this and be ready for the worst.

"Okay, Barb, you do the best you can. We really don't have a whole lot of choice anymore," he told Dr. Greshin. "I think I'd better spend a little time with his parents, make sure they really understand what the situation is. I'll go dictate his H&P after I've talked some more with them."

"You do that, Bob. Listen; be sure to check in with us now and then to see how things are going. We might need your help."

To his surprise, he found that Josh's parents seemed fully aware of the perilous state of their son's health. Janie must have detected a note of self-reproach in Dr. Gilsen's manner. "Dr. Gilsen," she said, gently touching his hand. "You and I know we've done the best we can. There's nothing we'd have done any differently, even knowing what's happened. We've just got to let the surgeons do their job and hope for the best. None of this is your fault."

What he wanted to do was give Janie a hug, but the chill down his spine commanded his attention, like a clear warning call from a long, cold distance.

As Dr. Gilsen walked on to the elevator on his way to the fourth floor and the operating rooms, he again thought back on the recent events and the things that made absolutely no sense. He couldn't shake the feeling of something impending, something both far off and near at hand. There seemed no pattern or explanation, and why the undercurrent of fear and anticipation? He had been through difficult times with patients and their families many times before, but he never felt anything like this.

The elevator stopped at the fourth floor, but it wasn't until the doors started to close again that Bob realized where he was, and leaped forward to catch the doors before they shut. He stepped out into the fluorescent green stillness of Surgery's domain, then turned left down the hall and into the surgeons' dressing room. He had earlier changed into scrub clothes, and in the dressing room found the locker he had borrowed, and hung up his lab coat. He then put on the paper shoe coverings, cap and mask, and headed through the inner door into the OR suite.

Josh's surgery was going on in OR number three, and Dr. Gilsen headed down the tiled hallway to the room with the bright white light and surgical noises. The atmosphere in OR three was palpably tense. Knowing better than to bother Dr. Greshin's concentration, he walked over toward Josh's head, and stood quietly next to the anesthesiologist, peering cautiously over the green drape. Unable to see anything meaningful between the heads and arms of the surgical team, he concentrated on the monitors set up by the anesthesiologist, but with Josh already on the heart—lung bypass, and with his core temperature cooled to a subnormal level, there was not much he was able to decipher.

After a silence of several minutes, Dr. Greshin eventually acknowledged his presence. "Hi, Bob. Glad you could come by. We're really just getting going, getting this old valve out. It's gonna be slow going. Things look just about like they did on your tape, which is not good, but so far no surprises. How did things go with his parents?"

"Actually, they seemed to have a real good grasp of the situation. They just said to do your best."

"Yeah, they're good folks, hope they hold up okay."

Dr. Gilsen stayed another fifteen minutes, then realizing acutely that there was absolutely nothing he could do to be helpful, excused himself, telling Dr. Greshin that he would inform Josh's parents that, for the present time, things were stable, and to please page him if anything major developed.

"Will do, Bob. Why don't you go get some rest? I reckon we'll need your help when we try to get him off the pump, but that's a ways off."

He left the way he came in, tossing his paper apparel in a large wastebasket in the surgeons' dressing room, and reclaiming his lab coat. He glanced at his watch, noting the time of 6:40 a.m. Thinking about it, he realized that he really didn't have much to tell Janie and Earl. Josh's heart and lung functions were being taken over by complex machines, and he was in the coma of general anesthesia. Somehow, despite all of this, he was still alive, though the border between life and death seemed rather indistinct. *Better talk to Janie and Earl,* he thought. *Can't tell them much, but at least they'll know we care.*

The surgical waiting room was one of the more depressing places in the hospital. The furniture was worn and faded, and the place smelled of years of smoke and perspiration. The carpet and walls were of a nondescript gray-green color that aged poorly. Janie and Earl were the only ones in the room when Dr. Gilsen entered. He let them know that, as far as anyone could tell, things were stable with Josh, and that, if anything changed, he would let them know. Janie thanked him, then told him that he was beginning to look rather haggard, and to go get some rest.

"Thanks, Janie. I'll try," he told her, then left to head back to the ER and find out what it was that Judy needed to see him about.

He had known Judy since his cardiology fellowship, when she worked as evening nurse in the Coronary Care Unit. She was new then, and fairly nervous, but always competent, and dearly loved by the desperately ill patients in CCU. The years had made some changes. By necessity, she had developed a "thicker skin", and was better able to handle the tough losses that go with the territory. Her competence became more apparent to physicians and the other nurses, and when major "staff restructuring" was felt to be needed, she seemed the logical choice for night supervisor in the ER. In the three years since she left the CCU, Bob had seen little of Judy, as he didn't venture into the ER very often after 11:00 p.m., and it was seeing her tonight, in the familiar setting of caring for the acutely ill cardiac patient, that reminded him of how much he had missed her. Bob had always trusted Judy completely, and had found her to be ever willing to hear him out when he had a gripe about patient care, or just needed a soul to share his thoughts. So now, after these years, in the middle of all the critical care and hectic doings of the past few hours, she had asked to see him. But it wasn't just that she needed to ask or tell him something. There was a strange tone of commanding urgency in her request that could not be denied.

Thinking about it as he headed toward the emergency room, Bob again felt the tingling icy sensation in his spine.

# Chapter Six

As the faint light of dawn reached the windows, Tom stirred himself awake, taking a few moments to orient himself to his surroundings. He was in a small room in Lady Vincente's chambers, and had been sleeping on the floor on top of some quilted cloths and under a woolen blanket. The air in the room was chilly, and a faint musty odor lingered. By the meager light coming in from the high window, he could see that the room was richly furnished and had been well used. On some oak shelves on the wall across from him were numerous large, old books. On a dark, heavy desk near his feet were more of the ponderous books, some piles of writing paper, quills, and what appeared to be items of commerce. A magnificent tapestry hung on one wall, depicting a knight on horseback under a flowering tree, with a flaming yellow sun and jagged mountains.

As a page, he found himself often within the noble houses, waiting to receive or deliver messages, and had developed the habit of lingering, as time would allow, to inhale the atmosphere of wealth and comfort therein. For sleeping quarters, however, he invariably found himself in a corner of one of the servant's rooms, usually a cold, hard, dark place shared with the local vermin. Last night had been different, very different.

The evening began for him with anticipation of great doings. The heightened noise and activity about the Council chambers had signaled to all the working pages that important and interesting errands were likely, and the talk suggested that even journeys might be coming up. There was nothing more enticing to an adventure-seeking page than a possible distant journey, and those lucky ones that had had the privilege often seemed to find themselves being promoted to higher duties. Though Tom was as excited as any of the other pages, he displayed a casual attitude, preferring to listen and absorb what he could of the talk and gossip, as the information might very well prove useful someday. Throughout the afternoon and early evening, as expected, pages were dispatched with regularity on business of the Council, but most of the errands were mundane matters of little interest or consequence. As the meeting ended, a few of the pages were asked to accompany individual councilors as they left, presumably to assist with unfinished business or personal tasks. This could either be an honor or sheer drudgery, depending on the councilor and his particular needs or whims.

As Councilor Rust left the great chamber, the pages involuntarily drew back, for it was no honor among them to be picked by "Old Carrot". As Tom was picked from the group, he could see slight jeering smiles on the faces of his fellows, but he chose to ignore them and pretend that this was, in fact, a high honor. At the time he did not realize that pretense would become reality in ways beyond his wildest reckoning.

"Come, page," the councilor had said, "there are matters of great urgency and delicacy I must attend to before tomorrow. I will need your assistance, and may need it for many hours."

He remembered they had gone first to the earl's own chambers, high above the great courtyard. Tom sat for over an hour in an anteroom within while Councilor Rust met privately with the earl. He could not hear what was said, but knew from the tone of their voices that the discussion was one of intensity and importance. At one point in their talking, Tom distinctly heard the name of Lord Vincente mentioned. He heard no details, but assumed that their discussion must have had something to do with the recent death of the beloved nobleman, and possibly the painters and potters. Rumor among the pages said that the deaths were related, and that foul play was suspected. Despite heightened effort, Tom could hear no more of the conversation. Nevertheless, he was determined to listen and learn whatever he could, for the evening was bound to be interesting, and very likely full of surprises. Rust came out of the meeting flushed and agitated, his awkward movements made more so by the tension visible within him.

"Come, page," he said "we must be off. There is much to be done, and the evening is already upon us."

They left the way they had come in, but much more quickly. As they walked out into the cold dusk air, the councilor gave Tom his first errand, to go to Lady Vincente's quarters, and inquire after the lady's health, and to ask, no rather to do all but insist, that the councilor be allowed a small amount of time to meet with the lady over matters of extreme importance to the council and all the people of the island. He was then to go straightway to Councilor Rust's quarters with the lady's reply.

"Mind you, these are issues of some urgency, son. Do not waste precious time. You will be rewarded accordingly."

"Sir, it will be done as you direct."

When Tom arrived at Lady Vincente's house for the first time that evening, he was met by Frieda, the lady's trusted old servant. "What is your business, boy?" Her manner was curt and defensive. "Don't ye know M'lady's ailing? She's not fit for business or visitors."

Tom was ready. "My good woman," he said, "I am sent on errand from Councilor Rust, who comes by way of the earl himself, with matters of extreme urgency. The good councilor has sent me to inquire of the lady's health, and further, to request that Councilor Rust be granted the honor of speaking briefly with the lady of this great house."

Frieda was somewhat taken aback by the eloquence and firm bearing of this diminutive page. Contrary to her initial purpose, she hesitated, then said, "I can only tell ye this, page, that I will convey your message to her lady-in-waiting. She shall then decide if M'lady is fit enough this night for a visitor. Come, it is bitter cold outside. Ye may await word within."

"Bless you, my good woman," Tom said, as Frieda let him into the hallway, closing the door quickly behind them.

As Frieda went to deliver Tom's message to Jeanne, Tom amused himself as he usually did when waiting in the noble houses, by taking careful note of the surroundings, matching what he now saw with what he had learned of the family through rumor, teaching and his own brief experience. His expression, as usual, was unreadable, his carriage alert but casual. Beneath that surface, though, Tom was intensely interested, actually excited. Within these walls was an air of learning, of adventure and creative energy he had not previously experienced. Somehow, he knew he would be coming back here, and that made the excitement more intense.

It was not Frieda, but rather Jeanne, who returned from within. She looked suspiciously at the page, who seemed to be standing rather complacently in the hallway. "Listen, page," she began, "my lady is ill, and not fit for meeting with lords and councilors. Frieda says though that you bear a message by way of Councilor Rust and the earl himself. If this is then true, you may tell Councilor Rust that he may see the lady, but only on these terms. First, that I will be in attendance with the lady, and that if I deem it necessary due to M'lady's health, I shall make the visit end at once. Second, that the time shall, indeed be brief, and I will keep a time glass within her chamber to ensure its brevity. Thirdly, that if what you or the councilor represent should be false in any way, M'lady will make complaint directly to the earl himself. Is this clear, page? Can you deliver this message to the councilor as I have given you?"

"I can, and I shall, mistress," Tom replied, and left to bring the message to Rust.

Tom and the councilor were back within the half hour, being let in again by Frieda, only to be told by Jeanne that the lady was too ill to accept a visit at that time, that perhaps later that evening or in the morning her state might be improved. Councilor Rust was clearly vexed, but he remained composed, apparently realizing that a show of indignation would not be very likely to gain him admittance to the lady's chamber. But there was something more that caught Tom's eye, a hint of what appeared to be genuine concern, mixed with what he could only think must be fear or dread.

The councilor never did get his meeting with the lady that night, though the two of them made three more trips to her chambers. Finally, it was decided to have Tom stay at the lady's house, and to send him with the message if the lady should be sufficiently recovered to receive Rust's visit.

Tom remembered the sudden air of panic later that night when Lady Vincente's condition took a turn for the worse, and being dispatched, not back to Rust's quarters, but rather to summon master Craycroft. It was a poorly kept secret that the master had himself been a page in earlier years. They knew that, even though he was not an actual member of the Council, Craycroft held more power and authority than any single member. Tom now understood why. True power, he decided, lay not in birthright or inheritance, but rather in the ability to gather and use knowledge.

It was knowledge in those books, Tom realized now, as he got up and began to inspect his surroundings. He had received a little training in letters from his father before he took ill. It was enough of a start to allow Tom to get further education in reading and writing wherever and whenever he could, to the point where he could now read most simple text, and some Latin. The light in the room was just enough to make out a little of the text in the books. He carefully and quietly paged through some of the magnificent volumes within the room. There were Bibles and other liturgical works, as well as books of regulations and what appeared to be law, but were too complex to decipher. There were volumes of history as well as stories and poetry.

He could not say why, but a single small volume caught his attention. There was nothing particularly striking about the book's appearance, merely a rather thin, gray, leather-bound volume, nestled between two larger, more magnificent books on the shelf at eye level. When he pulled it down from the shelf, Tom noticed the plain cover with no writing or design upon it, as well as the accumulated dust of time and neglect. Opening the cover, he discovered that the text was small, with handwriting unlike any he had seen; legible, but with no beauty or elegance, and with a peculiar backward tilt to the letters. The first page identified the subject matter with the following notation:

> Of powers and dangers learned in Eastern lands. Notes taken for the benefit of any who may be in great need.
>
> Drachma, the elder.

Tom stared at the open page with a mixture of awe, apprehension and unbearable excitement. His father had told him years ago of Drachma, the elder, his namesake. Local folklore spoke of a wild scoundrel, arriving with the wind, frightening the women and children, stirring up the youth with tales of magic and adventure, then disappearing with the moonless night when the king's men arrived, armed and dangerous. It was said that he eluded all efforts at his capture and might still be alive, somewhere in the great forest, never caught and never tamed. Tom's heart was pounding as he looked around to make sure he was not seen, then he slipped the slender book beneath his cloak.

The house was still, silent, and he was alone in the small room with the books. Despite his intense desire to do so, Tom did not feel he could afford to be caught reading the text he had just borrowed (or so he told himself he had done). Instead, he picked up his bedding, folded it, and then piled it on a chair by the door. By now his full bladder and empty stomach were both sending him signals he could not ignore, so he set off quietly in search of the servants' quarters, where surely someone would be awake, and perhaps direct him appropriately and be able to provide some bread.

The hallway outside his room was still dark, and he had no light of his own, so he walked along cautiously, touching the wall, heading for the dim light at the end, remembering that Frieda had seemed to go that way last night, returning apparently to her quarters. The relative warmth of the interior hallway was a welcome change from the chill of the room, but Tom shivered still, from emotion and anticipation. *I must get to my hideaway this morning,* he thought. *I cannot risk letting this fall into wrongful hands.*

"Good morrow, page." Tom started at the voice. It was Frieda, speaking from the room he had just passed. "It is yet early, and all the household is mercifully sleeping. Come, son, I'll show ye the pantry where there's to be some bread and dried fruit for ye. Jeanne asked as I look after your needs this morn."

Tom involuntarily felt under his cloak, reassuring himself that the book was still well hidden. "My thanks, good woman. Yours is a most generous house. What of your lady? Is she at rest? Is there need of Master Craycroft?"

"Aye, but not yet. M'lady appeared to be quietly sleeping when last I saw. Come, son I promised to take care. Ye have need of sustenance."

Together they walked down the hall toward the light, then turned left, then continued past two doors to the kitchen. A small oil lamp was burning within the kitchen, providing just enough light to see. Frieda found some loaves of yesterday's bread within the cupboard and some dried fruit in a storage bin. As she was getting the items together she turned to Tom. "I imagine ye'll have need to relieve ye'self. Just go down that way, the second door. It'll take ye out back. I'll start getting ye something warm to drink."

Tom found the door to the servant's entrance and stepped outside. The sunrise was, by now, magnificent, coloring the entire eastern sky and lighting up the bare trees of the forest. Knowing he was alone, he reached inside his cloak once more and pulled out the book to take just one more look. The pages were of a thick paper unlike any he had seen in the books commonly available, and had an unmistakable, subtle odor of the sea. He turned the pages, noting again the peculiar writing, and let his eyes fall on the first few paragraphs. As he read the opening lines and felt their warning, an unfamiliar sensation, a chill, distinct from the chill of the air, shot down his spine.

Be warned, ye who venture to read these lines, for there is much power of which we have little knowledge, and even less control. To summon forth the fearsome Powers that exist within the stuff of life, and within the Earth and Heavens, even in the times of direst need, is to put one's very soul at the mercy of Powers and Principalities beyond reach of human hands and human reason. Nevertheless, I endeavour, as I must, to record for the future generations of the Earth, what I have learned of these awful forces and how they may be sensed and perhaps called upon when the need is truly great.

Be further warned that knowledge contained herein is more precious than purest gold. The possessor of these secrets shall be at all times in mortal danger. The powerful of the Earth can and will sense the threat that this knowledge carries. If ye read no further, and replace this whence it came, ye may return to life as always, free of this danger.

This, then, is the final warning. Turn the page and all shall be for the reader as never before. Ye can never return!

Tom heard a sound from behind the door and quickly shut the book and slipped it back beneath his cloak. He ran down the steps, and quickly relieved himself, his heartbeat pounding in his head.

*Later,* he thought, *I must consider this later.*

Trembling from cold, excitement, and fear, he returned back up the stairs, through the servants' entrance, back to the kitchen where Frieda waited.

"My dear boy," she gasped, "what happened? The look of ye tells of great fear."

"Nay, dear woman, it was nothing. I was merely startled by an animal beneath the steps."

"Ah, likely the old fox we've seen about. Come, sit ye down and have some bread and drink."

Gratefully, Tom sat down at the old table and hungrily attacked the loaf of bread, his mind reeling at unimagined possibilities.

# Chapter Seven

The emergency room was quiet now, at seven on Saturday morning. Bob walked into the staff lounge, where he found Judy Morrison giving her report to the day supervisor, Alonza Chaves. Lonie was a good nurse, with years of experience and many battle scars, who listened now with casual alertness to her younger colleague. She was a little surprised to see Dr. Gilsen, and more than a little concerned.

"Hey, Dr. Bob," she said with cheerfulness that sounded a bit forced. "What're you doin' here at this hour on Saturday morning? Aren't you supposed to be sleeping, and letting the residents do the work? You look awful. Musta been a rough night."

"Hi, Lonie. Sure was a rough night, and kinda still is. Actually, as far as my end of it is concerned, I've done about as much hell raising as I'm likely to for at least the next few hours. I'm sort of on break, and I've come to see your lovely colleague. I see you're busy right now, though. Look, Judy, I'll wait up in the doctors' lounge on the fourth floor till you're done with report. Why don't you either come on up or page me when you're ready?"

"We're just about done, actually," Judy replied. "Just give me a couple of minutes. Why don't you just plant it in that chair over there?"

Bob sat down gratefully in the old stuffed chair in the corner, his fatigue now both visible and palpable. He found himself drifting comfortably into reverie as the nurses continued their report. He reclined the chair and propped his feet up, and as he did so he slipped quickly into dreaming, images of dappled forest floor in springtime coming to his mind, a sweet breeze carrying the scent of freshly turned earth. The image carried him far from the stuffy confines of the medical center and the city in winter, quiet, but alive with possibility. Yearning for something elusive, something sensed but not yet realized, he imagined himself taking the path into the forest, in the vibrant return of life and warmth.

"Bob, I brought you a cup of coffee. It looks like you could use some. You still take it black?"

Judy's voice brought him reeling back to the present. He shook himself back to alertness, with the forest image rapidly fading from his mind, leaving only the yearning. Judy was smiling down at him, with a smile both comforting and disturbing. Reluctantly, he sat back up.

"Thanks, Judy. I must have drifted off. You actually remembered how I like my coffee? Remarkable woman."

"Not at all. I remember a lot of details about the people I've worked with closely." Judy set the Styrofoam cup with coffee down on the table next to Bob's chair, then shuffled through her pocketbook, which she had retrieved from her locker. "Look, Bob, I'll wait 'til you're awake properly, then I've got to show you this note I got in the mail yesterday. It's in here somewhere ... ah, here it is." She pulled out of her purse a piece of yellowed paper folded lengthwise down the middle. "You know, I still think this could be some kind of crazy gimmick or prank, but I just don't get that feeling about it, especially after what we've seen here tonight."

"What in the world are you talking about? This has been a really strange night already, full of riddles and bizarre messages, and now I get the feeling you're going to make it weirder."

"Well, you're right about that, but I can't think of anyone better qualified to discuss weird stuff with," she said with a slight wink, remembering some long nights in past years, discussing life, love, death, fantasies and metaphysical questions, all the while attending to the ventilators, monitors, IV pumps and desperately ill patients around them.

"Oh, sure. And now we're going to solve yet another baffling mystery of the universe, right?" He smiled shyly back at Judy. "Okay, okay, now you've got my curiosity up. Let me see what you've got there."

Judy handed him the piece of paper. "Look, read the whole thing before you say a word?"

"Okay."

The paper had a peculiar feel, slightly rough to the touch, and was pale yellow in color, not the typical brownish discoloration of aged paper from old books, but old nonetheless.

"You said you got this in the mail. Do you have the envelope it came in?"

"No, Bob, it didn't come in an envelope. It just fell out of the pile of mail when I brought it in the house. Now just read the thing and tell me what you think."

Bob looked down at the paper in his hand, opening it with some care, as it seemed strangely fragile. Inside was a note, handwritten in black ink, in rather large, uniform lettering. The words were legible, plainly written, but in a peculiar script, with the letters slanted to the left. There was no date or any indication of origin. With just the slightest sense of fear and anticipation he read the words of the odd epistle.

Greetings!

Whosoever receives this message, know ye that it has come from a people in great need. I know not who will read this, nor where, but I trust in Providence that it shall be received in a spirit of trust and good faith.

My appeal shall be simple; that, good reader, ye should find it in your heart to take my message to one qualified and skilled in the arts of healing, as befits our most urgent call. Tell the healer, then, this simple fact: there shall come further messages to undertake a journey unlike any before. It is my most solemn request that ye make haste in delivery of this simple entreaty.

In humble expectation,
Drachma, the elder of the forest

Bob sat staring at the paper, unable to say a word, shivering uncontrollably. This was too much for one night. There was no way to prepare for such strange doings, and too many people depended on him being sane and rational. He wished he could believe this was all some prank, but Judy was right. It did not feel that way.

For a while, neither of them spoke. Finally, Judy broke the silence. "Bob, why don't you tell me about your night, and include all the weird stuff, then I'll tell you about mine. Then maybe we can figure something out."

"I don't know, I get the feeling there are too many missing pieces to figure anything out. And now you've thrown me into the midst of some fantasy I have no way of understanding. If I weren't so tired I might have reason to be afraid of what you're trying to pull."

"You may be right, but let's give it a go anyway. You start."

Bob though for a minute, his brow knotted as he frowned into his cup of coffee. "Okay, I'll tell you. Everything seemed pretty much normal till I got the call from Beasley, I think it was around three o'clock. Looking back on it, I can say that something about the call spooked me, though I really don't know what or why. After all these years, I've gotten used to calls at all hours, often in times of big trouble, but there was just something different about this one, like there was more to the phone call than you could tell from the words. It actually did scare me."

"Then, on the way in I fell on the stupid ice, trying to scrape it off my windshield, and was in a real bad mood by the time I made it down here. But you know what's strange? My whole mood changed when you smiled at me."

"Somehow, this isn't sounding like flattery. You want to explain?"

"Yeah, you're right, it's not flattery. It's probably nothing you were even aware of, but there was just something in that smile that caught me off guard, reminded me of something I couldn't put my finger on. Then just a bit ago, when you woke me up, I was actually dreaming, and that dream felt exactly the same as when I saw your smile."

Judy chuckled. "Now this is beginning to sound a little more like flattery. Please, do go on. I don't think I've ever been in anyone's dream before.

Bob blushed vividly, then stammered as he tried to go on.

"Oh, Bob, I didn't mean to embarrass you." Judy touched him gently on the arm, causing even more blushing. "It's just that you caught me off guard this time."

Bob took a minute to regain his composure. "Actually, Judy, you weren't in the dream . . . listen, this is kind of embarrassing; I don't make a habit of telling people my dreams."

"I can believe that, Bob. Okay, I'll try to behave, but you started, and you can't leave me hanging now."

"All right, I'll try. Just bear with me." He swallowed hard. "Anyway, this dream didn't directly involve you as far as I know. You see, I was walking by a forest in springtime. It was warm, and flowers were coming out on the forest floor, and I could smell them and the nearby plowed field. There was a path going into the woods that was dark, and kind of mysterious. I started to take that path. I wasn't really sure I should, but it was so compelling I had no power to resist. It was like being drawn by something more powerful, more wonderful than anything I had ever experienced, but at the same time I was afraid. I knew somehow that once I passed a certain point, there was no going back; then as I started walking on into the woods, I felt that exact same feeling as when I saw your smile. Then, of course, you were waking me up, and that feeling just faded away."

"Bob, now you're beginning to scare me a little."

"Why is that? Is there more to this than you've told me so far?"

"Yes, but you already know some of it. After all you were in the room at the time."

"You mean with Josh, just before his seizure?" Judy nodded.

"Now I'm really sure I don't want to think about it. That makes coincidence or a prank real hard to accept, doesn't it?"

"Yeah, it sure does. Up until that time I'd put the business with this letter almost out of my mind as some nutty prank."

"Wait a minute. If you'd done that, then why did you ask to see me? You did that before all the business with Josh."

"Oh, you're worse than some lawyers I've met. Okay, I guess I owe you some kind of explanation."

Dr. Gilsen winced, suspecting that this explanation was only going to make matters confusing and even more unbelievable. He was not at all sure he was ready. "Yeah, Judy, you better go ahead. I already feel in over my head, but might as well get the whole story. Maybe something will begin to make sense."

"I doubt it, but I'll tell you the whole scoop as far as I know it. You know, we haven't really worked together for a long time, and, in all honesty, I haven't thought about you for quite a while. It's not that I don't like you, 'cause I do. I think you're a real good doctor, and it was always kind of crazy and busy, but still fun working with you back in the unit. You know, in some ways I really miss the CCU even now, but that's beside the point. Anyway, I'm just going about my business as usual last week, working here in the ER, seeing our usual mix of the worried well and the walking disasters come through the doors, when in comes this old geezer—I mean really old, maybe a hundred or so. He comes in, he says because some dog had bitten him, and now it was looking infected. I noticed he seemed kind of odd, and had some accent that was different, foreign, but not like anything I'd heard before. As usual, we were asking him about his last tetanus shot. Through all this, he just sat mostly staring at his feet, kind of mumbling answers that didn't really make sense, but when we mentioned a tetanus shot, he sat back like he was scared stiff, and just repeated 'no shot, no shot, just treat the leg.'

"Then, when the aide stepped out of the room to get some supplies, he turns to me, stares at my name tag, then pulls me over and asked if I know a doctor of hearts named Gilsen (that's just how he said it). I said yes I did, but why did he want to know? He reached into his pocket then and pulled out a little box and handed it to me, saying I must give this to Master Gilsen, but that I was not to open it or let anyone else see it or know of its presence. You know, if it had been any of a number of other docs on staff here I might have thought it was some weird drug deal or something, but knowing you I knew that wasn't it, and for some reason I told him I'd find a way of getting it to you."

Bob looked puzzled. "You didn't recognize him, did you? He wasn't a regular patient of mine? Did you get his name?"

"No, I'd never seen him before. His name was Vincente, Carlo Vincente."

"No, the name doesn't ring a bell, and I'd remember one like that. I don't suppose you still have the box he gave you?"

"Sure do. It's been burning a hole in my purse since last week. And no, I did not open it, in spite of unbearable temptation. Here, let me find it." She reached into her purse and pulled out a small dirty brown wooden box, shaped about like a typical matchbox. Bob looked first at the outside of the box, noticing no marks, writing, or carving of any kind. It was lightweight, with the lid fitting neatly over the inside box. He opened it carefully. Inside was some soft dark blue cloth, and on the cloth was an ancient silver coin. Bob inhaled sharply.

"Judy, I know what that coin has got to be." He handed the box back to her.

"You do? What is it?" She picked the small coin out of the box, studying the markings, puzzling at the foreign writing and peculiar picture.

"It's a drachma."

"A what?"

"An ancient Greek coin. The name comes from the verb 'to grasp,' and has something to do with the number of arrows a soldier could grasp in his hand. Judy, I don't think you've got anything to be afraid of, but I'm starting to feel really nervous. If this is some kind of hoax, it's too complicated to have been conceived by anyone I know."

"But Bob, what if it's not a hoax?"

"Whether it's a hoax or not, I'm obviously someone's target, and that someone is apparently very clever, and probably very powerful. I have no experience with this sort of thing, I'm just a doctor, I just take care of sick people."

"Somebody seems to know that, and it looks like that's what they want."

Their conversation was interrupted by the overhead pager, calling for Dr. Gilsen. The page was for extension 4512, which, Judy informed him, was the OR.

"Jeez, no, it's too soon. That can only mean trouble." He picked up the nearby telephone and dialed the extension. One of the OR nurses answered, conveying the message that Dr. Greshin wanted him up there right away. A sensation close to panic hit him with unexpected fury. "Judy, sounds like trouble upstairs, I've gotta run. If I'm still around I'll call you sometime."

"Hey, look, you be real careful. It's been quite a night. Here, you better take this." She handed him the little box. "It's yours."

"Yeah, thanks," he said as he headed quickly for the hallway and the elevators, where disaster surely waited on the fourth floor.

# Chapter Eight

By the time Councilor Rust arrived at Craycroft's quarters, the master had already been up, had eaten, and had built a warm fire. It was still cold outside, but the little breeze that blew did not have the bite that it did the day before. When Rust knocked at the door, Craycroft invited him in warmly.

"Ah, good councilor, please enter. I have attempted to make my humble abode comfortable enough for our business today. We have much to discuss, you and I. Tell me, have you eaten yet this morning?"

"Aye, and well, thank you. Any word of the lady?"

"Nay, not yet this morning, but I left the page at the lady's place with orders to come at once should she require anything, or should her condition become more perilous. So, I take it as a good sign that I have heard nothing."

"That is indeed good news, Master Craycroft, but can you tell me anything of her condition of last night?"

"Only that she is gravely ill with the fever and catarrh, and I fear the worst. She is well attended, though, by her lady-in-waiting. Jeanne appears to be a most capable woman."

"Aye, she is that, indeed."

"Well, Councilor, let us go into my study while we await further word of our lady. I have no doubt that we shall hear something before long. I did leave strict orders to provide prompt reports of any changes, and further, to bring a report this morn of her condition no matter what her state."

Craycroft led the councilor through a narrow hallway to a room at the end, sealed by a heavy door. He opened the door, and the two men stepped into the master's small, cluttered study. Inside there were two desks, piled high with books, papers and odd looking boxes, jars and vials. A heavy table stood in the middle of the room, a lamp occupying the center, with more books and papers scattered about. The walls were covered with bookshelves containing an even vaster array of books, truly an impressive collection within a small space.

"I must say, Master Craycroft, you have a most remarkable collection of books, as befits a man of great learning. I have never before seen your study, but I can see now there is much substance behind your wisdom."

"Ah, Councilor, you flatter me. In truth, I am but a student, and a rather poor one, of the great minds that have produced these books. Alas, my memory does not retain all it should, so I must take voluminous notes of all that I feel might be of importance. Hence, all this clutter you see before you." He went over to the far wall and brought back a large, leather-bound volume from the shelf, setting it down on the table. "Come, Councilor, let us sit at the table. There is much we need to talk about, and I sincerely believe I shall be able to make your task, if not easier, at the least more effective and rewarding."

"Very well, Master Craycroft. I too consider myself yet a student, and eager to learn." The two men pulled chairs up to the table and sat down, the book between them.

Craycroft began, with an air of great patience. "Now, Councilor, this volume contains my written notes of all that I believe might be of importance as concerns the fearsome affliction visited upon our esteemed craftsmen. Much that is contained herein is fact, pure and simple, but much is also interpretation and supposition. For this reason, I would not ask that you read this text, but we may refer to it as need arises during our discussions. I shall be as forthright with you as I am able, and ask only that you be the same with me. What we are engaged in at the earl's request may have importance beyond our own under-standing and beyond our own lives." He caught a slight look of surprise in Rust's eyes.

"Ah, yes, I should explain that, prior to your assignment on behalf of the council; the earl had asked me to investigate, with the utmost discretion, events that have gone on to cause such distress, and to report to him what findings and conclusions may have come to light as a result. What I was able to report to the council was merely a simple summary of events with no attempt to give conclusions, and much more I have deliberately left out, also at the earl's request. You see, there are distinct advantages at times in having no official status with the council."

The councilor remained puzzled. "Why, then, would the Earl assign me a task that you had already been pursuing?"

"Quite simple, really. You see, if you investigate on behalf of the council, then two things can happen. First, the results can become official, and thereby reportable to the king's advisors. Second, if I have already done much of the work, the report can be ready sooner, and there should be little need for the king's men to do their own inquiry. Surely you will recall the last time we had the king's men disrupting our lives with an official investigation."

Rust nodded. "Only too well, I fear."

"Good, then you understand. With this in mind, then, might I suggest you tell me what you do know so far. It would be well to begin with common understanding."

"Very well, I will attempt to do so, but bear in mind that much of this is new to me, and I have not been privy to your information or even your sources thus far."

"I will, indeed, keep this in mind. Please proceed."

"From the little knowledge I have thus far been able to gain, it would appear that, beginning sometime in the late spring of this past year, three of our potters and four painters became ill and died, all without sign of ague or pox, and, as you have astutely noted, without afflicting their wives or families. If I am correct, there have been six or seven more of the craftsmen taken ill, of whom two are said to be near death, and others recovered. I fear I have little more than this with which to begin my investigation, except that, as you know from my report to the council, the people of the quarter have been stirred up by tales of curses, witchcraft and murder, and it would seem only a matter of days or weeks before word of such stories will be reaching the king's advisors. Then, as you well know, a royal inquest is sure to follow, with all the misery that would then be heaped upon our heads. Our hope, it would appear, lies in our ability to find, through our own efforts, a cause for this malady, and to have an official report ready for the king's men when they do hear of our plight."

"I would say, Councilor, that both your facts and inferences are valid, though understandably limited. I think, then, that we should begin by arming you with some of the information you will need in order to proceed with your more detailed inquiry." Craycroft opened the book, looking for a particular page. "Shall we begin, then, by building upon the information you already possess, and then proceed to establish a plan to continue the investigation into those parts of the story where much doubt exists, as time and conditions will allow."

"Indeed, that seems a most reasonable plan, in light of stories of witchcraft and murder, and it is my sincere hope that reason can be made to prevail."

"Reason, yes, but good Councilor, in my experience, we sometimes find that the truth, if it be known, may be stranger and more difficult to accept than fanciful stories of curses and magic."

Rust said nothing, but gave Craycroft a most puzzled look, as if to tease out of him what he might mean by such a statement. Craycroft, for his part, ignored the councilor's puzzled expression and, finding the page in the book he had been seeking, began his explanation of the events since last spring.

"I think it may be wise to begin by looking in some detail at the story of our first victim, as it both illuminates and confounds, and sets an example for the cases which follow." Craycroft pointed to the page in the book open on the table. "You see here our first victim was a mere youth of eighteen summers, named Alberto. It is reported that Alberto was in excellent health and good spirits throughout his young life. He had been apprenticed abroad, and became known, still at an early age, as a potter of exceptional virtue. He was brought here two years ago when the Earl had seen some of his craft while visiting his sister in Italy, whose husband had employed many excellent craftsmen, including young Alberto. Within our guild, Alberto was quickly accepted, as his manner and skill seemed above reproach, and he seemed more willing than most to do the extra work that was assigned.

"All seemed well until last spring, when his manner rather suddenly changed. Whereas he had always been a cheerful lad, he became sullen and quiet, then within weeks he became visibly weak and unable to take on the extra tasks. He would complain of pain within the head and limbs, and ask to leave work well before evening bells. His master became alarmed, and brought him to see me on one such occasion. At the time I saw him; I will admit there was little to see. His face was pale, and his eyes sunken, but this could easily have been from effects of the long winter and poor eating. I queried him about habits and appetite, and he noted only that eliminating urine seemed to cause him mild discomfort, and though there was to his breath a peculiar odor, he had not the look or smell of the diabetes mellitus, and there was neither ague nor pox upon him. His feet did appear swollen, and his belly unusually round for on so thin. I was not able to offer much help, and recommended a strong tonic at bedtime. I also requested that he be brought back to see me within the week.

"The week was little more then half over, however, when I was summoned to see him, as he was too feeble to come to see me. The sight that awaited my arrival was one for which I was ill prepared. Lying upon the cot was a sight so unlike the youth I had recently see that I had to make certain I had come the proper house. His pallor was extreme, and his lips and face were bloated almost beyond recognition. His belly protruded, and hands, feet and lower limbs were swollen grotesquely. Fluid oozed from the skin of the abdomen and legs. His breathing was rapid and full of effort, and an unmistakable death rattle was present. His sweetheart, to whom he was to be wed that summer sat quietly, weeping in a corner of the room. I will tell you, I ached at my own impotence in the face of such a tragic sight. His betrothed informed me that she had taken to his care, as he had no family. She had been giving him the tonic and brandy I had suggested, as well as fluids and purgatives her own mother had provided. For two days prior he had no urine, and had been falling into fitful sleep several hours at a time. I made careful note of the circumstances, but could offer little in the way of comfort or cure, and asked feebly if Father Henri had been called. Upon mention of the father's name the poor lass collapsed in a fit of weeping, and was inconsolable.

"Within the day, the young lad was dead, and a tremor of fear ran through the village."

In spite of himself, Rust was moved by unexpected feelings of fear, repulsion, fascination and pity. "A most remarkable tale, Master, and singular in my mind, as I have never heard before the details of this most unfortunate event. Tell me; were you able to conclude anything as to the cause of this young man's demise?"

"At first hearing of his death, Councilor, I concluded in my own mind that Alberto had likely been a drunkard, and had received rather too quickly the consequences of his habit. I made brief note of my conclusions, and thought little more about the matter until hearing of the next victim of what appeared to be a similar malady. Rather the second victim, a certain Robert of Bridgeport, had been a well-known drinker and gambler. I did not learn of my error in judgment until after the third person lost his life to this most pernicious of disorders."

"Pray, tell, what did occur, and why your conclusions changed."

"Well, Councilor, of all the individuals afflicted, the tale of the third was perhaps the most alarming, the most perplexing, and yet in some ways the most illuminating."

"The third was a painter, is that not so?"

"Correct, Councilor, a painter named Garza, a superb craftsman, trained in Florence. If I may say so, a man justifiably proud of his work. He had few friends, as he kept to his own affairs, but also no known enemies. That is why the note was so unexpected."

"The note? To what note do you refer?"

"Two weeks before he began to take ill, Garza received a most peculiar note, telling him that he would be next . . ."

"Master, you made no mention of this before."

"That is correct, Councilor, I did not, at the earl's insistence."

"What, then, of this note? Can you tell me any more?"

"I can, but I shall do more than that, as I have the actual note in my possession."

Rust inhaled sharply. The matter was clearly intriguing, but he could also feel himself falling into something bigger and more frightening than he had imagined. Craycroft was right. He would need an ally.

Craycroft went over to the desk to his right, and pulled from the drawer a small, flat box, bound with twine. He brought the box over to the table and opened it. Inside was a collection of papers and a few small artifacts. He brought out of the box a small piece of yellow paper, folded in half. He then opened the paper and laid it on the table in front of the councilor.

"Here, Councilor, is the note. What are you able to make of it?"

Rust picked up the paper and stared at it silently. It was written in a fairly large hand, with simple, unadorned script. The councilor read the note with a mixture of excitement, caution and dread. The message was, at once, both simple and confusing. He read:

Garza!

You are marked as the next. You know not what you have done but your time is at hand. All shall be made clear in due order. Know ye this, that your life shall be forfeit for a cause not yet come to pass. If there are affairs you must make straight, do so with no delay, as time is running out.

Do not destroy this note!

There was no seal or signature. Just the brief, fearsome message. Rust's hand shook slightly as he handed the note back to Craycroft.

"Master, this entirely changes how we must perceive the nature of these deaths and afflictions, does it not?"

Craycroft nodded his agreement.

"I would have to surmise that whoever wrote this letter knew of the cause of death of the first two craftsmen, and was, perhaps himself, the cause. It would therefore seem that we should seek out and find the writer of the note to obtain our answer. Do you not agree that that should be our course of action?"

A strange look appeared briefly on Craycroft's face as he answered, "Councilor, what you say makes perfect sense, and was, in fact, the approach I had myself taken when first I learned of this note. But let me direct your attention to this matter." He pulled from the same box another paper, a more formal letter, containing an official wax seal. He opened the second paper and laid it next to the first. "Now, Councilor, if you would look at these two pieces of paper and tell me what you think."

Rust stared at the two papers, side by side. A brief perusal was enough to draw the obvious conclusion. "Master Craycroft, they are written in the same hand."

"Precisely."

"Then whose hand is it that wrote the notes?"

"Look at the seal. Do you not recognize it?"

Rust turned the paper over and looked at the seal. A sudden recognition was followed instantly by a wave of nausea and pallor, "Good, God, no! This cannot be. Is there some mistake?"

"Councilor, I have taken the liberty of making a number of comparisons. The writing is all the same, and unmistakable. There is no mistake. It is his own hand."

Rust looked again at the writing, and then again at the seal. The seal contained, within a floral pattern, the letter V. Lord Vincente's seal.

"Master Craycroft, this is more than I had expected. More, I fear, than I am ready to undertake. I freely admit, I will need your guidance in the extreme, and I am willing to do whatever I must to assist you in this matter, but let this be your investigation, and mine in name only.

"Very well, Councilor, but you must also realize that I shall also need your complete attention to the matter. As well you might imagine, it is also too much for me to take on alone, which is why I asked the Earl for your . . ."

"Ah, so you asked the earl for my assistance?"

"Aye, I could think of none other more capable or trustworthy."

Rust's face became grave. "I give you my solemn pledge that I shall do my utmost to live up to your trust. I fear, though, that the consequences of our efforts will surely bring down about us powers over which we have little or not control."

"My fear is that there are powers such as these already at work, and we may yet become their unwary victims."

"Indeed."

For a full minute, neither spoke, each pondering anew their circumstances and their task. Rust, at last, broke the silence.

"Master Craycroft, there is obviously much I must learn, and little time, I fear, to adequately do so. I must trust your judgment to tell me what I must know. Perhaps then I may be of some help to you, and perhaps then we may be able to put a plan into action as regards this troubling matter."

"Very well, then, let us begin where we left off, in considering the circumstances of painter Garza. As you now know, he received this message some two weeks before feeling any illness. Evidently, he told no one of this note, but you may well imagine the turmoil he must have suffered. When he began to notice listlessness and aching in the limbs, also fatigue and loss of appetite, he was sent to see me. I saw, at that time, a young man, seemingly in good health, but in such a state of fear that he trembled. He told me of his aching and weariness, and also that the trembling made painting impossible. As he did not tell me of the note, and since the other two victims had been potters whom, I had surmised, had died of consequences of drunkenness and licentious living, I did not, at the first, realize that this young painter was suffering from anything more than a guilty conscience. I suggested to him that he see Father Henri and make full confession of anything that might be troubling his conscience, but to return should he become more ill. He told me he had already seen the father, but thanked me and went on his way. I thought little more about it until two weeks thereafter, when he returned, now a truly ill man. He told me of pains more severe in the head, limbs and back, and of difficulty breathing, as well as discomfort on urination. His pallor was alarming, and his belly round, and feet swollen. The smell of his breath was unmistakable, and I knew now that this was the same malady as had afflicted the two potters. When I asked about his habits, he told me he did not touch strong spirits, and rarely drank wine. It was then I suspected the beginning of what my old master would call an illness cluster, and took careful note of all details of what the poor man was able to tell me of his troubles. He did not then tell me of the note. Rather, on his deathbed five days later, he gave it to me with the promise that I would not mention it to anyone while he was yet alive."

"And have there been any more such notes?"

A knock at the outer door resounded through the master's quarters.

"Ah, that must be tidings of our lady." Craycroft got up to answer the door. "Await here, if you please. I shall return anon." Caycroft paused, then said, "if there be other notes, I have not seen them"

# Chapter Nine

*I hate these emergencies in open heart cases,* thought Bob, as he ascended in the elevator. *There's really never anything much to be done unless you're the surgeon with the heart in your hand. The patient's already on a machine supporting circulation and respiration. Heart rhythm, breathing and blood pressure are all meaningless, and us cardiologists just end up standing around looking and feeling useless. Why in the world would Greshin want me now?*

His train of thought was interrupted by the doors sliding open on the fourth floor. He stepped back out into the hallway leading to surgery, back into the surgeon's lounge, and back into paper booties and head covering. Donning a mask, he stepped out into the OR hallway, and down to the room where Josh's surgery continued. The room was as noisy and brightly lit as before, and, to all appearances, nothing had changed since he left.

Dr. Greshin noticed his entrance. "Welcome back, Bob. We've got us a real mess on our hands now, and I'm hoping you'll be able to help."

"Why, what's up? You having trouble with the tissues?"

"Yeah, but nothing I didn't expect. Anyway, that's my problem and I can handle that one. The reason I called you is 'cause his blood doesn't want to clot. We've got oozing everywhere, and this is no fun at all. His platelets, PT and PTT were all thera-peutic before surgery. You got any smarts about this kind of stuff?"

"I've learned a few things by necessity, but coagulation prob-lems aren't my strong point. Can you tell me what's happened?"

"Yeah, we started off Okay. Then, about two hours into this thing he started oozing from the sternum and the skin and you name it. It's just like somebody gave him some thrombolytic agent. I sure hope you know what to do, 'cause I sure as hell don't want to spend the next few hours stopping bleeders when we should be operating."

"Well, I know what we've done in the past for his bleed-ing problems, and it's worked." Dr. Gilsen had regained his usual composure. "We usually end up giving some Factor eight. The heme people seem to think he's got something like Von Willebrand's, not the typical form, but some cousin to that, and they've always said to give factor eight when he bleeds badly. It's worked before, and that's what I'd suggest right now. I don't think that would foul up your post op coagulation status too much."

"Fine, Bob, why don't you go ahead and take care of that, but please make it fast, Okay? It's getting ugly in here. I've never given factor eight to someone on a pump before." She turned to the anesthesiologist. "Richard, you ever given the stuff before?"

"Sure," he answered, "but not often. Usually for some hemo-philiac whose gotten into a wreck and is bleeding into his joints. It's no problem on the pump, actually should be somewhat easier."

Dr. Gilsen turned to the circulating nurse and asked her to have the blood bank send up two bottles of factor eight STAT. He was visibly relieved that the emergency, at least for now, seemed to be something for which he could provide some actual help. He turned back to Dr. Greshin. "How's the surgery been going, aside from the bleeding?" "Well, Bob, let me put it this way. It's no more of a nightmare than I expected. If we can get the bleeding under control, we might just be able to limp through this one with a live patient."

"Sounds real encouraging." Bob grimaced behind his mask. "You want me to tell his parents anything?"

"No, not yet. Really, there's not much to tell other than bad tissue and oozing blood. Why don't we wait and see how your factor eight performs then let the folks know?"

"Sounds Okay to me. I really don't feel ready to face them just yet. How you been doing with the valve? You been able to steer clear of the coronaries?"

A touch of annoyance crept into Dr. Greshin's voice. "Like I said, Bob, we'd be doing Okay if it weren't for this oozing. Since that started we haven't been able to do much at all but suck blood. There was a ring abscess, all right, but with a larger valve ring and some care, and just a bit of luck I think we might make it through the operation."

The sudden realization that Josh just might not make it this time hit Bob like a blow to the gut. Through all the previous illnesses and his first heart operation, the working assumption had always been that Josh would, as usual, pull through yet another one. From infancy to adulthood there had been repeated desperate illnesses, all capable of killing him, but those who came to know Josh came to believe that he would always recover. Dr. Gilsen did not feel that certainty now, and could not force himself to believe that Josh would recover. A cold sensation of fear came over him. He looked at the anesthesiologist, at the monitors, then at the surgeons. Nothing in their attitude had changed, and there was no visible change in the little he could see of Josh. Still, something had changed, and very suddenly. He felt an urgent need to find Janie and Earl, to see if they sensed anything. Maybe it was all imagination, and with all the strange doings of the night, that should seem likely.

"Barb, listen, I really think I should go talk with Josh's parents, at least bring them up to date. Just go ahead and give the two bottles of factor eight when they get up here. I'll check back with you in a little bit."

"Okay, Bob, have it your way. Thanks." Dr. Greshin did not look up from her work.

Bob turned and walked back out of the OR. He felt just a bit lightheaded, a little off balance. In the surgeons' lounge he retrieved his lab coat, and put it back on. He felt the reassuring presence of his stethoscope in the large right hand pocket. In the left was the small box Judy had given him. He hurried back out of the lounge to find Janie and Earl, presumably still in the surgery waiting room. His hand tightly clasped the box in his pocket.

Janie looked up at Dr. Gilsen as he entered the waiting room. Her face was slightly red, and eyes watery.

"Janie, I've just come from the OR, checking on progress with surgery. They've been having some trouble with bleeding. You know we've had this trouble before . . ."

"Dr. Gilsen, I don't think Josh is going to make it this time. I don't know, it's just something I feel. You know how he's pulled through all the trouble before, and every time I knew somehow he was going to be all right. Well, this time I just don't feel it."

Janie's manner was calm, but her voice cracked a little, and a tear ran down her cheek. Bob looked down, closed his eyes, and thought desperately of something to say.

Unexpectedly, Earl spoke. "It's Okay, Dr. Gilsen. We know you've done all you can, and you've always been there when Josh has needed you."

Bob swallowed hard. "Look, this bleeding is probably just like before. We should be able to take care of it without too much trouble. They'll call me if anything bad happens in OR." He reached into his pocket and pulled out the little box. "Listen, you remember me telling you about Josh mentioning something about Drachma, and Dr. Hurwitz explaining that it was a Greek coin?"

Janie and Earl both looked at him bewildered expressions, saying nothing.

"Well, the strangest thing happened. Apparently, some very old man came into the ER this past week and gave one of the nurses a little box to give to me." Janie and Earl both looked at Bob as if he was the strangest thing that ever happened. "Inside, of all things, was a little Greek coin, a drachma."

"What in the world . . ." Janie didn't know what to say or do.

"Here, let me give it to you Maybe some day you'll figure out what all this means." He held out the little box for Janie to take.

"Oh, no, Dr. Gilsen, I couldn't take anything like that. It's yours." Janie spoke with utter firmness.

"Well, at least take a look. It's kind of an interesting little item. Here, in this little box."

Janie examined the tiny box cautiously, then opened it with care. Inside was only the blue cloth, no coin.

Bob gasped. "My God, it's gone!"

Feeling like a total fool in the presence of these good people, Bob simply sat down and shook his head. He could think of nothing to say. He felt lightheaded again, slightly nauseated, and very confused. He began to wonder if this was all related to sleep deprivation. *This should all be a dream, but it's not*, he thought, *There's too much of the stench of reality about this place.*

Janie sat down next to him, touching him lightly on the arm. "Dr. Gilsen," she said, getting the words out with some difficulty. "What do you really think? Do you think Josh has a chance this time?"

Bob found her return to the matter at hand both disturbing and reorienting. *At least she doesn't think I'm a total lunatic if she still values my opinion*, he thought.

"Listen, Janie, as long as he's still alive I think he's got a chance." He didn't even convince himself of this. "I've got to be honest with you, though. One reason I came to see you now was because while I was in the OR just now, I got this sudden scary thought that Josh just might not make it this time. There wasn't anything rational about it, and nothing seemed any different in the room, including what I could see of Josh just a sudden weird feeling, that's all."

Janie said nothing for a few moments, then spoke, with tears streaming down her cheeks. "It's Okay, Dr. Gilsen, I'm glad you told me. I hate like all the world to lose him, but you're right, something changed, and I don't know what it was. How can you tell, though, how things are going while he's on the heart-lung machine?"

"That's a tough question, Janie, and I don't think there's any easy way to answer. Typically, we see how they do as we try to get them off the machine. That's usually where the real trouble shows up, when we can't get them off bypass. That's when we've got to make some of our most agonizing decisions."

As Dr. Gilsen was talking, Jane was mentally substituting "Josh" for "they" and "them", beginning to feel already the agony of trying to make some impossible decisions with profound consequences. She did not feel ready.

"I don't know, Dr. Gilsen, I just don't feel able to make decisions like that. I'll need your advice and help more then ever."

Dr. Gilsen didn't feel ready either. Normally, under these circumstances, he could be professionally detached and offer rational but comforting advice to grieving family members. Not so with Josh and his parents. It was all too much like family. Besides that, there were all the bizarre twists taken in these last extraordinary four hours. The more he thought about the coin, he suddenly felt like screaming. "Who in the world would go into the surgeons' lounge, early Saturday morning, find a lab coat hanging in a locker (Okay, it was unlocked), get a little box out of the pocket, take the little coin that was in the box, then replace the box in the lab coat pocket? It just didn't make any sense at all. "Perhaps," he thought, "it's not going to ever make sense."

Suddenly he remembered what Judy's strange letter had said about more messages to come. "Could this be," he thought. "No, it's just not possible. Things don't happen this way, not in real life." Somehow, he couldn't find himself a working definition of real life at that moment, "Maybe if I get back into the mundane, things will sort themselves out."

"Listen," he said to Janie, "I'm going to start making my morning rounds. They'll page me to the OR if anything more develops with Josh. I'll keep in touch with you, I promise."

"That's Okay, Dr. Gilsen. I know you've got work to do. You go ahead. We'll be waiting right here."

Earl reiterated, "You go ahead, Dr. Gilsen. We'll be all right here. Thanks for everything. We really appreciate all you've done."

Dr. Gilsen swallowed the lump in his throat "Thanks, Earl," he said as he got up to leave.

Rounds that morning certainly started off as mundane as anything Dr. Gilsen could have hoped for. There were no surprises in either the CCU or the Medical ICU, but enough details to attend to that Bob could keep his mind fixed on matters immediately at hand. The nurses kept his mind fixed on matters of immediacy. They did not seem to acknowledge either the cloud of sleepiness in his eyes or the fact that he was wearing a scrub suit. It all seemed to fit with the dreary winter Saturday morning.

After an hour and a half, he noticed, to his surprise, that he had heard nothing from OR. He began to wonder again how things were going down there. "Surely if there were problems they would call," he told himself. As he tried to continue rounds on the sixth floor, he found himself thinking more and more about the surgery, and finally gave into his need to know.

"Look, Karen," he told the charge nurse on the medical floor, "I'll be back in a bit. I've just got to go down and see how surgery's going."

"You could give them a call, you know."

"Yeah, I could, but it's not the same. Not in this case."

"Oh, who is it?"

"Josh Crabtree."

"Oh, Lord, is he back in surgery? Already?"

"Uh huh, and it's not good."

"No wonder you look like you do. Okay, I understand. You go ahead. Things on the floor will wait. Tell me how things come out will you?"

"Will do."

He got up to go, but at that moment he heard himself paged STAT to call the ER.

"Oh, God, what now?" He picked up the phone and quickly punched in the ER number. A woman's voice answered.

"Emergency Department, this is Brenda, may I help you?"

"This is Dr. Gilsen, I was paged."

"Yes, Dr. Gilsen. Dr. Beasley needs to talk to you right away. I'll get him."

There was a slight click as she put him on hold, then a brief pause before Dr. Beasley's voice came on. "Bob, this is Jerry. Sorry to bother you again, but I've got a guy down here with chest pain and pulmonary edema, big time, looks like he might code any minute, says he's a patient of yours and wants to see you."

"Sure, I'll be there. Who is it?"

"Wait, let me get his chart. Okay, here it is ... his name's Vincente, Carlo Vincente."

The chill that ran down Bob's back was so startling that he couldn't speak.

"Bob, you still there?"

He swallowed hard, then answered, "Yeah, Jerry, I'll be right down."

Karen caught his startled pallid expression. "Dr. Gilsen, what's the matter? Bad news?"

Bob shook his head. "I don't really know, Karen, it's too hard to explain." He sat with a look of utter bewilderment on his face, not moving.

"Doc, don't you need to get going?"

"Oh, yeah, thanks Karen. I'll be back whenever."

"Right, I'll see you when the storm blows over."

Dr. Gilsen got up once more and headed down the hall toward the elevators. He usually allowed himself a little pride in his ability to think and act clearly in emergency situations, but at the moment his mind was swimming and confused, with all the unexpected and inexplicable stuff happening. If he could only see an understandable pattern in all this it might begin to be less unnerving. As it was, things were occurring seemingly at random, but with a bizarre feeling of connection. He felt as if he were inside a complex building, looking for the way out, with instructions written on the walls in a foreign language he did not speak.

The elevator doors opened and almost closed again before Bob jumped in. He winced slightly as the elevator passed the fourth floor, realizing that any news of Josh's surgery would have to wait until this newest emergency was at least evaluated and some degree of treatment rendered. *But who in the world is Carlo Vincente, and why would he claim to be my patient? Surely I'd remember a name like that if he were someone I had seen before. I don't even want to think about all the other stuff Judy said about him. And that damned coin! Maybe if I just concentrate on treating his medical problems I won't have to contend with all the weird stuff, and maybe eventually a pattern will form. Then again, if he's already coding . . . No, better not think like that.*

The elevator doors opened back up, and Dr. Gilsen walked quickly out and headed toward the Emergency Room. He knew without being told to head for the cardiac room. Inside, where Josh had been a few hours before, on the exam table, was what appeared to be the oldest man Dr. Gilsen had ever seen. No, he realized, he had never seen this man before. A face like his was unmistakable. The man was very thin and his body appeared frail, but his face was one of immense power. In the center were eyes of pale blue, deep-set beneath white bushy eyebrows. His nose was hawk-like and commanding. His incredibly wrinkled face was encircled by a mane of pure white hair and a long, unkempt beard.

As expected, he had been attached to all the appropriate monitors, and all the usual tubes and wires emanated from his body at the center of the room. His cardiac rhythm was rapid and irregular. His respirations were deep and rapid. He was sweating profusely, and his color was extremely pale. Dr. Gilsen again found himself in familiar territory, quickly taking in the information available from everything visible and audible in the high-tech ambiance of the cardiac room. He glanced quickly at the man's chart, noting what had been recorded of his chief complaint and history, and his physical findings. A glance at the wall showed that his chest x-ray confirmed neatly what was apparent from Dr. Beasley's brief description of "big time" pulmonary edema—acute heart failure.

Dr. Gilsen walked to the center of the room, pulling his stethoscope automatically out of his pocket and hanging it on his neck. "Mr. Vincente," he said. "I'm Dr. Gilsen. I'm a heart doctor. I don't remember seeing you before. Do you know me?"

Carlo Vincente did a most unexpected thing. He smiled, and the smile froze Bob where he was.

"My God," he thought, "it's the same smile!"

As the inescapable rush of feelings swept over Bob, Mr. Vincente sat upright on the table, stared straight at Dr. Gilsen, and said in a loud, clear voice, "*Master Gilsen, it shall be today. Drachma, beware!*"

For an instant, all eyes were turned to Dr. Gilsen, standing in the center of the room, looking pale and stunned. Then the alarms screamed.

"He's gone into V fib! Quick, get the paddles charged up to 200, and call a code!"

Carlo Vincente had collapsed back onto the table, unresponsive. His cardiac rhythm had instantly degenerated into the deadly chaos of ventricular fibrillation. The experienced ER staff did what they had learned to do as a matter of course in these times of sudden catastrophe, mobilizing resources at their disposal in a coordinated effort at resuscitation. As the alarms went off, Dr Beasley quickly got the emergency paddles while a nurse placed the gel pads on Mr. Vincente's chest. When he was sure that the area was cleared, he pressed the buttons, sending an electric shock through Carlo's chest. His body jerked, and the paddles were withdrawn. All eyes turned to the cardiac monitor. Instead of the expected return to organized rhythm, the monitor showed a nearly flat line.

"Ah, hell, he's gone into asystole. Come on, let's get CPR started!"

The cardiac room remained busy with the resuscitative attempt for the next forty-five minutes, past the point where it was obvious that the effort was futile. Dr. Gilsen knew Carlo

Vincente was gone, and that his passing was somehow meaningful, but he did not know who this man was or why his brief contact made a difference.

"Listen," he said, "we might as well quit. We haven't had a recognizable rhythm since we defibrillated him, and it's been over half an hour. I doubt we'd get anything like a human being back even if we brought him back now."

Quietly and unceremoniously, the efforts stopped. The time was noted, and the participants filled out, returning to prior tasks. Dr. Beasley reassured Dr. Gilsen that he would take care of the paperwork, and Bob, for his part, let Dr. Beasley know that he had never seen Mr. Vincente before now, and that the medical examiner would need to be notified, as no one seemed to know anything about the man.

"I'll take care of it, Bob. Why don't you try to get some rest. You look beat."

"Thanks, Jerry, I'll try, but they're still operating on Josh. I've got to go find out how that's going."

"Yeah, well, take care. Let me know how that all comes out, Okay?"

"I'll do that. See ya."

Dr. Gilsen headed out of the ER again, profoundly weary, confused, and now notably hungry. He decided to stop by the cafeteria and pick up a roll, maybe some juice, and another cup of coffee before going back up to the OR.

Janie was a bit surprised to see Dr. Hurwitz come into the surgery waiting room. He was obviously fatigued, blood-splattered, and had been sweating. With no word of greeting, he sank noisily into a chair facing Josh's parents.

"Folks, it's been a long night, as you know. We're all kind of worn out. They're just now closing the chest, and Dr. Greshin will be out in a bit to talk with you. She wanted me to come out and let you know the operation's almost finished. It's gone about as well as could be expected. We ran into some problems with bleeding, but Dr. Gilsen baled us out of that one very nicely. After we got that under control, we got the new valve in, and it seems to be working fine. We even got him off the pump without too much trouble. His rhythm looks good, and, from what we can tell so far, it looks like a success, at least for now. He should be out in the Thoracic Surgery ICU within the hour. You got any questions?"

Janie didn't know what to say. *How could anyone bring good news so joylessly*, she wondered.

Earl spoke after an awkward pause. "You say he's doing okay for now? Have you told Dr. Gilsen?"

"We paged him, but found out he was down in ER helping with a cardiac arrest patient. We'll get word to him, don't worry."

"Oh, dear, the poor man," Janie said.

As she was talking, Bob walked in holding his cup of coffee. Seeing him, Janie sprang to her feet, ran over and embraced him, spilling some of the coffee on his lab coat and the floor.

"Oh, Dr. Gilsen, he's okay! They're just about done with surgery, and he's off the pump. He just might make it after all."

Bob flashed a brief, childlike grin. He looked toward Dr. Hurwitz, who nodded agreement.

"Janie, that's great! Listen, how are you holding up?"

"Worn out, but okay. Very relieved."

"I bet. Why don't you and Earl go get some breakfast? The cafeteria's open. I'll find you down there."

"Thanks, I'm not really hungry, but I could use some coffee. Earl, you want something to eat?"

Earl was unable to talk through the tears, but nodded.

"Okay, look, I'll just be a bit. I'm sure Dr. Greshin will want to talk to you as well. We'll find you. Now, go get a little something to eat."

Bob and Dr. Hurwitz headed off toward the OR, while Janie and Earl walked toward the elevators. On the way, Janie noticed the pay phones, and realized she should call her family with the news.

"Wait a minute, Earl, let me call Ma. I told her I'd let her know how things came out."

They stopped at the phones, and Janie fumbled in her purse, feeling for her wallet. She pulled it out, and opened the change pocket to get a quarter. The coin she pulled out felt odd and curiously heavy. She looked at it closely and realized suddenly that the writing was foreign. She gasped as the significance of this dawned on her. She looked, but Dr. Gilsen was out of sight, going toward the operating rooms.

# Chapter Ten

After he had finished eating and drinking, Tom turned his attention back to his surroundings. The light from outside was increasing, and he could better perceive his location, both within the kitchen area, and in relation to the bedchambers and the library where he had had the good fortune to spend the night. With the ever-brighter light, he realized, also came increasing exposure and risk. He was not sure now that if he did decide to return the book, that he could do so without being seen and raising an alarm. The palpable presence of the book, and its provocative warning, began to feel a little like a burden within his cloak. Still, he realized, eager curiosity was certainly going to win out, if only he were able to get the book to his secret sanctuary.

Frieda discovered, as Tom was looking about, that her young charge had completed his small meal. She came over and took his flask and small tray, and piled them with other dishes from the previous night.

"Come," she said, "let us inquire after m'lady's state. She might be needin' a thing or two. We shall ask Jeanne if she might be awake."

Tom nodded, got up, following Frieda's lead. "My thanks for the food. I was in need."

"Aye, not yet full grown. Ye'll need much sustenance."

The two of them walked back the way they had come, this time more easily due to the light. As they passed by the doorway to the study, Tom stole a glance inside, and as he did so he felt again the impact of the book's warning. For an instant, he thought about slipping back inside and returning the book, but the instant passed, and he kept going, walking a pace behind Frieda.

They turned down the hallway toward the lady's bedchamber, and stopped at the entryway. "Now, lad," Frieda said, "I shall go inside and ask how m'lady is doing, and whether she is in need. Wait ye here. I know in my heart we shall have need of your swift legs ere the morning is done."

"I shall wait," Tom replied.

Frieda slipped discreetly into the lady's bedroom as Tom waited in the entryway, much as he had done the previous night. It was only a short while before Frieda returned with the news that the lady was, for the moment, resting well and not in need of anything immediately. She would, however, soon need more aromatic oil for the mist apparatus Master Craycroft had provided for her use.

Tom saw the opportunity at once. "I shall go at once, as I am now certain where some more may be obtained." What he did not mention was that his secret enclave was near enough to the alchemist's that he could easily slip over for a minute without being missed. What he further did not tell her was that any excuse to run to the alchemist's shop was, to most of the boys, a real treat, and carried the breathless implications of danger and adventure. "I shall return anon with the oil. Is there anything else?"

"Nay, child, just that. Now bundle up. It's still bitter cold outside."

To his surprise, Tom found the servant's concern touching, and not the least demeaning. "Aye, I shall. I return in haste."

With that, he strode quickly down the hall toward the main doorway, and stepped back out into the chilly morning air.

En route to the alchemist's shop, Tom became sorely tempted to look within the book, but resisted, as it still seemed too risky. The sky was clear by now, but some cold mist lingered about the village below the hill on which the castle stood. Tom paused along the wall, and peered out over the battlement, looking down on the fog-enshrouded village. The early morning sun gave everything a slight orange glow, and a very faint breeze carried the salt smell of the sea. The transient beauty of the moment was enhanced by a newfound sense of purpose and opportunity. Tom felt with some certainty that his own adventure had indeed begun. He smiled to himself and, clutching the book beneath his cloak more tightly to his side, strode off again toward the alchemist's.

An unwritten rule within the earl's domain evolved which allowed pages to move about unhindered and unquestioned, regardless of rules affecting the movements of others. Pages, had become the vital communication link throughout the domain, and their free access to any persons and places of import was held nearly sacred. As a natural consequence of this, pages quickly learned not only the fastest routes between any two points in the castle or village, but also the most interesting routes. Each, of course, developed his own favorite pathways and sanctuaries, and jealously guarded his secret knowledge. For the more observant and politically astute among them, this acquired fund of information provided an avenue for personal growth and gain within the political structure. Master Craycroft, it seems, had become the best example of the growth of power and prestige that could be won on the basis of learning obtained as a page.

Having witnessed first-hand the display of skill and subtle use of power by the master, Tom became more intent than ever to learn the secrets of such success. He realized now how the provocative title and warning of the book had found him such a ripe target. As he scurried along the stone walkway usually reserved for the Guard, Tom thought back on the interaction between Master Craycroft and Councilor Rust, recognizing that hints of major personal and political power and influence had existed, and that the death of Lord Vincente, as well as the grave illness of his daughter, could mean major disruption in everyone's life.

*Then, what of the painters, and potters,* he thought to himself, *a connection surely exists to explain these deaths and illnesses.* Then a most startling thought sprang up in his mind, catching his imagination like a burst of lightning. *Could the author of this book, my namesake, be connected as well with these strange doings?* There was no rational reason to think so, but somehow, deep within his consciousness, he became convinced that Drachma, the Elder, was, in fact, still having an influence over the events of the past months, and further, that he himself needed to find out how and why.

Tom arrived at the alchemist's shop, and knocked loudly at the door, knowing old Falma was hard of hearing, and moved slowly. He waited, then after a full minute, the door opened slowly, and Falma cautiously let the young page inside.

"Aye, Laddie, you return. Come inside. It is cold indeed out there. I shall believe it to be a good omen that you have come, for it must mean the lady yet lives."

"Aye, Master, that is so, or it was when I left the lady's quarters just a little while ago. She is alive, but in need."

"Ah, yes. What does Master Craycroft require of me this time?"

"Simply more of the aromatic oil, as you provided last eve."

"Very well. I believe there is more that you may take, but please let Master Craycroft be aware that the oil is fast becoming scarce, and I shall not be able to make more until springtime."

"I shall tell him, but believe me when I say the matter is of some import and urgency. It is not at all certain what the lady's fate shall be, or whether she will live even this day."

"Lad, I understand this. I shall get what you require." The old man turned and shuffled back down the hallway, and turned into his laboratory. Tom followed quietly behind him, and watched intently as Master Falma drifted in among the counters and tables covered with all manner of bizarre bottles, flasks, tubes and solutions.

Tom sensed that the old man's appearance might be truly deceiving. He appeared the most benign, gentle and benevolent sort, a true grandfather. His hair was white, and hung in thin strands from his large, pale head. His lips were thin and parched, barely visible between beard and bushy moustache. His eyes, however, signaled great power held in check. There a dangerous gleam existed, suggesting knowledge beyond common understanding, as well as a spark of adventure.

The old man found, on a shelf at eye level, a small dark bottle, which he brought down and placed on the counter.

"Lad, do you have the little bottle I sent with you last night?"

"No, Master, it is still within the lady's chamber, and she was resting. I dared not ask for it."

"Aye, that is well. I shall find another." He pulled out a drawer, and rummaged about until he found a tiny-stoppered flask.

"Here, I shall pour a wee bit in this flask for you. Mind, you take care not to spill a drop of this precious fluid." The gleam in his eye was suddenly more obvious.

"I will be most careful, Master Falma." Tom found himself unable to look straight into the master's face.

"Good, Laddie. Your name, if memory serves me, is Tom, is that correct?"

Tom felt a slight tremor of fear, sensing that the old man was not just making conversation. "Aye, Master, but my given name is Drachma."

"Ah, well," said the master, betraying nothing more than the sparkle in his eyes. "Who might your parents be, then? Are they folk of the village?"

"Yes, they live in the village," said Tom, his voice faltering slightly. "My father is Eusebius, a gardener by trade, but he is ailing. My mother is Annabelle, a seamstress."

"Hmmm," said the old man, "I do know your father. You are their youngest child, is that not so?"

Tom felt an icy shiver run down his back. *Why would the old man know or care*, he thought. *I sense some deeper reason for his questions.*

He swallowed, then answered, "Aye, I am the youngest of four boys and five girls."

Falma turned his gaze directly toward the youth. Tom flinched, noticed that the old man was smiling sweetly at him. Something in that smile told him that there was no immediate danger, but that he was stepping into something that whispered of danger from afar.

"Come, Lad, I know you must return in haste, but before you go I must show you something you may find of some interest. Come, over here." He led the boy back to a tiny room off the laboratory, lit with two oil lamps. The room was dark and close, and in the center stood a desk and chair. The master went over to the desk and opened a drawer, taking out a small wooden box. "Here, Lad, I wish you to see this," he said, opening the box and holding it out for Tom to see.

Tom stepped closer and looked at the box in the master's hand. Inside the box, on a blue velvet cushion, was a small silver coin.

"Tell me, son, do you know what this is? Do you recognize it? Here, you may pick it up."

Tom gently took the coin from its cushion and looked at both sides.

"Nay Master, it is a coin of silver, but I do not know its value or origin. Its characters are foreign to me."

The master chuckled gently. "You said more than you meant when you told me you know not its value or origin. In truth, it is a coin of antiquity, of ancient Greece. It is called a drachma."

Tom now stared openly, his jaw dropping. He found himself unable to speak.

Falma laughed; a hearty, robust laugh that seemed to shake the room. Tom continued to stare silently.

"Here, Son," Falma said, after he ceased laughing, "I want you to have this. It is yours by rights, and I give it to you, asking only that in return you come back to see me when you may, so I may tell you more that is connected with this coin, your name, and your namesake."

He placed the box, with the coin inside, in Tom's sweaty hand.

"Now, here also is the oil you came for. You must make haste and return to the good lady's house. I know she is in need. Just remember to come back when you are able. There is much to learn."

Tom's voice finally returned. "Master, I know not what to say, but I shall do as you ask, and do so with eagerness. Your knowledge and generosity leave me ashamed and speechless, but I thank you."

"Good, Lad, now get about your business. You know the way out. Be certain you close the door securely as you leave."

Tom started to leave, but before he stepped out, he turned and looked back. Master Falma was in the doorway to his laboratory, and when Tom looked back, he spoke.

"Son, the book. It is too much for you now. I must recommend that you put it away securely for the present time. We shall discuss it when you return."

Tom stood, frozen to the spot, unable to utter a sound.

"Now, Lad get you hence. You have work to do."

The gentle command released him. Wordlessly, Tom stepped back outside, carefully closing the heavy door.

On the way back to Lady Vincente's house, Tom took a detour, which went past the unused winery. Through a half door in the inner wall of the winery, he entered a tunnel that ran below the outer wall of the castle, to a disguised exit near the marsh. As he felt his way through the tunnel, he cursed himself for not stopping by and dropping off the book on his way to the alchemist's.

*He must have seen the book beneath my cloak,* he thought with dismay, *but now in Heaven's name would he know which book it was, even if he were able to see part of it beneath my cloak?* Tom realized anew that Master Falma's appearance was most deceiving. He wondered how many were aware that, beneath what seemed a forgetful, slow, doddering, half-deaf old man, was a person of immense knowledge, wielding power beyond reckoning. Then there was the matter of the book itself. If nothing else, Tom's brief encounter with the master had been a vivid confirmation of the book's warning. Falma was obviously familiar with the book and with its author. That fact alone spoke of power and danger.

As he stepped out of the tunnel into the light beyond the castle wall, Tom was reeling from the unmistakable blow dealt him by what seemed to be fate or destiny. He had clearly been recognized and appointed by powers beyond his understating to a task he did not, in any way, understand. He felt suddenly small, inadequate and frightened.

Tom quickly ran over to the old copse of trees that marked his particular hideaway. There he stepped within the copse and found the old upturned wine barrel under which he had hidden some of his favorite personal possessions. He pulled out an old linen sack that contained a few small books and drawings. Looking through the contents to assure himself that the articles were safe from vermin, he took the book from under his cloak and slipped it inside the sack, along with the small box containing the mysterious coin. He then replaced the objects under the barrel and made sure the area appeared as natural as possible, and only then hurried back to the hidden entrance to the tunnel and back into the castle.

As he arrived, breathless, at Lady Vincente's quarters, he was met again by Frieda, who said little, and gave away nothing with her expression. She ushered him back toward the lady's chambers where Jeanne awaited. Jeanne's face suggested concern but not alarm. Tom took some measure of comfort from that.

"Here, Madame," he said, "I was able to procure some more of the aromatic oil, though Master Falma, in truth, did say it was in precious short supply."

Tom could not help but notice a very brief look of alarm that appeared on Jeanne's face at the mention of the master's name.

She looked down quickly, then, upon regaining her composure, took the small flask from the page's hand.

"You have done well, page," she said, walking into the lady's bedroom. "Come with me. I must tell you of our lady's condition so you are able to give Master Craycroft a full report of her state, as promised."

Cautiously, he stepped into the room behind Jeanne. The room remained warm, with a rather close, moist feel. In bed lay Lady Vincente, asleep, or at least not responsive to his arrival. He noticed a sickly sweet odor as he came closer to the bed, and could hear the deep rasping of the lady's breathing. He followed Jeanne's lead to the far side of the room, and listened attentively as she gave him a description of Lady Vincente's progress through the night.

"Mind you, lad, to tell Master Craycroft that I did follow his direction exactly, that the lady yet lives, but that life seems to be ebbing from her, even as we speak. She has not been in pain, and the terrible spells of coughing have lessened."

"I shall report what you tell me, Madame," he replied, "but please tell me also if there is anything at all the lady desires to have or to see. I should be obliged to do all in my abilities to find or provide such as she may need."

The page's thoughtfulness caught Jeanne by surprise. Here was no ordinary village urchin pressed into service, but rather a boy older and wiser than his years would suggest, and capable of seeing beyond the single task at hand. She looked deep into his wide, dark eyes. He did not avert his gaze, and Jeanne could detect no sign of pretense or guile.

At that moment Lady Vincente spoke, her voice barely a whisper, but carrying easily across the room.

"Come here, son," she breathed. "I thank you for your concern, and I do have two requests I wish you to honor." Tom and Jeanne slipped quietly to the lady's side. It was clearly a major effort for the lady to speak at all, but she made her words distinct and understandable.

"Pray, tell me what you wish my lady, and I shall do as you require." Tom answered.

Lady Vincente continued, "Firstly, I wish to see Councilor Rust. If he be not with Master Craycroft, find him and ask that he come to see me." Tom nodded in response. "You know there is little time . . ." Her voice trailed off weakly, and she seemed to lapse back into sleep. Tom waited in silence. He was about to speak when her eyes opened again and she continued. "Secondly, I would have you go . . . to Master Falma . . . the alchemist," her voice now barely audible, with her words coming at great personal expense, "tell him . . . from me . . . that he should proceed . . ."

"Proceed with what, my lady?" Tom asked after a pause.

"Just that . . . to proceed."

Her eyes closed again, and she appeared totally exhausted. Tom glanced at Jeanne, noting a look of near terror in her face, then turning back to the lady, he said, not knowing if she heard, "It shall be done as you asked, my lady."

Tom straightened back up, and turning to Jeanne, he noticed that her expression had returned again to normal. Silently, they both left the room. In the hallway outside the bedroom Jeanne spoke softly, but with urgency in her voice.

"Now, page, make haste to Mater Craycroft's abode, as M'lady has asked, Please, do not tarry."

"I am away, Madame," Tom replied, "and I shall return with the master and the councilor. I will not delay."

The brilliant sunlight stung his eyes as he stepped back outside, heading across the courtyard to Craycroft's quarters. He strode purposefully, knowing his own adventure had begun. Far off, from the village, came the sound of a trumpet, signaling the approach of a messenger.

# Chapter Eleven

"Bob, you wouldn't happen to have any idea where Jeff Reichert is staying down in New Orleans, would you? I've a notion to give him a call as soon as I get out of the OR, kinda fill him in a little on what's happened in his absence."

Bob could not tell if Dr. Greshin was being sincere, or trying to drive home a point. "No, Barb, I don't know for sure, but the meeting is mostly at the Hyatt. You might try there if you really want to call him."

The surgeon grunted acknowledgement, and continued working on the final touches of her supremely difficult and technically brilliant performance. Despite himself, Dr. Gilsen could not help but feel somewhat awed by the fact that she had accomplished what appeared to be a successful valve replacement under conditions so far from ideal. Any misgivings he might have about Barbara Greshin had nothing to do with her surgical skills. They were clearly second to none.

She finished the last stitch, then turned her attention back to Dr. Gilsen. "Listen, Bob, we've gotten through the surgery so far with a live patient, and that's great. And you know as well as I do that we surgeons usually get annoyed when you all start hanging around and messing with our patients at this point."

Bob winced, but tried not to show it.

"Anyway, this is no routine coronary bypass, and believe me, I'm gonna want and need your messing around this time. We've got to give this guy our best shot. This whole business has been something really complex, and I'm not ashamed to admit it's got me a bit nervous."

Dr. Gilsen savored this moment. While he had been standing in awe of her surgical expertise, Dr. Greshin was actually admitting that she would need his help. How very true that this was not routine.

He turned his attention to the middle of the room, to Josh. There, on the steel operating table, he lay naked, as the scrub nurse attended to his chest wound, and made preparations to move him to the thoracic surgery ICU. More helpless than a newborn baby, he lay still on the table, his heart beating regularly, but not yet breathing on his own. What was obvious was that the life that was there remained because of massive technological support, as well as the consummate skills, knowledge and training of the medical, nursing and allied staff. Bob realized, with a sudden glimmer of insight, that there was more. Somehow, looking back on all the craziness of the past six or seven hours, he caught a faint sense of purpose. There was nothing clearly defined or even fully recognizable, but an unmistakable sense that there was meaning, as if this were all a part of something larger.

He turned back to Dr. Greshin. "Barb, you've done a superb job, and I'll do everything I can medically to keep him going. I really do owe you for this one." There was no point in trying to explain his insight to the surgeon.

"Thanks, Bob. Why don't you come with me while I talk to Josh's parents? Are they still in that ghastly waiting room?"

"No, they should be in the cafeteria by now. At least that's where they were headed."

Dr. Greshin gave the scrub nurse some last minute instructions, checked with the anesthesiologist to make sure there were no further surprises in the immediate forecast, then headed out the door, Dr. Gilsen half a step behind.

An ever-increasing sense of fatigue began to settle over Bob as they walked down the hospital corridors. He would not allow himself to give in, but kept going, motivated by an inescapable sense of obligation, the driving force behind all the best physicians and students he had known. Still, he realized, this was all going to catch up, and probably soon. The task of completing rounds loomed larger and more onerous in his mind with each passing hour. The promise of a few hours sleep seemed infinitely far off.

He wondered to himself how he ever managed in training to keep up these hours week after week. True, he was older now, but not that much older. Somehow, though, long hours took a greater toll, and recovery was slower.

As he walked along, automatically, behind Dr. Greshin's purposeful stride, he found himself drifting again in his thoughts. His mind again took him far away from this place, away from corridors, buildings, and the city; away from the unspoken demands of the ill and dying. The smell of springtime and newly turned earth enveloped him as he found himself once more on the path to the woods. The yearning now was too strong to resist. His feet took him, without resistance, toward the inviting cool darkness of the deep forest. The path led him in among the great trees, their early leaves of spring dancing in the faint breeze. From the forests interior came the smell of moss and pine, and, very faintly, the sound of running water. The path led inward, and down a gentle slope. He continued on, drawn by the primeval voice he sensed but could not hear. As he entered the deeper woods, the sounds of birds became more hushed and distant, and the sound of water more clear. The stream had to be ahead and to the left, just the way the path seemed to lead. The forest floor had become softer, darker and moist. The trees, both hardwoods and conifers, were ever greater and more ancient. Bob glanced back to see the way he had come, but could not make out the path behind. The way ahead was clear, but the way back seemed to have been shut off. His throat tightened with fear, but still the yearning was more powerful, and he continued, following the path toward the sound of water.

"Ah, Master Gilsen, you have chosen, and you have been chosen. That is as it should be."

Startled, Bob turned toward the voice. An old man in a gray cloak stood beside him. He opened his mouth and tried to speak, but no sound came.

"Do not speak now. You are not able, but listen."

He did not recognize the speaker, yet the voice was utterly familiar. The old man continued. "I am Drachma, the Elder. You have been chosen by people in great need, though they do not know it. Your tasks will become clear in time. Heed well what I tell you now, as my time is short." Bob stood, awestruck and unmoving. "You may bring with you one instrument of your trade but no more. When next you hear my name, you shall have until the count of five to grasp in your right hand that which you would bring. I can tell you no more now, but wish you well in your endeavors. You have been wisely chosen."

The old man turned and began to walk away. Bob turned and started after him, but his foot caught a root and he fell forward. He could feel himself falling . . . falling . . .

A sharp pain in the forehead where Dr. Greshin was touching him woke Bob from his reverie. His head was swimming and there was a loud buzzing in his ears.

"Bob, are you okay? What'd you do, trip or something? Smacked your head pretty good, it looks like, on that cart."

Bob looked around, momentarily bewildered. He was lying on the floor of the hallway. Dr. Greshin was kneeling over him, and there were three others standing behind her. There was a stretcher next to the wall beside him. He sat up and shook his head. The buzzing decreased, but the pain in his forehead only got worse.

"Yeah, Barb, I'm Okay," he lied. "I guess I did trip. Getting clumsy in my old age." He stood, slightly shaky on his feet, and looked around to reorient himself. They were just outside the cafeteria. Janie and Earl were in the hallway, looking concerned and somewhat bewildered. Bob flinched as he caught their expression, realizing what a fool he must seem. It would be almost funny if things weren't so serious.

"What happened, Dr. Gilsen? Are you all right?" Janie's voice projected both alarm and concern.

Bob flushed visibly. "I'm okay, Janie, just tripped and hit my head on the stretcher."

She was unable to restrain her nursing instinct, and rushed to Dr. Gilsen's side. "You don't look too good. You're awfully pale. Come on, there are chairs in here. You better sit down. We should get you some ice for that bump on the head."

Bob found Janie's rapid patter oddly comforting, almost maternal. He relaxed, and followed her lead into the cafeteria, then sat down on the closest chair. Earl and Dr. Greshin followed closely. Dr. Greshin reexamined Bob's head wound, and, satisfied that there was no serious harm done, stepped back again, allowing Janie to apply the ice that someone had brought from the drink dispenser.

The atmosphere in the room was one of confusion and expectation, with no one knowing quite what to say or do. Finally, Bob broke the awkward silence.

"Listen, I'm fine. I just tripped and hit my head. Honest, I'll be just fine. I could use a cup of coffee, though, if someone could find one."

Earl moved toward the cafeteria line. "You take it black, Dr. Gilsen?"

"Yeah, Earl, thanks. I appreciate it." He allowed himself the luxury of leaning back in the chair and closing his eyes, holding the ice over his forehead wound. With his eyes closed, the image of the woods came rushing back to his mind. "No, not now," he thought to himself. "I can't drift off now!" With an effort, he opened his eyes and brought himself back to the reality about him.

He could see that Dr. Greshin was becoming visibly uncomfortable waiting for Earl to return with the coffee, so she could get on with the business of relaying news of the surgery to Josh's parents. Earl did return, and set the Styrofoam cup down beside Dr. Gilsen.

"Thanks so much, Earl. Look, why don't you and Janie sit down. I'm sure Dr. Greshin would like to tell you about the surgery."

The mention of surgery caught Janie's attention. She sat down and focused her intense eyes on Dr. Greshin. "Please, tell us. How did it go? How is Josh?"

Dr. Greshin responded carefully. "Josh is alive, and off the bypass. By now he is probably in the Thoracic Surgery ICU. He is on a ventilator, and will be, at least until tomorrow."

A dense veil of anxiety lifted from Janie's face at these words and she sighed.

"The new valve is in place, and actually, once the bleeding stopped, the operation went fairly smoothly."

She went on to describe the details of surgery, and what to expect over the next forty-eight hours. As she did so, Dr. Gilsen sipped his coffee, fighting a constant battle to avoid drifting off again. "Maybe making rounds would be just the right thing to keep my mind and body occupied," he thought. "This coffee's about enough to wake the dead, so maybe it'll help too."

The room was suddenly quiet, and Bob noticed that all eyes seemed to be pointed at him. It was as if they were all expecting him to say something. *Oh, great,* he thought, *now what?* He had no idea where the talking left off, or what he could possibly say that might fit the occasion.

He hesitated, and then stammered.

"What Dr. Greshin did, Janie, was one remarkable job. Considering the pre-op circumstances, the fact that Josh is not only alive, but off the pump, with a new functioning aortic valve, is truly an amazing piece of work. I can honestly say that I know of no one who could have done any better."

He thought, for a fleeting moment, as he glanced at Dr. Greshin, that there just might have been a hint of blush on the surgeon's face. It was gone in an instant, if were there at all.

"We're not out of the woods, by a long shot." Bob smiled secretly at the surgeon's strangely appropriate metaphor. "But Dr. Gilsen and I will continue to work very closely together to try to give Josh the best possible shot at recovery."

Janie turned her gaze downward, and the room was silent again. When she looked back up she was smiling through her tears. "Thank you, Dr. Greshin," she said, "you have no idea how reassuring it is to hear that. I know in my heart that Josh will get the very best care possible."

Bob found Janie's simple trust moving and humbling, as he knew all too well the limits both of modern medicine and his own expertise. He know how often things just seemed to happen, out of the control of any technology or human skill. He was also acutely aware of how often physicians created situations in which their patients became completely dependent for their very lives on the knowledge, skills, and technical support provided by their doctors. The image of Josh, naked on the operating table, his life supported both by modern medicine and by forces beyond control or understanding, came flooding back to his mind.

"Janie," he said, "you know, of course, that we can't provide any guarantee. There are things that can happen over which we have no control."

"Dr. Gilsen," she replied, smiling gently and touching his forearm, "after all these years with Josh, you'd think I might have come to understand that by now. I've had to learn to live with an awful lot of uncertainty."

"You're right, Janie, of course. I only meant that . . ."

"I know, Dr. Bob. Thank you."

He smiled, somewhat sheepishly. "Listen, I've got to go finish making rounds, but I'll make sure I see you again before I leave, and give you a progress report."

Janie nodded, and Bob got up from his chair, stood for a moment to make certain he was steady on his feet, and then headed for the hallway. The need to complete rounds now seemed an almost unbearable burden, but the task lay before him. There was no way around it.

He must have been quite a sight. When he arrived back on the floor, the first thing Karen did after noticing Dr. Gilsen's approach was to intercept him and whisk him off to the medication room.

"Listen, Dr. Bob, I'll not have you scaring all my patients making rounds looking like that. What in the world happened to you?"

Bob tried to explain his mishap as casually as possible, while Karen busily straightened his clothing and hair.

"Okay, I can see that this is going to take a while. Save the explanation for later. Look, I'll pull the charts of the patients you don't really need to see—just give me the verbal orders on them, then we can concentrate on the sick ones, or at least the ones that look worse than you do. I do believe we've got to get you out of here."

"I appreciate that, Karen. The idea of finishing rounds and getting out of here seems improbable, but highly desirable."

"Yeah, I bet it does."

They went out to the nurses' station and sat down. As Karen went through the charts of the less sick patients, Bob listened, more or less attentively, and added comments and gave orders as appropriate, Karen taking down the orders as he gave them. They then went off to see the sicker patients on the floor. Through force of will, Bob was able to concentrate enough to make what seemed accurate analyses and recommendations at each patient's bedside. Though they made progress, it seemed to Bob the kind of sluggish progress made by large committees with no agenda and no time limitations.

Between patient rooms, it took all Bob's concentration not to drift off again into reverie. The strange appeal of the woods grew ever stronger, and harder to resist. The rich, deep sights, sounds and smells seemed always at the edge of his awareness, and the yearning ever more powerful, almost painful.

Finally, after having seen the last patient, Bob and Karen headed back to the nurses' station, laden with charts and loose papers.

The page went out over the loudspeakers like a shout. "Dr. Gilsen, call 2547 STAT!"

"No, not again! I'm not at all sure I can take this anymore. That's the TSurg ICU, isn't it?"

Karen nodded.

"Look, why don't you leave those charts in a pile here. I'll come back and finish writing on them when I can."

"Sure, Dr. Bob. You go do what you have to. These charts will wait." She couldn't keep the look of worry off her face. "You take care of yourself."

Running on depleted energy reserves, Bob rushed off again.

The Thoracic Surgery ICU looked like a modern medical technology demonstration project. More than any other place in the hospital, the patients seemed lost amid the great, noisy overgrowth of machines. Josh was in bed five, and did not look good. Nestled in the middle of a great tangled network of tubes, wires, and machines was the patient. Around the bed and between the tubes and wires were the doctors, nurses, and technicians looking after him. Bob recognized Dr. Greshin, Dr. Hurwitz and one of the nurses.

With a practiced scan of the room and monitors, he was able to determine that Josh was, in fact, still in atrial fibrillation. His heart rate was 154, and blood pressure was too low, at only 84 over 40. The blood oxygen saturation was low (and apparently falling), and there was no urine in the catheter bag. The news from the monitors was not good. A look at Josh himself only served to confirm the dismal picture presented by the monitors. His color was ashen. The ventilator alarm signaled repeatedly, indicating high ventilatory pressures, evidently from fluid leaking into air spaces from pulmonary capillaries.

Bob turned to Dr. Greshin. "What happened? What went wrong?"

"Well, Bob, his pressure had been running kind of low, and his urine output fell off to nothing. We figured it would probably be a good idea to start some low dose dopamine. Well, that helped the pressure for a while, but about ten minutes ago he went into atrial fib, and you know as well as I do that he's not going to tolerate this fast a heart rate very well."

"What have you done so far?"

Dr. Hurwitz interjected. "We've drawn gases and 'lytes, and we were just getting ready to cardiovert him. Dr. Greshin though you should be here when we do."

Dr. Gilsen nodded, then looked toward the crash cart.

"You got the thing charged and ready, synchronizer switch on?"

"Ready when you are."

"Then go ahead, Mark. Why don't you start at sixty joules? See if that doesn't convert him."

One of the nurses applied the gel pads to Josh's chest as Dr. Hurwitz reached for the defibrillator paddles. He checked the settings on the defibrillator. "Okay, sixty joules. Synchronizer on."

He placed the paddles on Josh's chest, over the gel pads, looked around to make sure everyone was clear of the bed and connections. "Okay, all clear! Shock on five. One . . . two . . . three . . . four . . . five!" He squeezed the buttons on the paddles. There was a momentary pause as the defibrillator synchronized with the irregular heartbeat, then a quick jerk of Josh's body. All eyes turned toward the cardiac monitor.

A brief, half-second pause, then the chaotic return of atrial fibrillation.

"Didn't hold it, Mark. Better try again at a hundred twenty joules."

Dr. Hurwitz reset the defibrillator, checked again to make sure the synchronizer switch was on, then placed the paddles back on Josh's chest.

Dr. Gilsen heard a voice, and looked around to see if anyone else heard. Apparently no one did. The voice was clear and commanding, but from nowhere in particular.

"I am Drachma! You may come."

Bob's face lost its color as a sensation of utter panic gripped him. "No!" he thought. "Not now! I'm not ready."

"All clear! Shock on five."

He wanted to flee, but could not. His legs were frozen in position.

"One . . . Two . . ."

Without conscious awareness, Bob's right hand slipped into his coat pocket and gripped his stethoscope.

"Three . . . Four . . ."

Without thinking, his left hand reached for Josh's leg.

"Five!"

# Chapter Twelve

Tom did not have long to wait at Craycroft's door after he knocked. The master had obviously anticipated his arrival, and let him in hastily.

"Come in, Tom. You must have news to tell. Councilor Rust is within. Pray, come with me and tell us both of the lady's condition. I am led to believe, by your late arrival, that the lady yet lives. Is this not true?"

"Aye, Master, she lived while I was yet within her chambers, though life did seem to be slipping from her."

The two reached the study where the councilor waited.

"Come within, Page. Tell Councilor Rust what you have just told me, then please continue, telling whatever news you may have."

Tom blinked in the relative darkness of the study, and, looking around, noticed Councilor Rust seated in a large chair. Rust looked intently at the youth, then spoke.

"Ah, Page, we have eagerly awaited your arrival. What news of our lady? If there is life, then perhaps hope . . ."

"Good Councilor, as I told Master Craycroft, the lady yet lived while I was there, but, alas, seemed to be fast fading. I too hope, as you, that she is yet alive. If you would permit my impertinence, might I suggest that we proceed with due speed to the lady's chambers. I know not how much time she may have among us, but I should say that the lady herself bade me request your presence at her side."

The master and the councilor both were startled at the page's boldness, but said nothing.

"If you will," the page continued, "I can tell what I know as we go. I fear that time may be precious."

"Tom," Craycroft answered, "that is wise counsel. We shall do as you suggest."

"This is no common page boy," though Craycroft, as the three made ready for their excursion outside. "He carries the mark of great purpose. I must remember to ask Felicia about the book. Drachma, he said, is his given name. Could he be the reason?" The master fought back a tear as an uninvited flood of memories raced through his mind. Images of his own youth crowded his consciousness. The excitement and promise of those days! And springtime in Glen Oak Forest . . . the smell of newly turned earth . . . the sound of clear running water.

With an effort, he turned his attention back to the urgent matters at hand. Tom was correct. Time was precious, more precious than gold.

Cloaked against the chill wind outside, the three stepped out from Craycroft's quarters, headed down the steps, then across to the courtyard. As they walked, Tom told them what he knew of the night's doings, leaving out all mention of Falma and of Lady Felicia's second request.

As they walked, huddled against the cold wind, they were surprised by the sudden appearance of a rider, coming swiftly from the main gate. The horse and rider clattered to a halt beside the three. The messenger tossed back his hood, then leaned over to speak with the two men.

"Kind sirs, I have business of great importance to bring before the earl. Can you show me the way to his abode?" Rust pointed across the courtyard toward the earl's quarters, and indicated where he might tether his horse. "I thank you," he said, turning in the direction indicated, then turned back to Rust and asked,

"I am told there is an old loremaster named Falma that lives here. Is that yet true, does he live?"

Rust and Craycroft looked at each other, then at the messenger, taking note of his uniform and his horse.

Craycroft answered, "It is true that Master Falma lives, though he is becoming infirm. He lives across the courtyard and down the eastern walkway." He pointed in the direction, showing where to enter the walkway.

"Many thanks, good men, and fare thee well."

He turned his horse smartly, then rode off across the courtyard, toward the earl's abode. The three watched him ride, Tom most intently.

*Loremaster!* Tom thought. *Falma, a loremaster. What a rare bit of knowledge that is.*

"I was unaware," he said, turning to Craycroft, "that Master Falma was master of lore as well as alchemy. That is not common knowledge."

"I would say it had been a well guarded secret." Craycroft muttered. "At the very least, it was 'till this moment. I would caution you, Tom, not to make it common knowledge."

"Aye, sir, you have my word of honor."

"That should suffice. Come, now, we must continue."

The trio set off again, walking briskly toward Lady Vincente's home. Arriving at her door, the councilor knocked loudly. It was Jeanne this time who let them in.

"Thank God you have arrived!" she sounded breathless, and the atmosphere within the house reflected her sense of anxiety.

Craycroft spoke. "Aye, we have come. Tell us, Jeanne, how is the lady?"

"She is . . . yet alive, but . . . I fear . . . Oh, Master Craycroft, is there naught you can do?" Jeanne's resolve nearly broke, but she summoned all her strength, fighting back a torrent of emotion, held barely in check. "My lady, she is dying!"

The master reached out soothingly, and touched her forearm. His voice was deep and calm. "Come, Jeanne, take us to the lady's chamber. I do not know if there is anything to be done, but we must be at her side. Her need is great."

Tom trailed discreetly behind the others, remaining at the doorway as they entered Felicia's room. The atmosphere in the room was almost stifling, and the sickly sweet smell now obvious to the point of being almost overpowering.

On the bed, drenched in cold perspiration, Felicia lay, gasping for each breath. She seemed unaware of her companions' entry. Her eyes were half closed, her mouth open. The color of her lips was now a deep purple. Her cold, mottled arms lay at her side.

Craycroft came around to the right side of the bed, and knelt down at the head. He reached out and touched the lady's cheek. "Felicia, we have come. I am here with Councilor Rust and Jeanne."

Felicia's eyes opened slightly, and her head turned toward the master. She spoke, her voice barely audible between gasps. "The page . . . Tom . . . is he . . . with . . . you?"

Craycroft motioned for Tom to come in. "Aye, Lady, he is here."

The Master swallowed hard. "Lady, I must tell you, Tom's given name, is Drachma."

For an instant, her eyes opened fully, and in that moment Craycroft saw again the smile that pierced him in his youth.

"Dear Will," she said, softly, distinctly, "that . . . I already knew. The book . . . he must . . . have it . . . by rights . . ."

Craycroft nodded. "Where is it, Lady?"

"The study . . . the room with . . . the . . . tapestry."

Tom stood, motionless with fear and alarm. The color drained from his face. He wanted, more then anything else, to flee, but he had no power to move.

Lady Vincente turned feebly, her gaze directed toward the youth. Her voice was now barely a whisper. "Tom," she said, "my message . . . to Falma . . . you remember?"

Tom tried to answer, his voice coming out cracked and hoarse. "Aye, Lady," was all he could get out. He could feel the gaze of all the eyes in the room turned toward him. His head swam, his vision became blurred as his knees gave out and he sank to the floor.

Jeanne moved, quickly and gracefully, to the youth's aid. She cradled his head in her lap as he gradually regained his color and awareness, then sent Frieda, who had been quietly in attendance, to get a tumbler of medicinal brandy. As Tom regained his equilibrium, and was able to sit back up, attention returned to Lady Vincente.

Craycroft, who had remained at her side, noticed once again that she was trying to talk. "My Lady," he said, "what do you wish?"

"Rust, is he here?"

Craycroft motioned for the councilor to come over.

With a supreme effort, Felicia turned to Rust and breathed, "for the council . . . I ask that you . . . speak . . . for me. Falma . . . has summoned . . . help. I know not . . . how . . . or what. Listen . . . to . . . him . . ."

"Lady, I . . ."

Her head fell to the side, her breathing ceased, and the color vanished from her face.

An anguished wail leaped from Jeanne's throat as she ran to her lady's side.

"Lady, no, no! My lady, come back!" Heaving sobs came in uncontrollable paroxysms as Jeanne let go her emotional reins, "No, Lady, no, no! Do not leave!"

Craycroft slumped into the chair by the bed, buried his head in his hands, and wept. Silently, impotently, privately. The pain of this loss was more than words could tell.

The cold air stung his throat as he ran. He crossed the courtyard at full sprint, then slowed only slightly as he entered the walkway. Fear, alarm, unbearable sadness; all that, plus an overpowering sense of urgency impelled him. She had not given him the message with any feeling of hurry, but the mere fact that she repeated her message in the short time before life slipped from her under-lined its import, regardless of the fact that Tom had no idea of its meaning.

Tom had never before seen a human die.

He arrived at Falma's door breathless and shaking. His chest burned from the effort, and it took him several seconds to clear his thinking enough to knock at the door.

Falma found the youth at his door, bent at the waist, cough-ing and still panting from his effort. "Ah, Laddie, come in from the cold. Inside you can tell me what brings you back so soon, and in such a state as this."

Gratefully, Tom entered, and followed the old man down the hall, through the laboratory, back to the small candle-lit room.

"Now, Lad," said the old man, gesturing toward a sad old chair, "do sit down and tell me what manner of business brings you back in such a state to see me."

Tom caught his breath, sat down, and tried desperately to think of how to tell the master what had transpired.

"Ah, Tom, I perceive that you are yet searching for words. Very well, let me make this easier for you by telling you what I already know, and what I am able to discern from your appear-ance, then you may tell me if I am correct. Following thereafter, you may give me whatever message you may have brought with you. Am I correct in assuming that you bear an important message?"

Tom stared openly at the old man and nodded. "Aye, Master," was all he could say at the moment.

"Am I further correct in assuming that the message you bear comes directly from the lady herself?"

Tom swallowed hard and again nodded.

"Very well, then, let me tell you what I know so far." The old man sat down across from Tom, joints grating as he eased his body into the chair. "First, it is apparent to me that our dear lady must have died. That is an immense sadness to us all, and it shows plainly on your face, Lad. There have been none more worthy, and none more charitable than Felicia, Lady Vincente.

Alas, it is also a great personal loss for me, as I have known her since she was a mere lass of thirteen summers." He paused, reverently, looked up with eyes moist, on the brink of tears. "Ah, what a flaming beauty she was, Lad! None now can compare with her in youth. One look, one smile could melt the stoutest heart. I will not tell you that I was unaffected by her beauty, but I will tell you that to this day the lady and I have, as well as good Master Craycroft, remained the closest of friends."

Falma now had Tom's full attention. The old man's words fanned the ever-growing fire of adventure within his breast. Nothing, however, could have prepared Tom for what Falma went on to reveal.

"Now Lad," he continued, "you are the living witness of that which I must now tell you. You see, much as many a young man may have been smitten with ardor for Felicia, she herself remained gently aloof, save for the appearance of one gallant lad, arriving, as it were, with the wind, and changing her life forever."

"Who?" Tom asked eagerly.

"Ah, Tom, there were many who might have been." The master paused. "But that young man was none other than your namesake, Drachma, the elder."

Tom gasped. He knew it was not proper to ask further, but he could not resist.

"Master, what then did transpire, if I may be so bold as to ask?"

"I had intended to tell you in good time, but now that ill fortune has wrought these changes, I will do so, sooner that I had planned." Tom thought he detected a slight gleam again in the master's eye. "The tale is one of power, joy and sadness, but you, by rights, should know it, as you shall surely carry it forth and be its living continuation."

Tom could feel his heart skip a beat.

"Mind you, Lad, this story is for your ears alone. None other may know of it until the fullness of time permits. Do you understand?"

"Aye, sir, I do." Tom nodded, adding emphasis to his agreement.

"Very well, then, I shall tell you." Falma cleared his throat, then resumed. "Few here know or remember Drachma's first arrival on our island, or its circumstances."

Falma caught the puzzled expression on Tom's face. "Ah, aye, Lad, he has been here more then once, though most know or recall only his third arrival. Drachma was brought here by the present earl's father as a tutor for the young daughter of ambassador Gianni. His home had been on the Greek isles, and he had been well trained in classical Greek, as well as history, Latin and some mathematics. Despite his youth, he came, highly regarded as one bearing wisdom beyond his years.

"He provided lessons for young Felicia, then fifteen years of age, radiant in beauty and manner." Falma paused again, closed his eyes momentarily, shaking his head at the intrusion of a private, cherished memory. "Now, as you may well imagine, this young man, in his prime, given the opportunity to be in the close company of a lass of such effortless charms, was himself quite stung by Cupid's arrow. And Felicia herself, now in the presence of a man of unsurpassed learning and intelligence, also possessing charm and wit, and further, not much older than she, did find herself responding to his presence with emotions and sensations unlike any she had hitherto recognized; unbidden, but not altogether unwanted.

"What then followed, in the ensuing months, seemed easy and understandable, yet begat consequences beyond the understanding of any who may have been touched by the events and circumstances, be they innocent or otherwise." Falma paused and shifted his weight in his chair, leaning forward slightly toward Tom. "You see, Lad, as the warmth of spring arose from the land, what had been interest and amusement in the lives of student and teacher, blossomed along with the spring flowers into something of cherished beauty, fragrance and delicacy. In plain language, Lad, the two fell deeply in love. They became inseparable companions, sharing each other's joys, sorrows, worries (albeit few at the time) and hopes. As witness to the events, I must tell you, son, that simply to be near them was to feel some of their joy and delight, and to this day the memories of those times can warm me in the deepest winter." The old man paused again, lost momentarily in reverie.

Tom's attention remained firmly on the master. He said nothing, waiting patiently for Falma to resume his story.

"Alas, Tom, there came changes. One could say they came from within and without, both having effects well beyond the reach of reason. From without, came the ever-growing mistrust of the ambassador's wife, Lady Gianni. The ambassador himself seemed quite taken with the gifted young tutor, and saw nothing amiss in the growing friendship and intimacy that became evident. Lady Gianni, however, was of a different mind. She seemingly felt her daughter was suited for greater things than this teacher would ever be able to provide, and should marry a nobleman. Within months of first meeting Felicia's tutor, the lady had become busy arranging for noblemen to come court her beautiful daughter. Felicia saw and felt nothing of an attraction for these finely dressed and bedecked young nobles, and, in fact either ignored or privately scorned them, preferring to keep her attentions on Drachma. Mind you, Lad, she did remain polite and gracious, which many of the young nobles seemed to take as encouragement, and several did become ardent suitors, staying about the castle for weeks, like leeches on the earl's house.

"Well, Lad, it should be no surprise, then, that these suitors came to understand that their chief rival for the affections of the young lady was none other than her tutor. One young nobleman, by the name of Dulleston, of the house of Perrin, took particular note of this fact, as well as the realization that the Lady Gianni thought ill of the closeness between her daughter and Drachma. Possessing both sharp intellect and a charming demeanor, he soon gained the confidence of Lady Gianni. With her blessing and encouragement, he was able to put into action a plan to discredit Drachma's teaching, and force the reluctant ambassador to dismiss the young tutor, and banish him from teaching within the earl's domain. It seems that Dulleston came to find out that, within Drachma's possession were several volumes of writing from the destroyed ancient library of Alexandria, and that these volumes contained writings on matters of science and philosophy, and espoused ideas not in keeping with Church doctrine, and further, that Drachma had been so bold as to tell his young pupil of some of these ideas. So, when Dulleston and Lady Gianni presented their case to the ambassador, along with thinly veiled threats of exposure to Church authorities, Lord Gianni felt he had little choice but to confront and dismiss Drachma as quickly and kindly as he could."

Tom shifted in his seat. "And is that what came to pass?"

"No, Tom, not that way. You see, Drachma was able to learn of this ploy, and, angered though he was, saw the futility in any attempt to justify or defend himself. But Tom, you will recall that I also said there came changes from within, and here I must ask that you be as understanding as your young years will allow. What did transpire, within the growing flame of their ardor, was that Felicia, in passion, did conceive." Falma paused, realizing that Tom, did, in fact, understand what he had just said. "Now, I do not expect you, with your years, to fully understand the delicacy of Drachma's circumstances, but nonetheless recognize that, at about the same time that his beloved had told him of her pregnancy, he also had discovered the plan to discredit his teaching and integrity."

Tom looked down and shook his head slowly. Neither spoke for a moment, then after a pause, Tom asked, "What then did he do? Where did he go?"

Falma cleared his throat again, then answered. "For you to understand what he did, you must understand something of what torment existed in the young man's breast at this time. Imagine further that the employment which brought you so far from home, which had become a source of pleasure and honorable pride, was now, through little fault of your own, to be abruptly ended with no recompense. Above all, now imagine that your only friend and beloved companion was with child, which is certainly your child, and you must abandon her, without matrimony, to the powers of the world over which you have no control, some of whom have conspired against you and your love. To flee would seem to be cowardice and admission of guilt, to stay would almost certainly lead to loss of everything held dear. What, under these circumstances, would you do?"

"Ah, Master, I know not, nor can I imagine. I fear not even the Church Fathers would have an answer for this." Then, as an afterthought, he added, "I was unaware that Lady Vincente had ever had any children."

"Well, Lad, you are among the very few who are now aware. I will tell you more of that in a little while. But of Drachma, I will tell you that his actions befitted the man. He did not take the route of cowardice, nor did he foolishly stay to defend himself in a hopeless cause. Rather, he approached directly the seat of power and set forth a plan that cast long shadows through the years thence."

For reasons he could not have understood, Tom, sitting spellbound by the master's tale, felt again a sudden chill down his spine. The gleam in Falma's eyes was now unmistakable and just a little intimidating.

"What Drachma did," continued the old man, "was to go directly to the earl himself, and grant him an offer that he would have been a fool to refuse. It is well that the earl was receptive to Drachma's plan."

The youth's eyes widened as Falma's revelations seemed to take him ever deeper into a tale that he knew somehow would involve him. The feeling was as if he had passed another threshold from which there would be no turning back.

Falma continued, "Before proposing his plan, Drachma told the earl of all that had transpired, even including telling of Felicia's condition, and the proposed treachery of Lady Gianni and Dulleston. To his surprise, he found the old earl both attentive and forgiving. What he offered the earl was a source of fame and wealth for the nobleman's domain. He explained that a guild of potters and painters had been placed in miserable servitude, almost slavery, by the ruler of a powerful city whose wealth was great and whose ambition was yet greater. His own father had been among the potters, and had told Drachma, before the youth left, that, should he find a benevolent ruler willing to provide their needs, that the entire guild would come and practice their craft for the benefit of such a nobleman, offering both loyalty and skill in his service, and asking only fair treatment in return."

With sudden insight, Tom began to see the connection now that he had only viscerally sensed before between the mysterious figure of Drachma the Elder and of recent occurrences within the castle.

"Is it then Drachma we have to thank for having our guild, and all it has meant?"

"Aye, for that, and much more. In the past forty years, Drachma has meant more to the people of this island than any would realize, save those few of us who have lived close to the earl and Lady Vincente."

"I must assume, then," Tom continued, "that Drachma, in exchange for procuring the guild, had a private request of the earl; something, I would not doubt, related to Lady Vincente's circumstances."

"Your insight serves you well, Lad. Do not lose it. In truth, Drachma had two requests. This first was that the earl provide for the care and protection of Felicia and her yet unborn child. Understanding her tender nature and the likelihood of difficulties to come, and knowing especially that he would not be able to provide for her needs himself, he sought the earl's official protection, if, for no other reason, than to assuage the guilt he felt over abandoning his love in such a delicate state." Falma paused, then took a swallow from the tumbler on the table at his side. He continued, then, with cautious intensity in his voice, "the second request was more mysterious, or did seem so at that time. He asked that he be allowed to return within two years, and to stay for not more than one month. With the promise that he would break no laws, he asked that he would further be allowed freedom to keep company with any he chose within the castle. The earl, of course, was most curious as to the young man's motives for such a request, but Drachma said only that the purposes were for future protection of the earl and his descendants, and he could say no more at the time."

Tom could not resist asking, "What, then, did the earl decide? Did he grant Drachma's request and his terms?"

"Ah, Tom, the earl's choice was not an easy one, if you consider that this young man had asked the Earl to take a large risk for the sake of the ambassador's daughter and her departing tutor and lover. Now, you may well wonder how I have come to know as much about these circumstances as I have, and I shall explain. What the earl chose to do was tell young Drachma that he should return on the morrow for an answer. He then asked to confer with me, as I had oft advised him on delicate matters before, and he trusted my judgment. We did confer, and at some length, finally agreeing that the young man's wishes would be granted, with the proviso that he should have, within the castle, one person always to call upon in matters of need and communication, and that person would be me, as the earl was getting old and feeble, and might not live to see to fruition all that had been agreed upon."

"So, Master Falma, you have been close to Drachma's doings down the years? I would believe, from what I now know, that the tale must be an extraordinary one indeed, but tell me, what of Drachma's further doings, and what of the unborn child?"

"Ah, Laddie, the tale is too long to tell of now, but you shall hear it in time. As to the child, born in secrecy, and raised in conditions most unlikely, came to be your true mother."

"My mother! How is that possible? My mother is of age very close to that of Lady Vincente, and I am her youngest."

"Son, I shall try to explain . . ."

A loud knock at the door interrupted the conversation.

Falma stood up to go answer the door. "Come Lad, let us see who comes on such a day."

As the two headed down the hall toward the outer door, Falma stopped suddenly, and clasped Tom's arm. "Tell me," he said, "the lady's message . . . was it to proceed or not?"

"To proceed, Master." Tom did not stop to realize how strange it was that Falma would know, without being present, of the nature of Felicia's dying instruction.

The knocking repeated before Tom and Falma reached the door. Tom opened the door, letting in a blast of cold air. Outside was the messenger Tom had earlier seen in the courtyard. With a gesture, Falma bid him enter.

"Good sir," the messenger began, addressing Falma, "If you be Loremaster Falma, I am instructed to take you with me. I have just conferred with the earl and received his order."

"I am Falma, and pray tell, what is the nature of this rather rough business? I am old and do not travel well in winter."

"I can tell you only this much, for it is all I know. It would appear that a most alarming thing has occurred at the north edge of the forest, near Killiburn. It involves someone by the name of Drachma. It is not known whether there is danger."

"With Drachma there is always danger," Falma muttered. "Listen, I am old and feeble. I will need this young page to accompany me."

"Very well, if he can ride."

Tom nodded, noticing again the chill down his back, which was not from the cold.

# Chapter Thirteen

For a while, he could see nothing but white light, and hear nothing but loud buzzing. There was no longer the dark tunnel with its repeating geometric shapes, or the rush of wind past his ears; just the whiteness and noise. As the light faded, and the buzzing receded, he began to sense the coldness, like the cold of the outdoors. The faint smell of the sea reached him, along with the call of the crows from the treetops. As his vision cleared, the shapes of his surroundings became recognizable. He was definitely out of doors, lying on the hard ground. A forest loomed large above his head, with open sky beyond his feet. For several minutes, as his senses cleared, he was unable to move at all.

A cold, wet nose touching the side of his neck startled him into sudden alertness. As he sprang up to a sitting position, the hounds began baying loudly, surrounding him with activity, noise, and disorder. There were eight or ten dogs, circling him like some quarry, their barking made louder by the continued buzzing in his ears. His vision cleared further, and he could see, coming toward him and the dogs, three men and a boy, walking quickly up the hill, each carrying what appeared to be a bow. The boy, noticing the cause of the dogs' excitement, gesticulated wildly to the men. Two of the men drew their bows, and, as a group, they ran toward Bob, stopping ten yards short of where he sat.

While the two had drawn their bows held aim, the other man approached cautiously.

"Ho, stranger! Arise and state your name and purpose." Then he added with a chortle, "If ye'll be so kind, please also explain your dress." The others then joined in the mirth.

In total bewilderment, Bob began to stand up. As he did so, his vision again turned white, the buzzing became a roar, and he could feel himself falling.

He awoke again to find himself lying on a mat in the corner of a small, cloister-like room, with dense, smoky air and a musty stench. He found that his vision had cleared, and the buzzing had all but subsided. Lifting himself cautiously on his elbows, he surveyed his surroundings. A small window, high on the wall, let in enough light to see clearly. In the center of the room, there was a crude wooden table and two chairs. Next to him in the corner, on the floor, was another dingy cloth mat with a pile of blankets. On hooks on the wall by the wooden door were some rough wood and metal tools. Across from the door was a fair sized fireplace, with black iron pots hung on either side. Next to the fireplace, was a set of shelves with simple dishes and some objects he could not recognize or even describe. On the other side of the fireplace, sitting on a stool, and looking like part of the crude furnishings, sat an old man, attending to a large kettle hung over the fire.

For a while, the old man continued to tend the pot and the fire, taking no notice of Bob. Then, as Bob sat fully upright, the noise or movement caught the man's attention, and he turned.

"Ah, so you are alive and awake," he said, wheezing slightly. "That is good. They told me they had found you drunk, but I did not smell strong drink on your breath. Neither did your sleep seem natural. I asked that they leave you here 'till you recovered."

Bob was now fully awake, but completely disoriented. Trying desperately in his mind to sort out his surroundings, he let the old man rattle on uninterrupted, hoping that something he would say might give him a clue about his present circumstances.

"They knew from your dress that you were not from anywhere hereabouts and probably from a long way away. This much was obvious. However, much debate ensued over your most peculiar tools and weapons." The old man chuckled mildly. "I surely hope you do not take offense, but the earl's guard has been summoned, and one of them should come to see about you yet today."

It didn't help. The old man's prattling made things even more confusing. *Weapons . . . earl . . . guards, this doesn't make any sense,* he thought. *Where the hell am I? This doesn't even feel like dreaming.*

Eventually, Bob spoke. "Look, sir, you're going to have to back up and explain a few things. I don't know where I am or how I even got here." He paused and swallowed. "Last thing I remember, I was in the hospital ICU, helping out a patient having trouble after surgery, and now suddenly I'm here . . . wherever here is. Now, there were those three men and a kid, the ones with the bows, and all the dogs . . . did they bring me here?"

The old man stopped and stared, not comprehending, and not knowing what to say. His face registered caution and confusion, but also a hint of amusement. Some of the words from the stranger's mouth he understood, but much sounded like foreign gibberish. Then there was that particular accent, and that attire! Nevertheless, he did not seem dangerous, at least not immediately so.

Bob, for his part, noticing the man's puzzlement, decided to back up and slow down a bit himself. This was clearly nowhere he had ever been before. The old man's accent seemed vaguely English, but funny, somehow. He tried again.

"Sir, I don't know where I am or how I got here. My name is Robert Gilsen. I'm from the U.S. I am a doctor, a cardiologist . . . that is, a heart doctor. Do you understand?"

The old man did not look any less puzzled. "You are a heart doctor? From the ewe ass? What is a heart doctor, and where is ewe ass? I am Allen of Burridge. I am a carpenter by trade, but too old now to be of much service. This is my house, in the village of Clannach, near Killiburn. We are on Shepperton Isle. Is that of some help?"

Bob closed his eyes and shook his head. He had never heard of Clannach or Killiburn, let alone Shepperton. He couldn't look any more ignorant than he already did by asking.

"No, I'm afraid that's not much help. I don't even know where Shepperton Isle is."

"Ah, then you are truly lost; surely far from home. Shepperton is in the North Channel, 'tween Scotland and Ireland. This is the earl of Shepperton's domain. His castle is far on the other side of the island. But, pray tell, where is this ewe ass from whence you come? Is that the name of an island? I know it not."

"That's U.S. The United States of America . . ." Bob began to realize there may be more than just his location that had drastically changed.

The old man in turn shook his head. "Nay, I know it not. Is it far?"

"A whole, big ocean away. Listen, I guess it was those men with the bows who found me and brought me here. Did they say anything . . . what they found . . . where I was . . . was I hurt . . . anything?"

"Aye, it was the men, the hunters, who found you. They tell me you were at the edge of the forest, on the ground. They believed you to be either drunk or poisoned, and that you swooned as soon as you stood. They carried you to the village like some large game, then left you in my care whilst they went after the earl's guard."

It still made no sense at all, but Bob could feel himself relax ever so slightly, for at least communication seemed possible.

I should tell you, Robert of ewe ass, the earl's guard may arrive at any time, also that the hunters did take your weapon with them to show the guard. They told me they had ne'er seen anything akin to it."

"Weapon, what weapon? I have no weapons." Then he suddenly realized and reached for his right hand coat pocket. Empty! "Did you see what they took?"

"Nay. I did not, though they said it was a most marvelous thing, made of craft and material never seen in these parts. When I asked to see it, they said I must not, as it may have been made of magic or sorcery, and only a master of lore might pronounce it safe or dread."

Bob began to feel suddenly frightened. Wherever he was, he was a total stranger, lost and completely alone, disoriented in the extreme.

*I have to be dreaming,* he thought, but couldn't convince himself he was. *This is nuts! None of this makes sense.*

For a while, the two men said nothing, only sat watching each other. Eventually, Bob decided to stand up and at least take personal inventory. Looking down, he noticed that he was still dressed in surgical scrubs and white lab coat. His coat pockets were empty (thinking back, he realized that he had had a couple of pens in his top pocket, emblazoned with the names of familiar cardiac drugs, a penlight, also provided by some eager drug company rep, and several tongue depressors, each individually wrapped in paper). He felt behind, and found that his wallet was still in his pants pocket. What was most significant, though, was what was not in his right hand coat pocket, namely his stethoscope—his cherished Littman Master Cardiology stethoscope—the one the manufacturer had finally (in his opinion) designed and built right. Gone, too, were the beeper that had hung on the waist of his pants and his digital watch.

The old man, noticing Bob's sudden discomfiture at the realization of his missing equipment, tried awkwardly to provide some reassurance.

"My good man, your things, which the hunters have taken, will be brought before the earl's guard. I feel certain that, once satisfactory explanation has been given, and the items are deemed free of witchcraft and malice, they shall be returned to you. They are honorable men, the earl's guard . . ."

"Witchcraft! Malice, what are you talking about? The stuff is pretty ordinary medical equipment. I couldn't so much as scare a baby with that stuff, let alone do any damage."

The old man understood little of what Bob was saying, but enough to know that his loss of equipment made him uncomfortable.

"There is no weapon, then, among your things?"

"Good Lord, no! I'm a doctor, not some cowboy or gun nut. Look, do you folks have a doctor..." Bob hesitated. "A physician... somewhere nearby? Maybe he would understand some of those things."

"Ah, a physician, a healer. There is one within the castle, in the earl's service. Perhaps you shall meet him."

A sudden, half-crazy idea flashed through Bob's mind.

"His name wouldn't happen to be Vincente, would it? Or... or Drachma?"

The old man stared suddenly at Bob with a look of confusion and fear, then quickly turned his gaze downward.

"What? Did I say something wrong? Look, I'm completely lost here, but somehow those names seem to ring a bell with you. There must be a reason..."

"I am sorry," said the old man, still averting his eyes, "I think we may have said more than enough. We shall wait 'till the Earl's guard does arrive."

For the next half hour, Bob tried to engage the old man in conversation, using both direct questions and attempts to engage him in discussion of unrelated issues, in the hope of getting more information about their current situation and the strange events back at the hospital. Allen of Burridge, for his part, remained taciturn, answering only on occasion with a nod or wordless grunt, and offering no more information.

Eventually, finding his lines of communication shut off, Bob sank back into reverie, trying in his own mind to put together something sensible to explain his drastic change of circumstances.

*This makes no sense whatsoever*, he thought, *I know I was in the Unit, helping the surgeons with Josh's latest disaster, and suddenly this! Somehow, across many miles of ocean, I'm on some island I've never heard of, in some smelly old wooden hut with this freaky old man, who's babbling about earls and guards and weapons. I really wish I could convince myself this was all just a dream.*

"Look, Allen," he finally said, "can I wander around here for a bit, try to orient myself a little? You've got to remember, I'm completely lost here, and it would be nice to be able to get my bearings."

The old man understood little of what Bob said, except the request to wander about.

"You may feel free to wander," the old man replied. "Your things are in the keeping, by now, of the earl's guard, so I shall not worry about you wandering far. This is where the guard will come, I am sure, and it would be best for you to be close by, as I feel certain you would wish to reclaim your possessions."

"Sure," Bob answered, "I'll stay close by. I don't really figure I've got anywhere in particular to go. I just thought I might take a look around."

The old man nodded, turning his attention back to the pot on the fire. Bob stepped over to the door, paused to consider the peculiar latch on the heavy oak door. The mechanism was crude and awkward in appearance, made of wrought iron, and unlike anything he had seen before, even in trips to Europe and Asia. He grasped what appeared to be a gnarled handle of sorts and tried turning it, with no results. It would not twist in either direction. He tried pushing, pulling and sliding the knob with equal lack of effect. He then stepped back a pace and studied the door, seeing nothing else that looked like a latch or handle. He tried again, pushing, pulling, sliding and twisting harder. The door held fast.

He turned quickly when he heard the chuckling behind him.

"Confounded by the door, eh? That's a rue one, it is." Allen got up slowly, knees grating loudly as he stood, and headed toward Bob. As the old man got close, Bob recognized the source of the stench he had noticed earlier.

*I wonder how long it's been since he's had a bath*, Bob thought to himself. *I sure don't see any signs of running water. I'm going to have to look this place up on the map when I get home. Could the whole place be this primitive?*

As the old man reached the door, a loud knock resounded from the other side.

"Open at once! It is the guard. We have come for the stranger."

A spasm of utter panic shot through Bob. The man's voice on the other side of the door sounded large and intimidating, and not the least bit as amicable as the old man on this side of the door.

Allen, for his part, calmly kicked aside a doorstop that had held the door shut, then pulled firmly, letting in a cold blast of air, five men, and a boy. The two large men at the front of the group wore metal headgear, swords, and breastplates. Bob recognized the earl's guard without need of introduction. The larger of the two approached Bob, then roughly seizing his left arm, slipped a heavy leather and metal manacle over his wrist. Bob opened his mouth to say something, then seeing the look in the guard's eyes, thought better of it. Instead of saying anything, he just stood and shivered.

"Stranger," said the large guard, "you must come with us, and may I offer the suggestion that you come peacefully. Any resistance will be cause for severe punishment."

This did not sound to Bob like an empty threat. As disoriented and defenseless as he felt, he decided the safest course would likely be to stay quiet and comply. His years in medicine had taught him some unexpected things, including how to deal with police and other law enforcement types carrying weapons. He had found that they were always easier to deal with when they felt in control and their bristles were not up. In that setting, he had found that they tended to be at least benevolent, if patronizing.

After an awkward pause, during which he could see Allen conferring secretly with the other guard, Bob finally gained the courage to ask about his changing circumstances.

"Sir, if you could tell me, I would appreciate knowing what I might have done to deserve being taken prisoner. I'm not aware that I have done anything that could be called a crime."

The guard answered, rather roughly, "I am not the one to ask such a question, but I am certain you shall meet the right man, possibly today."

Bob nodded silently, realizing the futility of pursuing this line of inquiry.

"Tell me, stranger," the guard continued, "what is your name?"

"Robert Gilsen,"

"And, tell me, what is your trade? What do you do?"

"I am a doctor, a physician."

"Ah, I would not have guessed. And tell me, where is your home? Where do you reside?"

Thinking back on his recent conversation with Allen, he answered, "I live the U.S., the United States."

"And where, pray tell, is that?"

Bob was beginning to find the guard's feigned politeness as irritating as the manacle on his wrist.

"The U.S., it's a whole ocean away, all the way across the Atlantic Ocean. Listen, I better not say too much now, especially since I have no idea how I got here or what I did to get myself in trouble in the first place. I don't want to make it any worse for myself or anyone else 'til I know the rules."

The guard seemed genuinely puzzled.

"You say you do not know how you arrived here, and I am inclined to believe you, but tell me, how is this possible, for if you have come from as far away as you say, then the journey must have been long and arduous, surely not one a person would likely forget. I feel certain that the earl will wish to hear your explanations."

He turned his attention to the others in the room.

"Come, Michel, if you have heard the old man's statement, we must escort our guest to Killiburn and await the earl's further instructions. 'Tis a shame that our stranger is not better dressed for our winter weather, as we have no cloak to offer him."

Bob shivered at the prospect of going outside, remembering the blast of cold that his when the door was opened.

"Could you at least tell me," he said "how far it is that we'll be going?"

"Aye. That I can tell you. Killiburn is no more than two furlongs from here," he replied.

*Just great!* thought Bob. *What the hell is a furlong? Some part of a mile, I think. Maybe I better just keep the old trap shut from now on. It sure would help if I knew what was going on.*

At the guard's direction, they headed for the door. Before opening the door for the others, Allen paused and pulled on Bob's white coat.

"Listen, I have not a proper cloak, but you may take one of my blankets to wrap about you. It is too cold to go back outside dressed as thinly as you are."

Bob was touched, realizing just how little the old man possessed.

"I really appreciate that, Allen," he said. "If there is any way I can get the blanket back to you, I will. I honestly believe that generosity toward a stranger is never really forgotten."

He took the musty grey blanket gratefully from Allen, and, using his unmanacled hand, wrapped it around himself. Then the two guards and Bob, as well as the three men and the youth headed out the door into cold.

The wind cut through his thin clothing without mercy. The blanket, as thoughtful a provision as it was, seemed pitiful as protection. Only the brisk tempo of their walking made the trip to Killiburn bearable at all. The walk was actually not very far, and the path well worn, skirting the edge of a large forest that disappeared into fog-enshrouded hills. They arrived at the gate of the village of Killiburn still early in the day. News of the arrival of a stranger had spread quickly through the village, bringing a throng of curious children and a handful of adults to the gate. The crowd was not disappointed. None had ever seen anything quite like this before.

Bob found himself shaking, not just from cold, but also from uncontrollable anxiety, close to panic. He had not felt quite this combination of fear, embarrassment and overwhelming desire to disappear since he wet his pants in the fifth grade. His intense fear of being in the public eye had actually kept him from pursuing the potentially exciting academic career that had been encouraged by a number of the professors he had worked under during his cardiology fellowship. Now, as he was led, manacled, cold and confused, through the gate into Killiburn village, between rows of noisy children who were mostly pointing and laughing, his mind raced back to a moment of exquisite embarrassment from his residency.

The occasion was one in which one of the rheumatology professors was to give a special lecture to the second year medical students on the history of arthritis and its treatment through the years. As is common practice, it was decided that a good way to introduce the subject was with a case presentation using a live patient from among the hospital inpatients on the rheumatology service. The patient that was chosen was a young man with an acute septic arthritis who unwittingly agreed to have his case presented before the assembled students of medicine. As Dr. Gilsen was the resident in charge of the man's care, the task of presenting the clinical history was his. Being too busy and too nervous about his presentation to take into account the level of training and sophistication of his audience, Bob read from his collected 3x5 cards the pertinent features of the young man's history, including details of his sexual orientation and habits. Appropriate as the information may have been to practicing clinicians looking for causes of the man's arthritis, the very mention, in the public, of the young man's sexual activity seemed to strike the medical students as both irrelevant and funny. The chuckling that rippled through the audience caught Bob's attention and paralyzed his presentation. He glanced at his patient long enough to notice the man, sitting in his wheelchair, face bright red, looking down at the floor. The amount of acute embarrassment was so severe that all Bob could think of was how to get himself and his wounded patient out of that place as quickly as possible. He stumbled rapidly through the rest of his presentation, then waited impatiently as the professor, oblivious to the pain of the patient and resident, asked his probing and learned questions, then dismissed the patient with a very professional word of thanks.

Bob then quickly wheeled the man back to the safety of his hospital room. Neither Dr. Gilsen nor the patient ever mentioned what transpired, and activity on the hospital service quickly swallowed up any memory of the event or feelings.

Until now.

"Look, Elly, 'e looks like a jester! Ho, Jester, can ye make us laugh?"

"Sing! Can ye sing and dance? Dance for us now!"

Most of the shouts and taunts he could not understand, but the message was unmistakable. He now knew with utter clarity how his former patient, manacled to his wheelchair, had felt.

He was almost grateful to his captors as he was led briskly away from the silly throng, to the guards' quarters.

# Chapter Fourteen

The messenger, wearing the uniform of the Forest Guard, led Falma and Tom to the earl's stables, where horses had been readied for the journey across the island. It had been years since Falma had ridden (though in his youth he had spent many hours on horseback), and he did not like the prospect of getting on a horse for a long, wearying ride through hills and forest in winter. His mood was quiet, almost sullen, and he seemed wrapped up in private thoughts. Tom, though not an experienced rider, had been on horseback a number of times in his short life, and relished the idea of starting his adventure with a ride, which was certain to be filled with unexpected delights. For the moment, his sense of wonder and adventure transcended his recent experience of sadness and shock. Sensing Falma's mood, however, he resisted the inclination to chatter, keeping his excitement just under control.

When they arrived at the stable, the guard bade them wait at the door as he went in and briskly approached the grooms, to make sure adequate provisions were on hand, in accordance with the earl's directive. Seeing that everything was made ready, he signaled Falma and Tom to enter the stable and get ready to ride.

"Will the earl be coming with us?" Falma asked.

"Nay," the guard replied, "he informed me that there was cause for him to remain, and that you would know what must be done. He also told me that you should act freely in his accord, and whatever you would wish done shall be considered his direct order."

Falma said nothing, but muttered inaudibly, looking rather distraught over this added responsibility.

Tom understood as well as Falma that the Earl would certainly have been referring to Lady Vincente's uncertain condition, and that by now he must have heard about her death. Falma's and Tom's disparate moods were made even more so by preparations for the trip. While Falma grieved to remain and see his friend Craycroft in this time of sorrow and intense need, Tom could not wait to get started and find out what his namesake had done to cause such a sudden stir.

The horses were large and heavy, well suited for carrying supplies and men at arms. To Tom, perched high in the saddle, the bay mare he was now sitting on seemed immense, almost ridiculously so, considering his own small stature. Her slightest movement seemed like the moving of an entire building. For the moment he was glad that he would be following another rider's lead and not setting out on his own. Controlling horses of this size seemed a task for much larger men. He looked behind him to check on the progress of the others, and saw that Falma was just now mounting his gelding. For a man of his age with creaky joints, he mounted with surprising ease and grace, taking the reins with calm authority.

The guard, whose name was Kerlin, checked quickly to make sure Tom and Falma were secure on their mounts, then, reassured, mounted his own grey, and then led the other two out from the stables, through the courtyard and out the gate.

Though still cold outside the castle gates, the wind had died down, making the weather somewhat more tolerable. The three wound their way down from castle hill, through the trodden village thoroughfare, attracting little attention, then across the fields toward the forest. The riders were silent at first, each absorbed in his own thoughts, Kerlin leading the way, with Falma's and Tom's horses following instinctively.

Falma eventually asked, "Tell me Kerlin, how was the way? How are the woods this winter? I trust you are taking us back the way you came."

"Aye, that I am," he replied. "The forest was calm as I came up. The path by Croftus Knob and Lough Teagle was a mite bit treacherous under foot, but the rest of the Eastern Riverway was easy travel."

"Ah, that is some comfort to an old man with the rheum. I do not remember the last time I rode a horse."

Tom could not help asking, "How long a journey shall we expect? Are there hazards of which we should beware?"

"Ah, son," Kerlin answered, "the length of our journey will depend upon the forest. There are hazards too numerous to name, but little that I should call deadly peril. Most are merely obstacles that can be avoided or surmounted. These are good mounts, and I should think that they are equal to any task we would ask of them."

Tom pressed, "and you know the route well?"

Kerlin chuckled. "Well enough, I would say. Beyond Croftus, I know the routes as well as if they were lines on my own hand, and on this side we have well trodden pathways. To proceed past Croftus would likely be our only difficult passage, and that not very challenging at this time of year. Tell me son," he continued, "have you traveled through the forest?"

"I do not remember ever going through the forest, though as a young child I might have, within the care of my mother." He added slight emphasis to the words "my mother", and glanced toward Falma to see if he had caught the reference to their prior conversation.

Falma said nothing, and his expression was unreadable.

"Well, son," the guard continued, "there are many stories of the forest, most containing bits of truth and much fancy. What tales you hear are likely the same ones I heard as a child, and have since learned that their truth had been greatly distorted in the telling, usually to serve the purpose of the teller."

Tom noticed a change in the guard, as he was no longer the

taciturn, cold henchman he had seemed, and by talking about his favorite subject, he now waxed eloquent and animated.

Falma's expression remained a mask. He did not even seem to be listening, except to his own hidden thoughts.

As the three riders now entered the forest, Tom turned his attention back to Kerlin and asked, "and what of Drachma? Is he yet alive in the forest?"

"Oh, aye, Laddie, he is very much alive. His name was told to me with the message that the earl and Master Falma would know of him and of what import he might be as regards to events at the other end of the island." He continued, with a cautious note in his voice, "of those events, however, I have little knowledge and am not at liberty to even tell the little I do know."

"That is well, for now," interjected Falma, unexpectedly.

Tom and Kerlin looked at the master, somewhat chagrined that they had been speaking as if Falma had not been present.

"Knowledge of Drachma's doings has always carried a certain risk to those that possess such."

"With what little I do know thus far, I have already come to understand that to be true," said Tom.

While they had been talking, Tom had let his horse come along side of Kerlin's, but now, as they entered deeper into the forest, the path became narrower, forcing them to again ride single file and keep conversation to a minimum. Tom began to sense ever more the close quiet of the forest surrounding him, and found his thoughts returning to Drachma. Almost all the stories he had heard of him until today had had something to do with the forest. There were tales of magic and sorcery, of wild beasts tamed for strange tasks, of hunters becoming lost and returning weeks or months later ravaged and mute. He had never before really believed the tales, but could now begin to sense that there must have been truth in at least some of the stories. He could not put it into words. It was simply a sense that the feeling of the forest matched precisely the feeling of hearing the tales for the first time.

After an hour of riding in near silence, they came to a clearing, surrounded by ancient hardwoods. In the distance to the east, they could hear the sound of rushing water.

*How strange*, thought Tom, *I definitely hear running water, but this is a cold January, with the rivers frozen over.*

Kerlin halted his horse and the others followed suit.

"We should stop here for a rest and food," he said. The next clearing of any size will be hours away, and I am charged with your safe conduct."

As they lit and tethered the horses, Tom thought, for just a fleeting moment, that he heard a whisper. He turned in the apparent direction of the sound, but could see nothing but the forest itself.

"The forest does seem alive, does it not?"

Tom whirled to see Falma right behind him.

"It is more so at nightfall," Falma continued. "both the noises and the silence are deeper."

"Did you hear it?" asked Tom.

"Nay, but it is apparent that you heard something, and I know this forest well enough to believe that it was not merely your imagination. If it be any comfort to you, you should know that this part of the forest has thus far not proven to be dangerous."

Tom muttered an inarticulate reply.

Kerlin, in the meantime, had brought down the sack of provisions from his horse, and began dividing portions of bread, dried fruit and dried meats for the three of them, as well as wine for Falma and himself. For Tom there was a flask of water.

"Come, we should eat," he said, noticing Tom and Falma's attention directed elsewhere. "We have much traveling yet to do, and shall need our strength.

"I truly hope you are not expecting strength from me," replied Falma with a wry smile, "for I am an old man, stiff in the joints and well past my prime."

Tom listening to the banter, suddenly got the uneasy feeling that Falma was likely playing Kerlin for some hidden purpose. He already knew better than to believe Falma's professed humility. There was strength in this old master that had nothing to do with joints and sinews.

*It must be close to midday,* thought Tom. *The sky has clouded over. If it should snow, our way could become difficult indeed.*

Quietly and gratefully, he ate his bread and meat.

Sensing Tom's unexpressed question, Falma asked, "Can you tell how far we should be able to ride today?"

Kerlin took a swallow of wine, then answered, "I truly cannot say. The forest and the weather might create an answer for you, but we should be able, at the very least, to reach the shelter of Croftus before nightfall.

"That would still leave a good journey for the morrow, would it not?"

"Aye, but one well known to me. That is my domain, if you will. There is little in that part of the wood that I have not encountered before, and I feel certain we shall be safe."

"By what you say do you imply that we might not be safe until we have reached Croftus?" Tom could not help asking. "Are there real dangers in this forest?" His voice conveyed more excitement than fear.

Kerlin paused and studied the page, as if seeing him for the first time. There was more to this slender, wide-eyed, curly headed youth than his first impression implied.

"How old are you, Laddie?" he asked. "You do seem old beyond your years. You cannot have seen more then fourteen summers."

"Aye, I am but thirteen years of age. However, this is my third year as page to the council. I began early. I believe my father knew someone upon the council who made my way for me."

Tom had spoken openly, before realizing that he had done so to a stranger, and one likely to carry some influence. He regretted his actions, but could not take back what he had said. He glanced at Falma to see if there was disapproval in him, but Falma's expression gave away nothing.

"To answer your question, Lad, there are dangers. I cannot say much now, but some of the danger is a reflection of the reason for our hasty journey."

Tom was about to ask for further details, but caught Falma's sudden change of expression suggesting caution, and held his tongue. Kerlin, too, noticed the change in expression and instinctively looked about, his hand on the hilt of his sword. For several minutes no one spoke, each listening intently, sensing something, but hearing nothing but the far off sound of running water. The air was absolutely still, but in that cold stillness Tom sensed that there was something amiss, something intangible but powerful.

It was then he heard the whisper again, more distinctly this time, coming from the right side behind him. He turned in the direction of the sound. Falma and Kerlin too looked in the same direction, but heard nothing.

"Falma is right" thought Tom, "this forest feels alive. It seems there is a malign purpose at work, and we may be the unwitting targets."

Silently, Kerlin stood up and motioned for the others to get up and prepare to move on. Under Kerlin's watchful gaze, they quickly packed the horses and mounted, getting ready to ride out of the clearing and back into the forest proper. As they did so, the fog engulfed them, a cold, wet shroud rolling down from the hills. Within minutes, the fog became so thick the riders could only see as far as the horse in front. Kerlin continued to lead the way, carefully picking out the path just in front of his mount. Behind him rode Falma, then Tom. The three remained silent, concentrating on keeping together in the dense mist. The sound of rushing water faded into the distance, and even the heavy steps of the horses became muffled in the grey-white stillness.

Tom began to feel as if he were drifting in a dreamlike state, lulled almost to sleep by the quiet sameness about him. But then the whispers started again, and all his former enthusiasm vanished into helpless quiet terror. He felt like crying out, but no sound came from his throat. He could tell that there were words being whispered, but he could not decipher them, and he could no longer tell from where they came. There was no wind, but the sound came like the rush of air through the trees. He became very light in the saddle, as if floating and he could feel himself spinning, then falling, falling.

More than a mile down the path, as the fog lifted enough to see about them, Falma and Kerlin looked around, and then looked behind them to see Tom's horse with its empty saddle.

Falma moaned in disbelief, as Kerlin turned his mount and tried to peer back into the blankness.

"Ah, this is most foul!" Kerlin spat. "Did you hear anything at all to suggest when we might have lost him?"

"Nay, not a sound, nothing." Falma sounded full of dismay.

"This is simply more than I can bear. We cannot lose this page. His future is too important to all of us."

"I hope you will be able to explain what you mean, sometime. At the moment, though, I must try to find the lad if I am able. I need ask that you remain here, mounted, and not drift off the path, not in the least. I will go back along the path we took to see if I am able to find any sign of him. I shall return in a very short while, with or without the youth."

With that, Kerlin took his horse back down the path. His hand held the hilt of his sword. His horse, sensing something amiss, snorted and shook his head, but went as directed.

Falma remained seated on his horse, his hands trembling, his stomach knotted. Strangely, he felt no fear for himself, but was distraught over this terrible turn of events. He was absolutely convinced that it was something of malice that took Tom off his saddle.

*How could anyone have known of his importance or his whereabouts at a time like this?* he wondered silently. *And why would the earl have chosen me to act in his behalf now? I am old and tired, and have no longer either wit or wisdom for such as this.*

"Oh, Drachma, you are both a blessing and a curse!" he said aloud, but quietly, with whispered intensity. "Few know of your power and influence, your love and disdain. Surely you must know something of this!"

Eventually, he looked up again to notice that the fog had cleared further, and he could see that the path skirted the edge of a rather steep hill. The forest here was mostly evergreens of varying sizes and ages. Pine cones and needles covered the path, along with some old, trampled snow. The quiet dissolution of this place, as well as his recent losses, produced within him an overwhelming sense of loneliness that ached like his old bones.

"My old friend, you seem distressed. Sorrow hangs about you like the fog."

Falma started at the voice, and turned to see an old man seated on a small black horse.

"Drachma, it is you! What in the name of heaven are you doing? Do you know of the youth? Did you see him?"

"Ah, Falma, it would be safest if you did not know all at the present time, but to answer your anguish, yes, I know of the youth called Tom, and I will assure you that he shall be returned safely to your good care on the other side of the island. Know this much only that he is in less danger in the company of my men than he would be in the open with you and the Forest Guard."

Falma sighed, swallowed the lump in his throat. Shaking his head, he said, "then it is as I feared. There are powerful and malign forces at work here again. Drachma, I am too old and weary for this."

"Aye, then you do understand. He is better now in my care. Be assured, my friend, I am fully aware of his value and importance. You, of all people, should know that," Drachma paused, listening. "My friend, I must away. Do not tell the guard of this. It is safer this way, if you do not know or say any more."

"True, I see your point. I shall say nothing."

"Then farewell. We shall meet again soon."

Drachma then turned his horse, and almost without a sound, disappeared into the mist and trees.

Despite his age and aching bones, Falma felt within himself a sensation of youthful excitement, which he tried to suppress. *After all, I am really much too old for this,* he thought, *and Tom is yet too young. Perhaps Drachma will succeed again, but he too is getting old. I hope that we will, indeed, have the chance to meet again. There is much we need to talk about.*

His train of thought was interrupted by Kerlin's return up the path. The guard's face was grim, his manner alert, cautious.

"I fear," he said, "that young Tom has been abducted. I cannot say with certainty, but less than three furlongs back there appear to be fresh hoof prints that converge on the path, and trail back into the trackless forest. The mist would not allow a more careful inspection. Alas, I think he has been taken, and by whom and why I could not venture to say."

Rather than reveal his newfound knowledge, Falma directed his question away from the central issue slightly by asking, "Then what do you propose that we do? Is there anything we can do?"

Kerlin was taken aback by Falma's seemingly matter-of-fact tone, but then answered, "By ourselves, nay. It would be very risky, but I feel sure that, when we are able to travel past Croftus, there we shall be able to send a message to the other Forest Guards and have a party sent in search of the youth." He paused, and looked quickly about. "My desire would be to stay and search, but my reason tells me we should proceed with some haste. There are foul doings about in the wood, and you are most needed on the other side of the island in safety."

"Your counsel is most reasonable," Falma answered. "I too would wish to stay and know more, but I have no desire to face sharp swords and arrows unprotected in this forest. Let us be gone, then. The fog has lessened, and our way should be somewhat easier for the present."

As they set off again down the path, Falma added, almost as an afterthought, "I do fear for the safety of our young page. There is the mark of some greatness in him, and I do believe we would all suffer the loss if harm came to him."

"Aye, Master Falma. You speak the truth."

The path wound back into the denser forest, and as they entered the darker domain, the sound of rushing water could again be heard off to the right. Distinct from the sound of water, though, Falma was sure he heard whispering.

# Chapter Fifteen

Judy Morrison tried to sleep, but could not. It wasn't worry exactly, but felt about the same. She lay in bed, staring up at the ceiling, perplexed. Why this need to try to make sense of things? Most days, she would return to her apartment after the night shift, make herself a snack while listening to Morning Edition on public radio, then settle down in bed and drift off to sleep reading, without any crazy need to find reasons and explanations.

Not this morning. Her mind teemed full of unfinished business. The events of the previous twelve-hour shift stuck to her morning routine like a misplaced piece of chewing gum.

Lots of mysterious and inexplicable things came through the emergency room in the course of a month or even a week on duty. They were interesting to remember and speculate about philosophically, but they did not, as a rule, disturb Judy's sleep. There was a random or chance quality to those events that made them somehow acceptable in the normal flow of life and work. Last night's encounters were different. There were hidden connections and a striking lack of randomness that gave a numinous quality to what had transpired. No matter how she tried, she could not shake the sense that a plan or purpose lay behind all the crazy stuff with Josh and that Mr. Vincente. Somehow, too, it seemed tied in with the peculiar note, and with Bob Gilsen, and with all that nonsense about some ancient coin.

Bob Gilsen! The very thought of him made her sad beyond anything she had known. He looked like a man in the deepest need, but unreachable; as if he were doomed, but was the only one who wasn't in on the secret. Remembering the look in his eyes as he took off for the operating room brought tears to her own eyes.

A sensation of the utmost urgency took hold of Judy, and she sat upright in bed, then reached for the phone. For reasons she did not understand, she felt an urgent, impulsive need to try to contact Bob. She quickly dialed the hospital number, then waited as it rang an inordinately large number of times.

"Good morning, Memorial Hospital."

"Yes, this is Judy Morrison, night ER supervisor. I need to talk to Dr. Gilsen. Can you page him for me?"

"Let me see if he's still signed in. Yes, his light's still on. I'll page him for you. Please hold."

Judy could hear the intermittent clicking sounds of being on hold. She began to feel vaguely annoyed as time elapsed. The operator came back on after several minutes. "Who are you holding for?" she asked.

"Dr. Gilsen. He hasn't answered yet."

"I'll page him again for you. Please hold."

More clicks. Judy could begin to feel her throat beginning to tighten as she shifted uncomfortably on the bed.

After several more minutes, the operator came back on. "I'm sorry, but Dr. Gilsen has not answered. You might try his office."

"Yeah, okay." Judy tried to sound calm, but her voice cracked. "You got that number?"

"One moment, please . . . It's 389-4227."

"Thanks. Listen, if he does answer in the next few minutes, would you have him call me? I'm at home. The number's 983-5271."

"If he answers I'll give him the message."

Judy hung up, and thought about what she was doing. This was crazy. It wasn't rational. Still, her compulsion was stronger than reason. She reached inside her bedside table and pulled out the phone book, hoping that his home phone was listed. It was not.

Frustrated and just a bit agitated, she went ahead and dialed the office number.

After five rings a female voice answered, "Dr. Gilsen's answering service. May I help you?"

"Ah, yes. This is Judy Morrison, ER nurse from Memorial. I need to speak with Dr. Gilsen. Could you beep him for me?"

"Certainly. I'll have him call the ER."

"Ah . . . well . . . could you have him call 983-5721?"

"Very well. What was your name again?"

"My name's Judy, Judy Morrison," she said in a croaking whisper.

"Okay. I'll beep him for you."

"Thanks."

Now, on top of feeling frustrated, she felt acutely embarrassed. If Bob were still tied up with emergencies, the last thing he needed was to get beeped by someone who couldn't even explain why she was calling. If he did answer his beep, what would she say? She hadn't even thought about that before.

Realizing that she was definitely not going to go to sleep now, she got up and walked over to her kitchen. Not looking for anything in particular, she opened the refrigerator door and stared inside. This infernal diet she was on had left her refrigerator distinctly free of goodies. She closed the door in disgust and turned on the burner under the kettle to heat some water for tea.

*What will I say now if he calls?* she thought. *How can I explain this without sounding totally goofy?* She made herself a cup of tea and sipped it as she watched the clock. Five minutes, then ten minutes went by without a return call. The more she tried to reassure herself that all was okay, the less reassured she felt, until the sensation became one of near panic. Getting back up, she paced the floor for several more minutes, then went back to the phone and dialed the hospital number again. This time she asked for the ER, and specifically for Lonie Chaves.

"Yeah, Judy, what in the world do you want? You're supposed to be sleeping." Lonie's tone was more soothing than her words.

"Listen, Lonie, I need Bob Gilsen's home number. It's not listed, and he didn't answer his page. You haven't seen him around your neck of the woods, have you?"

"Naw, I haven't seen him since you gave me report. Okay, let me see. I've got his number somewhere here . . . hang on . . . Okay; here it is . . . 359-6202." She paused, then added, "I sure hope it's important. He looked like he could use a week or two of sleep himself."

"Thanks, Lonie. I owe you one."

"You betcha. You know I'll collect."

"Yeah, I know. Thanks again. I'll see you soon."

Judy hung up the phone and glanced at the clock. Nine thirty. Not stopping to think about it, she dialed Bob's home number. It rang repeatedly with no answer—six, seven, eight times. She let it ring for another minute, and then hung up. When she did so, she noticed her hand was shaking, her chest hurt, and she felt close to crying.

*What am I doing?* she thought to herself. *This makes no sense whatsoever! I'm a rational, intelligent person. I don't act on crazy impulses. Why do I even care? This is no affair of mine.*

She reasoned with herself, but couldn't shake the growing agitation within her. Something was terribly wrong. She knew it as surely as she knew her own name, but couldn't put her finger on what it was or why. It had something to do with all that stuff last night and with Bob. Maybe if she could just talk with him it might clear things up a bit, then maybe not.

Realizing just how irrational it seemed, she nevertheless got dressed, ran a brush through her hair, then put on her coat and gloves, and headed for the door. This was one of those times when she was truly grateful that she was no longer with Greg, having to explain everything she was doing, logical or otherwise. She carefully closed then latched her front door, and turned and walked down the hallway toward the bitter weather outside. All the way down the hall, she tried to convince herself that she really didn't need to do this, that everything was Okay, and that she was just being impulsive.

*But I'm not an impulsive person. I don't do things like this. I should just turn around, go back in and go to sleep.*

She kept walking. Something stronger than reason impelled her. Stepping outside almost did it, almost turned her back to the warmth and security of her apartment. What had been frozen drizzle had become blowing snow. Another inch had fallen since she got home and the temperature had dropped. Fortunately, she had found a parking spot close to the apartment building. Cursing her inexplicable actions, she found her car, started it up, and began dusting off the new snow, enough to see to drive.

The drive to Memorial Hospital was slow and treacherous. Judy cursed herself the whole way there. She was tired, but not sleepy, running on unnatural energy. Twice she lost control of the car at intersections, but avoided hitting anything by pure luck. By the time she pulled into the hospital parking lot, her overwhelming sense was that she was being pulled in a direction she had no intention of going and all this tromping about in the cold and snow had definitely not been worth it. The cold, the wind, the ice and snow . . . it just didn't make any sense. If someone had asked her what she thought she was doing driving back to the hospital in this weather after already completing her shift, there was no way she could have given any semblance of a logical answer. Fortunately, no one asked.

Pulling the hood of her coat close about her head, she quickly shuffled along the snow-slicked sidewalk and slipped into the northeast entrance of the hospital, then headed down the long hall toward the ER. The ER was bustling with activity, enough so that no one noticed Judy's unexpected presence. She was able to go into the nurses' lounge, hang up her coat, and sit down by the phone while attracting no notice whatsoever. She let escape a quiet sigh of relief, then picked up the hospital directory, and found the number for the OR. Judy dialed the number, and when the nurse in surgery finally answered, she asked if Josh Crabtree was still in surgery. She was told quite curtly by the nurse, who obviously had more important things to do, that Josh's surgery had been completed, and that if she wanted more information, she should just call the T Surg ICU.

"Thank you," Judy muttered, and hung up the phone.

*Well,* she thought, *I might as well make a total fool of myself and go on up there. I'll at least find out more in person than on the phone.*

Leaving her coat hung up in the nurses' lounge, she walked out into the hallway, and turned toward the elevators. The other people in the hospital went about their tasks, and took no notice of the tired, tousled nurse in street clothes.

As she walked the hallways she thought, *It sure would be easy for some maniac to go around in a hospital doing terrible things as long he just blended in and didn't make a scene. Nobody really notices anyone or anything except their own immediate concerns. No wonder we can have deranged nurses slipping ICU patients curare, and weirdoes dressed up like doctors and writing orders and such. It's actually surprising those things don't happen more often. Maybe we all get so focused on one or two things that we miss all the big stuff. I wonder if there's some major drama being played out under our very noses that we're completely oblivious to.*

The thought made her shiver, visibly. The orthopedic resident, riding in the elevator with her, half noted her tremor, then retreated back into his own professional shell.

The elevator chimed, stopped, and opened, and Judy got out, quickly heading for the double doors which marked the Thoracic Surgery ICU. Despite her years of working in this hospital, now she was out of uniform, the sign on the door noting "authorized personnel only" caught her eye and made her feel just a bit awkward. Her hesitation was short lived, thought, and she stepped inside.

At the moment she did not feel like a nurse. The noise, the machines, the tubes, the wires, all connected some way to sick and dying people caught her off guard. She felt ill at ease, and actually a little physically sick. She looked awkwardly about, trying to find a familiar face. Everyone seemed busy, intent on their appointed tasks. No one noticed Judy's arrival. Coming up to the nurses' station, she did recognize Sandi Harman, a nurse who had worked CCU with her.

Judy approached Sandi at the desk and caught her eye. "Hi, Sandi," she said "Look, I don't mean to bother you, but they told me Josh Crabtree had been moved here, and Dr. Gilsen was involved in his case. I need to get a hold of him, and he didn't answer his page."

"Well, Judy, long time, no see. How've you been?" Sandi seemed genuinely delighted.

"Fine, busy . . . still working ER nights. I've been fine, really. And you?"

"Pretty good. This isn't all that different from CCU, just the docs are more demanding. Anyway, I don't have Josh, Jennifer does. She could probably tell you. We don't see Gilsen up here very often. Look, I'll get Jennifer for you."

Sandi got up and walked around the corner, then came back with her coworker.

"Judy, this is Jennifer. She's got Josh today." She turned to her fellow nurse, "Jenny, Judy and I used to work CCU together. She's looking for Gilsen. You seen him or know where he might have gone?"

"Oh, Hi, Judy. Nice to meet you." She smiled quickly. "No, I haven't seen him since Josh had that last run of A Fib. I know he was here then, I saw him. It wasn't very long ago, less than a half hour. Wait, Hurwitz might know. He's been working with Gilsen."

"Hey, Mark!" Jennifer yelled across the noise of the ventilators, monitors and sundry machines, "over here. Someone needs to ask you something."

Mark Hurwitz ambled over, looked at Judy quizzically, "you're out of uniform, you look different. Whatcha need?"

"Well," Judy replied, flushing slightly, "I'm looking for Dr. Gilsen. He didn't answer his page, and I was told he might be around here with Josh."

"Funny," he said. "You know he was here when we got ready to cardiovert Josh this last time. Then we looked, and he was just gone. It seemed kind of spooky at the time. We paged him. Haven't seen him since. I wonder if he went back to talk to Josh's folks. They could be anywhere … surgery waiting room, cafeteria, ER, almost anywhere. Sorry." Hurwitz paused. "You know, too, he could just be trying to catch a nap. He looked beat. You could try the doctor's lounge on four."

"Thanks," Judy replied, as a wave of nausea and apprehension spread through her body. Now she really felt torn. If she did find Dr. Gilsen resting, asleep, or involved with some emergency, she would really feel guilty about disturbing him. On the other hand, the need to find him, or at least find out about him became ever more intense and irresistible.

Unfortunately, Judy didn't even know where to begin looking now. Dr. Hurwitz was right. He could be just about anywhere—the doctors' lounge, the surgical waiting room, the cafeteria, the medical floors. Who knows? Maybe the best thing would be to start in the doctors' lounge, and if he weren't there, then page him again.

She turned to leave, and as she did so, Sandi added, "Listen, Judy, if we see him, we'll tell him you've been looking for him."

"Yeah, thanks, Sandi. I appreciate that."

The tiredness was getting worse as Judy walked back out into the hallway toward the elevators. Before she got there, through, a sudden compulsion seized her and she walked, almost ran back to the ICU, in through the double doors, to the nurse's station.

"Sandi, while I'm up here, I thought I'd like to see Josh, if that's okay, just briefly."

"Sure, Judy, that's fine. He's around the corner in bed five."

The sight was truly pitiful. There, in the ICU bed lay the thin figure of Joshua. He was literally surrounded by tubes, wires, probes and monitors, all registering the facts that his body still pumped blood, circulated oxygen, moved air in and out of his lungs with the assistance of the ventilator, and made urine. That was all well and good, but the body in the bed did not respond to voice or to touch. There did not appear to be any perception or understanding of his environment. Seeing him this way made Judy want to run and hide. She knew it was not her fault, but nonetheless she felt guilty by association.

She found she couldn't bear to look at Josh, so she concentrated instead on the monitors registering vital data. Looking intently at the EKG monitor, she thought for a fraction of a second that it flashed. She looked quickly around to see if anyone else had noticed anything. Satisfied that no one did, she stared back at the screen.

For no more than a tenth of a second, the screen went black, then as it came back on Judy saw, or thought she saw, in the lower right corner of the screen, in small figures, the number 4277. She blinked, and as she did, the screen reverted to normal. Again she looked to see if anyone else had seen anything amiss. Evidently they had not. Everything was back to baseline, no beeps, no alarms. Josh remained insensate in the bed, the noises and sights of the unit continued uninterrupted.

Realizing that no meaningful interaction with Josh was possible, Judy turned and walked back out of the ICU, back toward the elevators and to the doctors' lounge on the fourth floor. The walk down the corridor seemed abnormally long, and vaguely futile. She arrived at the door to the physicians' lounge, and again felt the unease that comes from being out of place and out of uniform. Judy hesitated before knocking at the door, thought about what she might say to Bob should he be inside.

There was no answer to the knock. She knocked again to be sure. Still no response. She went ahead and opened the door and stepped inside. The room was stale and deserted. The furnishings were dull, functional, and modestly comfortable. On the coffee table by the couch a newspaper was left carelessly abandoned, along with a plastic wrapper and a nearly finished Styrofoam cup of coffee. The phone sat on a table next to a grey stuffed chair. Beside the phone was a note pad and pen, which caught Judy's eye. She walked over to the table and picked up the note pad. Someone had evidently taken a phone message, and written hastily on the pad the cryptic scrawl:

Judy sat down and stared at the message on the note pad, and felt suddenly very uneasy. She had a good head for numbers, and remembered that that was the number which showed on the ICU monitor screen briefly, and also remembered that Dr. Gilsen's office number was very similar at 4227. The sense of connectedness was there again. This was just too much to be mere coincidence.

For a while she just sat in the chair and stared straight ahead, pondering. She then picked up the telephone and put it to her ear with the aim of dialing, but then thought better of it for the moment, and put the phone back down.

*Why am I doing this?* she thought. *I am making no sense, even to myself. I've driven back out to the hospital in the middle of a snow-storm, risking my life and car on the street, for no reason that I could put into words, when I should be sleeping. But here I am anyway. I might as well follow through with what little information I do have, weird as it is.*

She looked again at the note pad. The handwriting was not any she recognized at a glance. It was definitely not Bob's writing. His scrawl was easy to spot. The numbers could be a phone number, possibly a hospital extension. "Dr.," she assumed, referred to a doctor. Objectively, there was no reason at all to think it had anything to do with Bob, but the strange feeling within that impelled her to leave her warm and safe apartment told her that it did.

Somewhat hesitantly, she dialed 4277, then waited as the phone rang. It rang six times before someone answered.

"Hello."

"Uh, hello. Who is this?" Now Judy was really embarrassed.

"This is Mrs. Crabtree, Janie Crabtree. Who were you trying to reach?"

"Oh, Janie. This is Judy Morrison, the night ER supervisor. I was actually looking for Dr. Gilsen. You haven't seen him recently, have you?"

"Oh, no, Judy not in quite a while. Not since before Josh was moved to the ICU."

"Oh, well listen, Janie, tell me where you are. I would like to come talk to you anyway."

"Why, in the surgery waiting room. Isn't that where you called?"

"Ah, well, actually I just had the number ..." Judy paused, then resumed. "I just saw Josh a bit ago. This must be very difficult for you. I'll come over. We can talk."

"That would be nice, Judy. We'll wait for you."

"Okay. See you in just a bit."

When she hung up the phone, Judy knew for the first time that day that she had done the right thing. She did not understand at all, but simply knew that it was right.

Without consciously thinking about what she was doing, Judy slipped the top page from the note pad into her pocket as she left the doctors' lounge, heading for the surgical waiting room. As she walked down the corridors, she found herself no longer resisting the internal pull of the large, subtle purpose or plan about which she had no understanding, but for which she now possessed a true visceral sense of participation.

# Chapter Sixteen

The guards' quarters, located along the east wall of Killiburn Village, were in a low, dull gray stone building. The dark inside contrasted sharply with the rapidly brightening day outside. There was just enough light coming in the small, vertical windows to see that inside it was divided into two sections, one clearly designed to house a half dozen people in relative comfort, with simple cots and a large fireplace, the other section a more austere, open area, presumably set aside for the various regular functions of members of the guard.

Once inside, Bob was taken to one of the cots and offered a seat. After he sat down, his manacle was removed by Sean, the larger of the two guards.

"Well, Robert of Ewe Ass, you may move about freely within these quarters until the earl's envoy should arrive. I know not when that shall be. Have you need of drink or sustenance?"

"No, nothing now, thank you," Bob replied, fighting nausea. Two things had struck Bob as he was led into the building. The first was the musty darkness within. The second was the repugnant odor of sweat, smoke and human waste. He could feel neither hunger nor thirst with wave after wave of nausea overtaking him. "If I may, I'd just like to sit here for a while. I don't really feel very well."

"As you will. Michel will remain on guard for now. If you do have need, ask. We have simple provisions, but adequate. I shall attend to the throng outside." Sean hesitated, then added, "I would caution you not to attempt to leave or to cause a disturbance. Neither Michel nor I wish you any harm."

Bob knew immediately that this was not an idle threat.

"Believe me, I won't. I wouldn't even know where to go if I wanted to."

As the guard left, Bob sat on the bed, holding still to avoid the waves of nausea, hoping faintly for something to ease his confusion, disorientation and fear. Except for the muted chatter of the crowd outside and the cooing of pigeons, all was quiet. The terrible chill gradually eased as he sat inside on the bed, wrapped up in the pitiful blanket given him by the old man.

Bob tried again to sort out in his mind what all this was about. Nothing made sense! Not this place, this time, these people. How or why he got here was almost too weird to think about. Somehow, through, there had to be a link, and it surely had to do with that strange coin and that strange old man who died, and this one who called himself Drachma. The very mention of that name seemed to set off a reaction as sudden as flipping a light switch. Perhaps in time the connection would become clear, but here and now, in this cold, dingy barracks there did not seem to be a lot of answers.

As Bob sat, absorbed in his thoughts, Michel went over to the fireplace and began stoking up a fire from the embers that remained and some kindling from a basket nearby. The two men remained silent as the fire gained momentum and took hold of the logs Michel has placed over the kindling.

Noticing the radiant warmth, Bob left his blanket on the cot and walked over toward the fire. The two stood next to each other, close to the blaze, still saying nothing.

Eventually, their silence became irritating, and Bob broke the barrier.

"Tell me," he said, "your fellow guard had mentioned some

things of mine that you are holding. Do you know where they might be?"

"Aye," Michel replied, "but I am not at liberty to tell, insofar as the earl's envoy has not yet arrived. After that, I feel certain they shall be returned to you unharmed if they be not works of sorcery."

"Sorcery! Oh, good grief, no! They're just common everyday doctor things. If I'd had any sorcery at my disposal I sure would have used it to help out my very sick patient. That might be just about the only thing that would help poor Josh at this point."

Michel stared at Bob blankly. He might as well have been speaking in Arabic for all the sense his words made.

"I'm sorry," Bob said, noticing the guard's incomprehension. "I don't mean to rattle on. I'm just confused, disoriented and very, very, tired."

"Aye, the tiredness does show on your face. But, tell me, what do you mean by 'disoriented'? I know not what that word means."

"Ah, well" Bob hesitated, tried to think of some way to explain. "The word describes the circumstances of a man in a foreign country, not knowing where he is, how he got there, or even the local language."

Michel considered for a moment what Bob said, then ventured to ask, "and is that, then, the circumstance in which you find yourself at present?"

"That's it exactly," Bob replied.

Both men warmed their hands by the fire, saying nothing.

After a time, Michel asked, "then you truly do not know how you came to be here or whence?"

"That's true. Even when I try to think about it, it still makes no sense. No, I really don't know how I got here or why." He caught himself just in time before blurting out the name Drachma again. Realizing that perhaps, at least for the present time, it might be better not to say too much or give too much away, he let the subject drop, then returned to the silent activity of hand warming by the fire.

As he stood impassively by the fireplace, Bob was reminded of the old man in the forest he had seen in his reverie. The old man's words came back to his mind, clear as ever, along with the smell of forest in springtime.

"You have been chosen by people in great need, though they do not know it. Your tasks will become clear in time."

A loud pop from the fireplace brought Bob back from this latest daydream, again somewhat begrudgingly.

*I wonder who these people are that have chosen me,* he thought, *and why would they have done it without knowing. I'm sure that whatever my "tasks" might be, there would certainly be better people to do them, maybe even some who knew what was going on. I still wish I could convince myself that this is all a strange dream, then turn over and go to sleep.*

Bob noticed now that his waves of nausea had been replaced by low-level swells of somnolence, sweeping him into a state of transition between waking and sleeping worlds. The warmth from the fire only barely able to keep himself erect. He left the sheltering warmth of the fire, then staggered back to the cot, put the blanket back around himself and sat down.

"Listen, Michel," he said, "I'm very sleepy. Would it be all right if I laid down for now, at least until these Earl's men arrived? I really could use some sleep."

"As you wish. You may sleep if you are able."

As Bob lay down, he found himself hoping that, with sleep, he would wake back up in his own familiar environment, either home or in the hospital, at this point it didn't matter, just somewhere where he knew who and what he was, and what he was supposed to do.

It did not take long for Bob to drift off into deep, dreamless respirations. When Michel was sure Bob was sleeping, he took the opportunity to inspect his strange charge more closely. Never had he seen anyone like this before, not here, nor on travels to the mainland. He did seem to be in good health, though not stout or fit for hard labor. His hands were smooth, not those of a soldier or laborer. Likely he spoke the truth about his occupation as physician, but he did not have the garb of any physician Michel had ever seen. His garments, in fact, were not like any he had seen anywhere on anyone. They were thin, of cotton or linen, sewn with unbelievable precision, and very clean, too clean and thin for this winter weather.

Michel had never seen a sorcerer before, but still could not believe that he was looking at one now, despite what Sean had said. This was a tired, lost traveler, far from home, not a wielder of powerful dark magic. True, the objects found upon him by the hunters were of a craft that defied any explanation, and perhaps his power depended upon having the objects in his own hands, but instinct still rebelled at the thought that this might be a man of malign purpose. Certainly as he slept peacefully on the cot he appeared no more a threat than a newborn babe.

*Whence came you and why*, thought Michel, *is there a purpose behind your presence here?*

Michel's thought and Bob's slumber were abruptly interrupted by a loud, shrill sound from the far corner of the room, followed by a high pitched voice that was not quite understandable, and sounding not quite human.

Bob sat back up, dazed, then, as the sound continued with the hiss of white noise, memories returned.

*My beeper!* he thought. *Where is it?*

Michel, never having heard anything like the sound of an electronic beeper, stood frozen, momentarily paralyzed by an unnamed fear. Then the obvious realization dawned on him. *A banshee! Sorcery indeed!*

He shot for the door and the bright daylight, slamming the door shut behind him as he leaped out, leaving Bob, sitting on the cot, groggy and confused as ever.

Upon hearing the sound of the beeper, and before consciously realizing what it was, Bob had reached for his side automatically as if to silence the alarm. He felt his side empty, then became aware of what the sound was, and then did he open his eyes, and was shocked to find himself still in the dark barracks, with his guard fleeing for the doorway. He sat on the side of the cot, trying to think. He was still sleepy, but coherent enough to realize some of the importance of this moment.

In his mind a debate raged between his need to find his beeper and other "stuff" and his need to stay alive and not incite his captors to violence should they find him rifling through the confiscated equipment. It didn't occur to him to think that Michel was running for the door out of abject terror. Neither did it occur to him to think that the beeper going off at all was unusual in his present surroundings. Finally, the persistent hissing of the beeper left on persuaded him to search it out.

He got up and crossed the room toward the sound, emanating from a large wooden box in the corner by a simple sturdy table. Then the disembodied voice came on again, as usual, repeating the message. This time he could make it out.

"Dr. Gilsen, please call Judy Morrison at 983-5271." The voice was actually fairly clear this time.

Then the strangeness of it all really hit him.

*How in the world . . . ?* he thought. *Wherever the hell I am, it's sure to be out of beeper range. This just isn't possible!*

The beeper began hissing again as he tried to open the box, but found it was locked. A clumsy but sturdy metal lock held tight the lid to the oak box of about the same size as a laundry hamper. There was no way into the box without either the key or some solid tools. Bob made a feeble attempt to pry open the lock, but realized quickly that it would be useless to try, and probably quite risky as well, considering the demeanor of his captors.

Recognizing the futility of trying the box further, and resigning himself to the fact that the beeper would just have to go on hissing inside the box, Bob decided to try exploring his environs further. Somewhat nervously, he began looking about himself, pacing back and forth in the room. He found little of interest in his surroundings, mostly crude tools and what appeared to be edible provisions, but which smelled as unappetizing as rotting fruit. As he paced about, finding nothing of particular interest, he began to get bored, and then, as before, progressively sleepy. With some hesitation, he returned to the cot and sat down. He heard again faintly the sound of the pigeons, and the crackling fire. He couldn't fight it anymore, so he let himself fall back onto the cot and drift back to sleep, dreamless and profound, no forest, no voices, just sleep.

Within the forest hut, nearly hidden amid the gnarled trees, a man of indeterminate age, with white hair and flowing beard, sat at his table, writing on a small piece of yellowed paper. The man had the appearance of both ancient wisdom and youthful vigor. He wrote with sure purpose, a look of undeniable intensity on all his features. The writing was clear, unadorned, and with a peculiar slant to the left. Of necessity both the paper and the message were compact. He glanced up as the youth stirred in his seat by the fire.

"Ah, Tom, it is well that you are here for the present time. Your services are needed and shall be needed by more than just Master Falma. Rest assured, you are safer with my men and me than with the Forest Guard. We shall return you safely to Falma's service, but your route will be different. There are forces about these woods for which you would be a prize booty indeed, and my men and I know of safer, lesser known pathways by which we may escort you." He paused, noticing the youth's concerned look. "Fear not, son. Falma and the guard travel with the earl's seal of surety, and it would have to be the most foolhardy of villains that would cause them harm. Further, the old man would not be perceived either as a threat or as anyone worth molesting."

Tom could see the logic in what the man was saying. Though he could not imagine why anyone would consider him booty, he was afraid to follow that line of questioning lest he learn of something that would make the forest yet more fearsome. He nodded as a signal of his understanding.

"Tell me, son," the man continued, "do you know anything of the purpose of Falma's Journey? You may speak freely, for I am in the earl's loyal service."

"Only that there has been something of import that has happened near Killiburn Village, and that Drachma was named."

"Ah, and what, pray tell, do you know of this Drachma?"

"Alas, much that I had learned I did so from stories of dubious origin. Yet today Master Falma has told me more of the truth, or so it would seem, as he has known Drachma."

There was a smile on the man's face and a gleam in his eye. "Aye, he has known Drachma as well as any man alive. That much is true." He then fixed his glaze directly at Tom and said in a voice barely above a whisper, "Tom, I am he. I am Drachma."

Tom swallowed the lump in his throat, unable to speak, unable to hold the man's gaze. A cold shiver shot through his back, and he trembled.

"Be at ease, lad. I am not what the stories would have me seem. Furthermore, your safe conduct is my main concern for the present." He paused, then continued, "tell me, son, do you read?"

Tom, still unable to speak, nodded.

"Very well, then, come hither."

Tom stood, then moved over to the man's table.

"Look, here," he said, handing Tom the paper on which he had written, "do you recognize the script?"

It was not an innocent question and Tom knew it. He glanced down at the paper and noticed the familiar handwriting. The message was brief, stating clearly:

> Guard well the stranger who has come among you. No harm shall come to him or lives will be lost.
>
> Drachma

Tom handed the note back and said, realizing the futility of any attempt at concealment, "Aye, I do recognize the hand."

Drachma nodded, said nothing. He took the small piece of paper, folded it in two, and then rolled it into a cylinder, which ten fit neatly inside a capped hollow reed.

"Come, son, this you should see," he said, getting up from the table and heading for the back door. The two stepped through a tiny hallway to the door, then out to a small shed in which there were cages with six or seven pigeons. Drachma took out one of the birds and gently clipped the reed with the message to a ring on the bird's leg. Then, with a word of encouragement, let the bird fly into the forest.

"A messenger pigeon, son. It will return home with the message, to be received by the guard for whom it was intended."

Tom stood in awe and admiration. The elegance and simplicity of such a system of communication carried staggering implications that he could only begin to comprehend.

Drachma laid a hand gently on his grandson's shoulder, then guided him along the path to the stables. "Come, lad, I must speed you on your way. There is much for you to learn. Both Falma and I will tell you of things you will need to know. There will be time for that, but not now. Matters are urgent, and you are needed."

Tom burned inside with a mixture of excitement, anticipation, fear and surprise. He had never before felt important, and now, suddenly, he seemed a part of something grand and dangerous.

# Chapter Seventeen

Croftus Knob, the bare, rocky high point of the island was now, as it commonly was in winter, obscured by fog. Lough Teagle lay nestled between the two arms of the ridge that formed the knob. The place had a forbidding beauty that haunted the memories of those who had seen it. Gazing out of the high window of his observatory toward the distant promontory, the earl thought about those he had dispatched in that direction.

"Ah, Falma," he thought, "would that you were younger! But you alone can I trust with such a mission, and with so little instruction or explanation. Your wisdom and insight will be needed more than ever before. Craycroft would be a worthy companion, but my need of him here is too great, and Rust knows too little to be of use yet. And the page—such a bright gem among youth! My old friend, take care of that boy. We shall all have need of him." He came away from the window, and walked back over to the table and chairs in the center of the room. He looked again at the piece of paper bearing the message that had started all this fretful activity. It was a small piece of paper, smaller than the palm of his hand. Beside the paper was the tiny cylinder that had contained it. The handwriting was familiar, and the message direct.

The one summoned shall appear. Arrive near Killiburn on the morrow. Send envoy in haste.

Drachma

The earl sat and drew out a piece of paper, cutting the edges with a sharp knife to similar proportions, then wrote his reply.

Envoy dispatched. Provide all necessary protection.

Shepperton,
The Earl

He then rolled the paper, fitting it into the cylinder, and sealed the end. Getting up, he went over toward the door and pulled on the heavy bell cord hanging from the ceiling. While waiting for the page to answer the bell, the earl went back to peering out his window, his brow knotted with concern over his charges.

*Too much is at stake,* he thought. *Drachma may be correct, as he is most often, but the powers he might be invoking are beyond our ken and beyond our reach. I fear for consequences for which we have no means of preparation.* At times like this, he felt most keenly the burden of rule, and wondered how his father had remained so calm and sure throughout all the crises of his own office. He did not feel well, and had not for a week, but hoped that it was nothing more than his delicate nature under the strain of these difficult times.

*I can only hope that the king's advisors do not become aware of our doings. That would spell certain disaster. Mercifully, great affairs of state have kept their eyes in directions other than our isle. I do not wish for crises, but perhaps this once some minor clash or schism will keep their attention elsewhere.*

The earl's efforts gave way to a terrible fit of coughing. He brought out his kerchief, and spit out some vile looking material, then he sat back, to catch his breath. He noticed the page at his door, and quickly gathered himself. He felt just a bit lightheaded, but then the spell eased up.

"Good, it is you, Marcus. I have two tasks for you. Firstly, I will have you take this pigeon message to Herschel, and have him dispatch it with haste to Drachma. As usual, be discreet, and let none question you. Secondly, I will have you escort Master Craycroft here. There are matters of utmost importance that he and I need to discuss. He is likely weary, and perhaps reluctant to leave his charges, but use whatever gentle influences you may have to appraise him of my need to see him without delay."

"Understood, m'liege. I shall make haste."

"That is well, Marcus. Here, take the message."

The earl handed Marcus the tiny cylinder, which the page placed carefully in a leather case. With a quick bow of the head, the youth turned and was off on his appointed tasks. The Earl, then, left the observatory himself, and headed toward his meeting rooms. On the way, he passed by the servants' quarters, where he paused to order a small repast with some good brandy to be delivered to his meeting rooms for himself and his friend and physician.

Marcus did not have to search for Craycroft, as he met the master walking toward the earl's abode. The look on Craycroft's face was enough to quell any thought of conversation, let alone any attempt at coercion.

The page said simply, "The earl does request your presence, Master Craycroft. He sent me to accompany you."

Craycroft nodded glumly, saying nothing, and continued on his way. Marcus turned and walked two paces behind the master, sensing that protocol and courtliness were not on Craycroft's mind at the present. The master walked quickly, but, at the same time, as if the world's burdens were on his shoulders. The two made their way across the east end of the courtyard to the earl's abode and entered through the large front doors.

Once inside, Marcus promptly assumed control. This was his own domain, where he became the voice, the eyes and the ears of the earl.

"Come," he told Craycroft, "I will show you to the earl's chambers. He will expect me to bring you there. And further, he did say there were matters of great import he wished to discuss with you."

Craycroft, having been a page of the inner circle himself, saw through the ploy, recognizing the youth's attempt to gain the upper hand in these rather awkward circumstances. He said nothing, but allowed a wan smile to appear momentarily on his otherwise dour face. Marcus led him up the spiral stone stairway to a long hallway leading to the earl's chambers. Though Marcus and Craycroft both knew that these surroundings were as familiar to the master as to the page, they tacitly agreed to follow protocol, and have the page lead Craycroft to the earl's inner chambers and be announced upon entry.

The earl was both pleased and surprised to find that Marcus had brought the master so soon.

"Ah, my old friend, please come in. I am delighted to see you. Do take a chair. I am sure you are weary." He paused to look at Craycroft. "There is more than weariness on your countenance. Tell me, what has happened?"

Craycroft sat heavily into a large cushioned chair, a great sigh escaping him as he did so. Both men turned and noticed that Marcus was still in the doorway.

"Marcus, I thank you for bringing Master Craycroft. You may leave now."

With an obvious look of reluctance, the youth turned and left the doorway, heading back into the hallway, toward the servants' quarters.

"My friend, Craycroft," the earl resumed, "I can see by your face that there is grief beyond measure in your heart. Is it the lady?"

Craycroft nodded, swallowing back the latest flood of emotion.

"Aye, m'liege, she is dead." The earl somehow knew, but still the message hit him like a blow. This lady was no mere subject of his domain. This was a person of incomparable importance in all their lives. She had been the symbol and personification of all that was beautiful. Steadfast and meaningful, she had complemented their meager existence with her mere being. She was its history made flesh, coming as a stranger and staying to make all their lives more full and joyous.

For a time they sat in silence, each contemplating what Felicia's loss meant personally. Then, unbidden, the thought came to both at once, and the earl voiced it: "Drachma," he said, "he must be told at once. But how? I do not have another messenger pigeon to send him, as I have just dispatched the last that would go to him."

"Is there not a trustworthy rider you can send?" asked Craycroft. "Surely one could deliver such a message with little delay."

"My best is now, as we speak, dispatched for other reasons, escorting Falma and the page, Tom. Their mission is, in fact, the reason I did summon you."

"In truth, m'liege, I was already on my way hence when I encountered Marcus." Then the realization struck him. "You sent Falma, on a mission in the middle of winter!? Ah, m'liege, this must be of the gravest importance. I fear for the old man. He is quite frail."

"Of that, I am fully aware, my friend. And aye, the mission is fraught with peril. Nevertheless, its urgency and significance are of the highest order, and shall, in time, involve you most certainly."

"And where have you sent them, sire?"

"Toward Killiburn."

"Ah, that would be through the wood and past Croftus Knob. They would then likely encounter Falma or his men."

"Indeed, they shall. I did dispatch a pigeon message that will make that a near certainty."

"Well, I would venture to say, then, that Drachma will get the message as regards our lady, and soon, as the page, and likely Falma, too, are aware of her demise."

The earl nodded, and both men sat quietly, pondering and grieving.

"Tell me, m'liege, what is this matter of such portent that you have sent poor Falma out at peril?" Craycroft asked at last. "It cannot be a matter for the council, as surely you would have summoned a meeting if it were anything that could be made public. Further, it would appear certain that our friend Drachma is involved in the matter. His name does seem to ring loudly whenever great doings are to occur without council knowledge or approval. This much I did learn from years with your father."

"True, friend," the earl replied. "That is, above all, why I have called for you. I may only discuss this with one whom I trust implicitly, and one who has the breadth of experience that few here possess. That could only be you and Master Falma."

"Ah, m'liege, I understand." Craycroft paused. "Please proceed, then, and tell me what you will. I am, as always, wholly in your service."

"Aye, that you have no need to prove. Listen, my friend, as you well know, this matter of the deaths and illness of the painters and potters I have asked you to investigate, has taken on aspects completely unforeseen either by you or myself. When you made me aware of Lord Vincente's knowledge or involvement in the matter, I began to understand that it might threaten the very fabric of our lives on this isle. You know, as well as anyone but Falma, how our prosperity through the years has depended on the work, overtly and covertly, of both Lord Vincente and our mysterious benefactor, Drachma."

Craycroft nodded, indicating his understanding.

"You know, as well," the earl continued, "how both my father and I have come to depend on Drachma's connections and influence when matters of extreme delicacy have arisen that required prompt and effective action."

"Aye, that I also understand."

"Well, then, with the knowledge you were able to provide, and the dangerous implications that it suggested to my heart, I sought out Drachma's counsel in this matter."

"And what did you tell him, m'liege, if I may be so bold as to ask?"

"Certainly, you may. I told him I knew of the matter, which was nigh unto one month ago. He listened with his usual dispassionate countenance; that is, until I told him of the note, and that it was written in Lord Vincente's own hand." The earl paused, then continued. "As I told him of this, his brow darkened, and his expression changed. The look was not one I had ever witnessed, and I cannot describe it to you except to say that I, ruler of this Isle and commander of men-at-arms, felt fear within me as I had not since I was a small child."

"I have heard tales of such, m'liege. It is said to be most unwise to provoke him when his visage has darkened thus."

"That would likely be true, and I did not. Neither did I question him regarding the meaning of the note, nor of Lord Vincente's apparent involvement in the matter. For his part, however, he insisted that the note proved Lord Vincente had invoked the powers that lay beyond reason, and we must be prepared to do the same."

"Ah, that could be a most fearsome thing to do. Have any in authority ever invoked that power that we know?"

"Nay, not within my memory or within our history."

"Fearsome, indeed." Craycroft paused. "What, then, did you do sire?"

"Naught, at that time. I did tell Drachma that I must confer with Falma and possibly others before making a decision. His face, then, began again to darken, but did lighten once more before he spoke. He said, then, that I must make a decision within the fortnight, and that he would be expecting my reply."

"I must assume, m'liege, that you did, then, confer with Master Falma about these matters."

"Aye, that I did do. It is most curious, though, what Falma suggested."

"Sire . . . ?"

"He said that he must confer himself with Lady Vincente, and that she had within her possession a book that might yield the necessary keys to proceeding as Drachma had suggested. This book, he said, was written by Drachma himself and was in safekeeping at Lord Vincente's, and that Drachma was aware of this fact. Furthermore, he said that he would need Lady

Vincente's approval to release the book and to invoke the powers of which we had spoken."

To Craycroft, the memories of Felicia's final hours came rushing back, most notably her conversation with Tom, having to do with a message to Master Falma, as well as her final instructions to him to release the book to young Tom. He knew without asking that the message had something to do with the earl's prior conference with Drachma. He thought about the book and what its release might mean. It was clear that he knew more about it than the earl.

"Ah," he said quietly, to himself, "most curious, most curious."

"What is it, my friend?" the earl asked. "It is obvious that I have touched upon something you have seen or heard."

"M'liege, it is simply that, in her final hours, our lady did send to Master Falma a message, through our page, Tom. I know not the nature of the message."

"I see," the earl nodded, pondering what Craycroft had just said. A knock at the door caught their attention.

"Ah," said the earl, "that would be the food I requested. It would please me if you could take a small repast with me."

"As you wish, m'liege, though I have not felt much hunger of late. Please, stay seated. I shall let the servant in."

Craycroft rose, then let in the servant, who silently brought in his laden tray, set it on the table before the earl, and then, just as quietly, left with a bow. The master then uncovered the dishes to find a small but elegant array of meats, fruits and bread, along with a flask of brandy and two glass tumblers.

"Ah, m'liege, the food is excellent, I am sure, and I would normally find it most appealing, but allow me to serve you some. I will be content with a small sip of brandy."

"Nonsense, friend. You must have at least some bread. I insist."

"Very well, I shall." Craycroft selected for the earl some fine spiced meats, fruits and bread, then poured brandy in the two tumblers. For himself he took only a small quarter of a loaf of bread and the lesser of the two portions of brandy. After serving the earl, he took his bread and brandy and sat back down heavily. The earl ate without obvious enjoyment, while Craycroft nibbled perfunctorily at his bread. The two said nothing as they ate and drank, each enveloped in his own cloud of thought and emotion.

With his own meal almost untouched, the earl spoke again. "Come, my friend, the meat is truly well prepared. Have a little, at the very least."

"Thank you sire, but no. The bread is more than sufficient for me."

"As you will. Tell me, Craycroft, what do you know of this book?"

The master swallowed hard, thinking of what to say to his liege lord. He decided the truth would probably be better than any foolhardy attempt to try to discern what the earl would want to hear. True, any knowledge of the book alone might carry a burdensome price, but any effort at evasion would have the effect of forfeiting the trust that the earl had bestowed upon him.

"Well, m'liege," he began, "the book you mention is a most extraordinary thing indeed. Drachma himself wrote the book while yet young in years, but following extended travels and considerable study at the feet of great masters in eastern lands. It contains much insight as well as keys to great power. At its opening, however, Drachma penned a warning to any who might open the book, which states that all who would be so bold as to read it shall be irrevocably changed."

"Tell me, friend," the earl said, with a note of caution in his voice, "how did you come to know of this book?"

"Ah, that is a tale unto itself, m'lord. But to answer your question as briefly as I may, it was through my lifelong friendship with the Lady Vincente that I came to know of its existence. She, rather than Lord Vincente, had been entrusted with its care."

"That, based upon what I do know of their history, makes perfect sense," the earl added.

"Aye, m'liege."

"Tell me, then, did you or the lady, either one of you, happen to read this dangerous text?"

"She did, m'lord, but I, though sorely tempted, did not. She did tell me of some of what it contained, but I have not myself read more than the warning inscription which begins the book."

"Ah, well, tell me then, do you know where this book presently resides?"

"I believe that I do . . ."

"And Falma, does he also?"

"Most likely, m'liege, he does as well. Lady Vincente, only a very brief moment before she passed on, did indicate to me its location."

"Hmm, that is curious indeed. For what reason did our lady tell you of it?"

"It seems, m'liege, that she intended for me to give it to the page, Tom."

"The page? The very one I have sent with Falma and my guard toward Killiburn?"

"Aye, that is the one."

"Pray, tell, Craycroft, what do you know of this page boy?"

"Until a few short days ago, m'lord, I knew nothing. But now, it seems, I have learned much of who he is and what he may yet become."

Craycroft knew very well that the earl had learned much that his questions did not reveal, and that he was likely trying to build upon what he already knew or suspected; and that what light Craycroft could shed on the matters at hand might illuminate facts and rumors new and useful way. His years of service to the house of Shepperton had made the master well accustomed to devices used by those in authority to gain that which they needed most, namely, reliable information.

"Please continue, my friend. Do tell what you have learned. I am most eager for this knowledge."

"As well you should be m'liege." Craycroft's manner became, quite unconsciously, very deferential, almost unctuous. "What I have come to learn, from a number of sources, is that this young page boy is far more than he would seem at first acquaintance." The earl nodded, knowingly.

"His name alone, m'lord, carries much history with it, his given name being Drachma. When he told me of it, I took the opportunity to investigate what was recorded of his lineage. This, unfortunately, was mostly sham, and it required several more hours of searching to uncover his true past, which I believe I now do understand."

"As always, my good friend you seem not to rest with doubt, and will ever search until you have grasped a kernel of hard truth. It is well that I have appointed for you the tasks I have."

"Sire, you do know me well."

"Of course. Pray, continue. What did your search reveal of the youth's history?"

"I am sure, sire, that you are well acquainted with the doings of Drachma the Elder while he was yet young among our people."

"Of course, that is familiar history to this family."

"Then you know that, while I was yet a page myself, Lady Vincente, then the daughter of Ambassador Gianni, whom we knew and adored as Felicia, and Drachma, her tutor, did find mutual love and comfort in each other's arms, and brought forth, under the cover of discretion, a child."

The earl nodded, indicating familiarity with the story. His coughing started again, and he became somewhat winded. Craycroft got up to assist his earl, but was waved off. After another brief spell, he seemed to recover, and Craycroft continued.

"Well, few here on the isle have learned of this, but the daughter born of Drachma and Felicia grew to womanhood upon the Isle, sheltered as it were from history. She did, in fact bear a child, who grew up in obscurity, and who then did herself die while giving birth, while the infant that she bore did live. He was given the name Drachma, but was raised in the village, by common parents, and was made to become a page early on. That is none other than our page, called Tom."

"You were able to discover this upon your search? I was not aware that this matter had been recorded anywhere."

"Only upon the hearts of those who needed to know, m'liege. The lady herself had told me of this in years past, and I pursued it no further. Nay, my search did not tell me this, but rather it told me of what became of the babe that Felicia's daughter bore."

"Ah, well, do continue your tale."

"Certainly. It seems that the young woman, whose name I have only recently discovered was Maggie, did have a dying wish that her son should be reunited in time with his grandparents. This, as I feel certain you understand, presented difficulties in the extreme, considering what had transpired in regard to matters of your family, this island, and of Drachma the Elder. Your father did learn of the woman's wish, and felt moved to honor it, and, in his wisdom, did assign Master Falma, his trusted advisor, the task of carrying out Maggie's wish in such a manner that the House of Shepperton's honor would not be tarnished."

"You have learned much, my friend. This is not common knowledge, and those who share it are very few."

"In truth, m'liege, I learned some, and have surmised much that would fill in the gaps of knowledge."

"That has always been your way, has it not?"

"True, it has."

"What, then, did become of this child? Did you find out more with any certainty?"

"Aye, which does bring us full circle in this tale to the present time. It seems that this infant, named for his grandfather, was entrusted to the care of a man and wife of the village, he a gardener and she a seamstress. They were known to be loyal workers, and had within the month, lost a son of their own in childbirth. Master Falma was able, in a way, to bring back the woman's lost son. She was instructed simply to raise the child fully as her own, but at an age of reason, he would be given a position of work within the castle. Only in the fullness of time would he be told of his true heritage, for with that knowledge would come power and a mission he would not be able to deny."

"This, then, is our page, Tom."

"Aye, m'liege, the very one who is now most certain to meet his grandfather and namesake; the very one sent upon your perilous mission with Master Falma."

"Aye, Craycroft, you have discovered much in little time. It is all as you have surmised." The earl paused, considering his words carefully. "Listen, my good friend, I must tell you now of the nature of Falma's mission. But pray tell no one of this save Falma, Drachma and young Tom. What we have embarked upon I fear more that any battle or plague, for it is truly venturing in uncharted waters."

Craycroft noted that his earl seemed just a little out of breath, and that his coughing sounded hoarse.

"My liege, I shall provide some syrup for your catarrh, if you would like," said Craycroft, as he looked at the uneaten tray of food on the table.

"Ah, thank you, but no. It is but this winter weather."

# Chapter Eighteen

To anyone walking in, the surgery lounge would hardly seem a place for quiet or serious conversation. Simply put, it was ugly and it reeked. What it smelled of was years of dirt, sweat, smoke, disinfectants and worry, the combined effect of which was acrid and rather nauseating. The walls were a faded grey, the carpeting a dull shade of green, and the vinyl-covered furniture a mixture of vague neutral hues. When Judy arrived, Earl and Janie rose quickly, and greeted her with such enthusiasm that Judy was almost literally taken aback.

"Oh, Judy, we're so glad you came! I know you've been up to see Josh, and really, that's very touching that you would care enough to go see him in your off hours."

Janie's usual pressured speech carried undertones of pain and gratitude. Sensing this, in contrast to her own confused reasons for coming back to the hospital, Judy blushed and stammered a little.

"Ah . . . er . . . actually I really came to see—"

"Oh, come on now and sit down," Earl interrupted. "You're probably tired."

"Thanks, Earl, I will. And actually, I am kind of beat."

The three sat down, Earl and Janie on a coach and Judy in a large stuffed chair. After a moment of awkward silence, Judy spoke.

"Listen, I know this must really be hard on the two of you right now. You've got to be going through some kind of hell. Believe me, I know just how big and impersonal hospitals like this can get. Like I told you, I've been up to see Josh in the ICU. I don't know what the nurses and doctors have told you so far, but it really doesn't look too good at the moment." Judy swallowed, pausing to try and form the right words. "You know I've seen Josh a number of times, when he's come through the ER, and even when he's been desperately ill, there's been kind of a spark of life to him that seemed like a signal to us taking care of him that he wasn't done yet, that he had more to do and say, to tell us not to give up just yet."

Janie and Earl nodded, their eyes moist.

"Well, when I was up there looking at him just a bit ago, I didn't see it, and that frightened me. He was peaceful, not in any kind of pain or anything, but there was something missing, something important. It was like that spark had been given away." Judy paused again, "I just couldn't get out of my mind the notion that Josh himself gave it away, released it. That must really sound crazy, but I can't help but feel it's true."

Janie stared, saying nothing, a solitary tear gleaming on her cheek.

"I'm sorry, maybe I shouldn't be telling you this, it's really not my place. I tried to find Dr. Gilsen, but no one seems to know where he's gone. I'm so sorry . . ."

Judy reached across the small space and touched Janie's hand.

"No, Judy, I'm glad you've come and told us." Janie hesitated. "It's something I also sensed. And too, I do think somehow Dr. Gilsen felt the same thing. I'd love to talk to him, but as busy as he is, I sure don't want to go bothering him over something like this that I couldn't even put into a good question."

"I wonder," said Earl, unexpectedly, "if this isn't just our way of trying to come to terms with failure." Judy and Janie both stared at him. "I mean, after all, there have been all these unexpected victories with Josh, and now are we finally failing, and trying to explain it away?"

"No, Earl," Janie chided gently, "I don't think that's it at all. There's just something different, and you know, I can't help but think Dr. Bob knows too, maybe not in a way that can be put into words, but knows nonetheless. Don't you remember he said something about that himself?"

"Yeah, I do remember. That was when he came down and was talking about that funny coin that wasn't in the box. Right?"

The memory of that conversation, and of later unexpectedly finding the coin in her purse, caused Janie an involuntary gasp. She hadn't said anything to Earl about having the coin. What could she have said that made any sense? No one could possibly have put it there. She had had her purse with her the entire time they had been at the hospital, and hadn't fallen asleep or left it lying about.

"A coin?" Judy asked. "You wouldn't happen to mean an ancient Greek coin?"

Janie and Earl both stared at Judy, dumbfounded.

"You mean, you know about the coin?" Janie asked, incredulous.

Judy got the feeling again that she had stepped into something from which there was no retreat, sort of the way Bob had described walking down that path he had no power to resist.

"All I know is this coin is tied in somehow with Dr. Gilsen and Josh, and what Josh said before his seizure, and with a very old man who died in the ER early this morning."

"I don't understand," Earl said, "this is getting to sound kind of weird. I'm not a believer in magic and stuff, but all this is starting to seem a bit like the sort of mumbo-jumbo you read about, with spells and incantations and the like."

"Now, Earl," Janie chided again, "you can't go thinking things like that. I'm sure there's some logical explanation or reason, even if we don't understand it now."

She did not sound convincing.

"Tell me, Judy," she went on, "what do you know about this coin? Have you seen it?"

"Well, actually, I have."

Judy thought carefully about what she should or could tell about the inexplicable events of the past two days. There seemed to be nothing to gain by holding anything back. She considered for only a moment, then went ahead and told Janie and Earl about the curious letter, about her encounter with Mr. Vincente in the ER, and about her conversation with Bob, during which he had opened the box to find the Drachma."

Earl and Janie sat in puzzled silence, understanding little, but coming to accept that somehow their son, now desperately ill, had unwittingly become part of some mysterious and powerful chain of events which defied explanation and resisted understanding.

"Does Dr. Gilsen know or understand what's been going on," Janie asked.

"I doubt it," said Judy. "The last I saw or talked with him, he was as puzzled as me, maybe more so, seeing as how he hasn't exactly had a good night's sleep."

"You know, I really would like to talk to him," continued Janie, "but I'd just hate to bother him, especially if he's finally getting some sleep."

"Yeah, I know, but still . . ."

"You think we should try getting a hold of him?" "I don't know, I just don't know. Through the years I've known him, though, he's never once seemed upset when I've had to wake him for something. Maybe we should try paging him, just this once."

Judy went over to the phone and picked it up to call. Thinking about it, she put the receiver back down.

"Wait a minute. Now, what in the world are we going to say if he answers his page? I already feel more than a little foolish doing this."

"Well," Janie suggested, "we could tell him we've got his coin to give back."

"What do you mean?" Earl sounded shocked. "You have the coin, the one that was supposed to be in his box?"

In answer, Janie opened her purse and reached inside, rummaged briefly, then pulled out a small silver coin, about the size of a nickel. She held it in the palm of her hand as Judy and Earl studied the object with a mixture of awe and fascination. Judy touched it gingerly, and turned it over in Janie's palm.

"Yeah, that's the same coin, all right. There wouldn't likely be two of them running around here. How did you get it? Did he give it to you?"

"Well, that's the strange part, Judy. Actually, he tried to give it to me, and said that maybe some day I'd figure it all out. But then, when he opened the box, it was empty! He was just mortified, I could tell, but I didn't know what to do or think at the time."

"But you've got the coin now," Earl interrupted. "How did you get it?"

"You're not going to believe it, and I really don't quite myself, but when I stopped to call Ma on the pay phone, I reached into my purse and pulled out what I thought was a quarter. Only it wasn't a quarter, it was this coin. I swear, I have absolutely no idea how it got there."

"Oh, Janie, that doesn't make any sense at all. That's not possible, just not possible!"

"You got any ideas, then? Earl, you've been with me this whole time. The purse hasn't been out of my sight."

"No," he answered thoughtfully, "I don't have a single idea, good or bad. But maybe you're right. Maybe we should try to page Dr. Gilsen."

"I'll do it," volunteered Judy, "I already tried once before. No harm in trying again."

"Did he answer?"

"No, Janie, he didn't, but then I left for the hospital, and he might have called after I left."

Judy picked the phone back up and dialed the operator.

"Hello . . . yes, this is Judy Morrison, night ER supervisor. Could you page Dr. Gilsen to call 4277? Yeah, that's 4277. Thanks."

The page went out over the intercom, and the three waited for an answer. Several minutes passed without the phone ringing. Judy picked the phone back up.

"Look, I'll call his office number and have the answering service beep him."

She repeated the request when the answering service picked up the line.

Five minutes passed, then ten, still with no response. Waiting became increasingly awkward, and a sense of futility began to pervade the little room. Feeling a need to do something, Judy began calling all the places in the hospital that she thought Dr. Gilsen might possibly have gone, all with the same result—no one had seen him recently, and he had left no messages as to where he might be going."

"It's okay," Janie said, finally. "We better leave things be. If he's sleeping, he must surely need it. It's been a trying day for everyone. Why don't you go back and get some rest? We can talk later, or tomorrow sometime. Josh is in good hands. Everyone's done all they can do, and whatever happens is going to happen."

As she spoke, Janie's eyes were dry, but the depth of sadness in her voice was more than Judy could bear. She excused herself with a word of thanks and a handshake, then turned and left the room.

Judy did not consciously think about where she was going when she left the surgery lounge, only that she needed to go somewhere. She was not through searching, but her tangled mixture of feelings was hardly ideal for making rational decisions. She was tired, but on edge, energetic, but with no reserve, as if she were running on the last of her fuel. More obviously, she was worried, almost to the point of panic, but could not name the source of her worry. Beneath it all, though, was a feeling she did not wish to recognize, a deeply powerful sensation that seemed to stem from ages past, and against which she had no defenses. It was illogical and dangerous, unwanted, and did not belong.

Running on pure nervous tension, she arrived without realizing it back at the ER nurses' lounge.

*Now what?* she thought. *Maybe if I just sit down and try to relax, I'll think more clearly.*

As she sat down in the stuffed chair, she realized her left had had been clenching tightly. With an effort she relaxed her hand. In her palm was a moist, wrinkled paper along with another object that fell out of her hand and rolled across the room. She got back up and walked over, stooping to pick up the small silver coin.

For an instant, as she looked at the coin, there was the sense of being away, outside, with the smell of spring and newly turned earth, the feel of warm sunlight filtered through pale green leaves. She closed her eyes, felt the pull of something unnamed and far away, then with a conscious effort resisted, opened her eyes and reoriented herself.

"Judy! What the hell you doin' here, girl? You're supposed to be home sleeping. You got family sick or something?"

It was Lonie Chaves, who had found a few spare minutes to retreat to the nurses' lounge and search out the refrigerator.

"Oh, hi, Lonie. No, it's not family exactly, but I couldn't sleep. There were things running around in my head over this business with Josh and his surgery and all. I came back to check on some stuff."

"He really got to you, huh?" Lonie smiled and patted Judy on the shoulder. "All the years I've known you, I've never seen you get involved after hours like this. It's not like you. What's the difference this time?"

"I wish I knew. If I did, I might be able to go back to sleep. I mean, I've seen all kinds of heartbreak stories come through this ER, some that would just melt your resistance, but after the shift's over and the patients are taken care of, I could always just leave it at that and go about my business. This time it's different, I don't know, just got to me, I guess."

"Ah, Judy, you're talking about the patients. That's not what I was talking about."

"No? What do you mean . . ."

"Well, girl, you just figure that one out for yourself. I'm sure you will someday. Now, you get yourself back home and try to get at least a few hours' sleep before you gotta be back here."

Lonie poured herself some cola into a cup from the can she took from the refrigerator, took a long swallow, then headed back into the ER. "So long, Judy. You be careful out in that blizzard."

Mention of the weather brought reality screaming back down upon Judy's awareness. The thought of going back out into the blowing snow and ice, and driving the miserable distance back to her apartment was more than she thought herself capable of handing at the moment. The alternative of finding some place in the hospital to sack out for while, though, was just about as unappealing.

With an effort, she heaved herself out of the chair, got up and put on her coat, hat and gloves, then walked on out of the ER toward the exit. The door to the parking lot resisted when Judy tried to open it, due to the fierce wind blowing from the northwest. Pushing with her shoulder, she was able to get the metal door open enough to slip outside. She regretted it immediately. If anything, it was colder than ever and blowing harder. The exposed flesh of her face was stinging, and it was hard to keep her eyes open against the wind and snow.

*Damn you, Bob Gilsen,* she thought as she trudged out to her car. *Why in Heaven's name did you make me come out in this weather, chasing some fantasyland coin with a mind of its own, and a kid dying after open heart surgery? I should have been in my nice warm bed, sleeping.*

When she got to her car, Judy looked back and noticed that most of her footprints had already been covered over with new blowing snow. She fumbled in her coat pocket, found her car keys, then got back into her car gratefully. After several attempts, the engine roared to life. She sat in her car, rubbing her hands together, letting some feeling return to her face before deciding to go back out and scrape the windshield clear. After five minutes of scraping and cursing, she had cleared enough from the windshield that it seemed safe to try driving, so Judy got back into the driver's seat and pulled her car out of its parking space and headed for the street, somewhere out there.

It took more than half an hour to get back to her neighborhood, find a parking space, then trudge back up the steps to her apartment. On her way in, Judy picked up the daily paper and her mail, which had, incredibly, already been delivered. An overpowering sense of fatigue washed over her as she crossed the threshold and closed the door behind her. It was all she could do to deposit the papers on her kitchen table, dump her coat, hat and gloves on a chair, and the rest of her clothes on the floor of her bedroom before collapsing on her bed.

Conscious awareness gave way, and as it did, Judy found herself on a path heading into a forest. It was warm. The smell of flowers and newly turned earth, the sound of a flowing stream . . .

# Chapter Nineteen

The clouds were low and dense above their heads as Falma and Kerlin made the climb toward Croftus Knob. An ominous breeze began blowing from the northeast, cutting through their winter clothing. Falma's hands and feet no longer ached, they were numb.

"This would be such a formidable place to find ourselves caught in a winter storm," he said to Kerlin, "I would feel more assured if we were closer to the earl's hunting shelter. By my recollection, though, we are yet hours away."

"Aye, that is true. We are at the very least three hours away if we continue our present pace. We have strong mounts, though, Master Falma, and with a sure storm approaching, we might goad them along faster."

"Let us then try. I would rather hurt from hard riding than risk this fearsome weather's clutches."

They had little difficulty encouraging the horses, which were bred and trained for hard riding with armored men on their backs. Progress was good for the next quarter hour, before the storm hit. Light, blowing snow swirled around the riders for several minutes, then, as they rounded a great curve on the mountainside, the winter storm's fury engulfed them. There was nothing to see but the whiteness, no path, no mountain, no trees.

There was nothing at all to hear except the panting of the horses, and nothing to feel except the stinging cold of the driven snow.

*The Island's need would certainly justify the earl's action,* thought Falma, *but to send an old man out to his death in a winter storm—the council will want an explanation, and that might prove most difficult. I hope he will have the chance to talk with Craycroft.*

Falma realized, after a silence of some minutes' duration, that he could only hear his own horse's panting. Kerlin should be just ahead, but nothing was visible nor audible. Fear suddenly clutched at his throat, and his heart began racing.

"Kerlin!" he cried out. "Are you there, Kerlin?"

He reined in his horse and listened for a reply. There was only silence, cold and white.

"You see the order there before you quite plainly. We are bound by duty and must obey. You know as well as I that any message so received has the earl's seal of approval a priori."

"But how are we to provide protection to one empowered by magic, and in the company of banshee?"

"Banshee, indeed! You saw this, did you?"

"Nay, but I did hear it. Its voice arose from where we locked up his weapons."

Sean nodded, but his expression was skeptical. "And what, pray tell, did its voice say?"

"Say? Nothing I could tell, but it did make an ungodly scream, not unlike a tortured cat."

"Ah, so you say." Sean looked even more skeptical. "You do not suppose, perhaps, that it might have been nothing more than a cat which you heard? Perhaps one of the village boys at a prank."

Michel felt exasperated, but held his tongue in check, remembering his rank. He said simply, "you would not have said what you did if you had heard it."

"Ah, well, perhaps not," Sean replied, patronizing in his tone.

"Nevertheless, our duty remains. We must provide protection, whatever the cost. The earl's envoy must not find us remiss."

"So be it, then, but might I suggest we not provoke our charge. We know not, nor do I suspect do the earl or even Drachma, what power's he may wield."

"Very well, though I have not seen anything that would make me fear for my safety. He does seem, if anything, a small and timid sort."

"So I thought as well."

The two guards had been discussing their newly arrived dispatch in the eastern tower where the messenger pigeon had returned, bearing Drachma's terse note. Michel took another look at the note, as if to reassure himself that there was no mistaking the message. It was as plain and concise as ever.

> Guard well the stranger who has come among you.
> No harm shall come to him or lives will be lost.
>
> Drachma

After coming to their hesitant decision and returning the bird to its cage, along with food and water, they descended the inner stairway back into the village, then turned back toward their quarters. By this time a little crowd had gathered, following the sight of Michel, the brave man-at-arms, as he bolted from the quarters in absolute terror. Walking back now, the guards could see the amused and excited faces of the young ones in the group as they pointed, chuckled, and made whispered comments among themselves.

As if in answer to their implied derision, Michel clasped the hilt of his sword, set his gaze sternly ahead, and walked with as firm and commanding a stride as he could. Unfortunately, the effect was that of a parody which caught the crowd's fancy, and the smirking and giggling only increased. Michel's neck and face reddened from embarrassment and barely suppressed rage, but he walked on, eyes held rigidly forward, saying nothing, but wanting more than anything to draw his sword and rush into the throng of jeering villagers.

*Laugh now, you fools,* he thought, *I shall see your mocking turned to fear ere long.*

The guards stopped at the door of their quarters. The crowd that had followed at a safe distance noticed their hesitation, and then began jeering with renewed interest and energy. Whatever or whoever had driven the man-at-arms running from the building earlier must still be inside. To the boys, who had discussed the matter eagerly among themselves, it seemed inconceivable that the oddly dressed stranger, whom the guards had taken manacled into the quarters less than two hours before, could be the source of Michel's terror. Still, there was no other prisoner. And then there was the shriek that some had heard just before the guard had bolted, unlike anything heard before in the village or forest. Whatever the explanation, there was sure to be fighting, possibly bloodshed, and likely more armed men with horses. None wanted to miss seeing anything this thrilling.

Sean, in answer to Michel's mute question, decided to peer inside himself, while his partner remained at the door. He opened the heavy door as quietly as he could, then stepped halfway inside.

As his eyes adjusted to the dimness, he could see Bob's still form on the cot in the middle of the room. Stepping all the way inside, he could see the slow, quiet chest expansions indicating slumber. Something, though, was amiss. After several puzzled moments, Sean realized what it was. The room was not silent. Rather, a hissing sound was present, not loud, but clear, and seeming to originate from the region of the locked box.

Sean stepped back outside to speak with Michel.

Whispering, he said, "he is sleeping, and soundly, it would appear. There is a sound in the room, a quiet, blowing noise . . ."

"Did I not tell you? It is magic, and surely foul. We should not provoke any disturbance."

"Aye, if all remains still, it might be best if we would remain here without. That would surely honor our duty. But, whatever happens, we must not flee or leave him unguarded."

Michel nodded his begrudging assent.

For the next two hours all did remain quiet, with the two guards pacing about in front of their quarters. The quiet hissing could still be heard from within if they strained to listen. After about one hour, the crowd of children began to disperse out of boredom. It was agreed among them, though, that some would stay "on guard" and signal the others should anything change.

The weather was the first to change. Clouds began to roll in, low to the ground, coming from the forest and hills, and bringing a northeasterly wind that grew in intensity. Light snow began to drift about the trees and buildings.

To Sean and Michel, the prospect of staying outside in the gathering winter storm gradually became more onerous than facing the unknown magic within. Dangerous or not, there was at least a fire inside and shelter. The snow became mixed with stinging tiny pellets of ice, driven by ever stronger winds. The guards could no longer see across the yard to where the children had been keeping vigil, and, in fact, could barely see each other.

"Michel, you may stay without if you wish, but as for me, I would rather take my chances with banshees than this blizzard. I am going inside."

Michel said nothing, but followed Sean inside, quietly closing the door behind him. Inside was warm, dark and still, except for the continued quiet hiss from the box and the sound of wind through cracks and windows. Bob remained soundly asleep on his cot. The fire, which Michel had earlier fed and stoked, blazed quietly, shedding its warmth through the stone building. Sean walked over to the far corner to relieve his full bladder as Michel walked silently over to the fire to tend it further.

The shrill scream of the beeper going off in that dark, quiet room commanded immediate attention. Bob was roused from his deep slumber, instantly alert and listening for the message. Sean, terrified, in mid stream, turned, grabbed his sword from its scabbard and faced the source of the sound, urinating down his leg. Michel, recognizing the terror, dropped the log he was carrying on his foot, and then fainted from pain and fear.

"Dr. Gilsen, please call Judy Morrison at Memorial, extension 4277. Please call 4277."

The harsh, tinny voice rang through the stone-walled room. To anyone not used to listening to mechanical voices coming from beepers the words would be completely unintelligible, but to Dr. Gilsen such transmissions had become as routine as listening through a stethoscope, and he had no trouble understanding the message. The problem, he realized as he sat up, was someone was paging him (now twice), and he had absolutely no way to respond.

To Sean, the problem was much more profound. As he understood his present circumstances, he was now trapped in a room in a blizzard with a mysterious stranger whom he was duty-bound to guard and protect, who had just magically released a banshee into their midst. He had been through battles and skirmishes, through bloodshed and torment, but he had never faced numinous terror like this before. He stood in his corner of the room, shaking and speechless, eyes wide and mouth agape, frozen to his spot. The fact that his fellow guard lay unconscious by the fireplace only made things more terrible.

It took Bob a few moments to regain his bearings. He then looked about and saw one guard passed our on the floor, the other staring blankly in his direction, standing in a puddle of urine. These the same fierce men who had brought him shackled to this dingy, stinky old building. He couldn't help himself, it was to much; he began laughing, first a quiet chuckle, then building to full blown uproarious laughter.

*Oh, God, preserve me*, thought Sean, *the wizard has released his banshee, and now laughs! I have no power over this. If he seeks revenge, I am lost.*

Bob stopped laughing. An idea sprang up in his mind, unbidden, that suddenly clarified some of this utterly improbable situation. He quickly walked over to Michel, unconscious on the stone floor, bent down and observed that, his breathing was regular and unlabored. He gently felt the guard's neck to find that the pulse was strong, slow and regular, and that there was no obvious blow to the head.

"Well," he said, "I am quite certain that I can silence that awful noise, as well as help revive your friend, but I will require your cooperation."

"My cooperation?" Sean stumbled through a clumsy pronunciation of the obviously unfamiliar word.

"Yes," Bob continued, "if you will unlock that box, or give me the key to do so, I will retrieve my tools and silence that sound."

Sean listened, thought about the prospect of opening the box and facing the dreadful sound and what it might represent, then made his decision.

"I shall give you the key as you request. I would ask that you remember that Michel and I do not wish you ill. We were merely doing our duty."

*How familiar that sounds.* thought Bob. *The age-old argument.*

Sean warily reached to his side and removed an iron key from a ring attached to his belt. Very carefully, he placed the key on the cot next to Bob. He then backed up several paces as Bob picked up the key and studied it.

Remembering the acute embarrassment he suffered over his recent attempt at opening the door in the old man's hut, Bob was relieved to find that the key looked fairly straightforward. As he got up and walked over to the box and its continued hissing, he noticed the pale, fearful look on the guard's face, and incompletely suppressed a grin.

The crude, unpolished iron key fit easily into the large iron lock that secured the box. The lock opened with a clunk, and Bob turned to look at his captor before opening the lid. The temptation to perform some mumbo-jumbo while opening the box was strong, but he resisted, thinking that the consequences might be more than he bargained for. Instead, he unceremoniously lifted the lid, looked inside, and found he could barely make out the contents in the dim light. He reached inside and found his penlight, then, turning it on, found he could see his other belongings lying on a colorless cloth in the bottom of the box. He reached back in and took his beeper, pushed the small button on the top and silenced the hissing.

Sean stood where he was, transfixed. When he saw the stranger reach into the box, he held his breath, feeling utterly paralyzed with dread. Then the light rose out of the box!

*Oh saints preserve us, a ghost for certain,* he thought.

Then the noise ceased, the light went out, and the wizard turned toward him, carrying his unearthly weapons.

Sean's head began to swim, his vision blurred, and he had to reach down and clasp the edge of the cot to keep from falling. But the wizard did not come toward him, rather toward his prostrate comrade."

"Oh, please sire," his voice came out half croak, half whisper, "do not harm him! I swear by all the saints that we truly meant you no ill."

Bob smiled as he knelt down to attend to the fallen guard.

"Relax," he said, "just stay where you are. I'm a doctor. I know what I'm doing. Your friend will be all right. I won't hurt him."

Sean quivered and watched helplessly as the stranger put the small ends of his weapon in his ears, then applied the other end to Michel's chest, under his armor. The wizard's eyes were closed, and he appeared to be concentrating intently, as if casting a silent spell. He then removed the black snake-like weapon from Michel's chest, and turned his attention to the guard's face. He then took one hand and opened one of Michel's eyes, and pointed a small white stick toward it. Then, all at once, a light leaped from the stick to Michel's eye, and the guard awoke, fearful, but alive and well.

Miracle or sorcery, he couldn't tell which. The moment would be burned in Sean's memory for life.

*What good are swords and spears,* he thought, *against powers such as these?*

# Chapter Twenty

Craycroft sat alone in his study. A stout log burned quietly in the fireplace, and an oil lamp provided light enough to read and write, but he could do neither. Between the burning grief he felt and the earl's latest revelations, his mind and heart were too chaotic to let him record his thoughts in logical order. The paper lay blank on the table as he refilled his tumbler with dark red wine.

"The earl is right," he thought. "This is more dangerous than warfare, for these things we have done are beyond any knowledge and beyond our control. We have thrown a feeble old man and a mere lad into the winds of fate, and to what end we could scarcely guess. Ah, Drachma, you have always seemed to play easy in these games of chance and come away victorious. For all our sakes I pray your fortune and wisdom hold true again.

"What a chance the earl has taken! If the king's advisors were to hear of this it could be the end of his rule and our safety. He is right, though, to try to protect the painters and potters, for without our craftsmen, there would be no wealth or security on this fair isle, king or no."

He took a sip of his wine, savoring the dark, sweet flavor and warm glow that rose from deep within his chest. It did not really ease his sorrow and fear, but did give promise of numb repose.

"This has truly been a bitter winter thus far, and there are more than two months yet to go before the equinox. Somehow I fear there will be more grieving to be done before the healing warmth of spring is upon us."

He stared into the fire, trying to remember clearly all that the earl had told him and how that might affect what he had already learned or surmised about their present crisis. His thoughts did not stay on any logical progression, but seemed rather to wander or leap from idea to memory to emotion and back again. The more he tried to force coherence in his thinking, the more disjointed his thoughts became. Repeatedly, his mind came back to Felicia, and to his great loss.

"I know what the earl and Drachma are doing is right for our isle, but I cannot bear the thought of losing Master Falma and Tom as well to dangers unseen and unimagined.

"And what of Lord Vincente? Was it treachery? I cannot believe that of him. Drachma must know more of this than he has told the earl."

Craycroft thought that if their efforts should fail now, who knows what the consequences of such power unleashed would be? The earl said that even Drachma himself had never before uttered the 'Lux de Mortis Concentis' of which Felicia had spoken. That book, with its shroud of mystery and implications of power, had repulsed and intrigued Craycroft for years, but he had resisted the temptation to read it, claiming, with some justification, that it might only hamper his efforts at healing and aiding the sick through more "normal" means.

"I am plodder, not a magician," he had claimed on more than one occasion of debate. "I could not wield such power with any grace or dignity. Let me proceed in my own humble, stumbling way."

Felicia had chided, saying he had no idea of his own strengths and purpose, and that there was none more suited to power than he who did not wish for it.

His thoughts continued, randomly touching past and present events, always tinged with sorrow and regret.

Realizing, finally, that he was not likely to make sense of things the way he was feeling, Craycroft resolved to try to accomplish at least some little task that would not require mental effort. So doing, he decided to go again to Lady Vincente's quarters and seek out the book which had suddenly seemed to take on such import.

"In the study," she had said, "the room with the tapestry."

*Yes, I remember the room well,* Craycroft thought. *Many memories are contained therein. I should find the book and keep it safe for young Tom. M'lady, I do as you wish.*

With effort, he pushed himself up from the chair and rose to retrieve his cloak and hat. He toyed briefly with the idea of finding Councilor Rust, to discuss matters further, but quickly discarded that idea. He was not ready to discuss anything with anybody, not yet.

Stepping outside, Craycroft was a little surprised that it was still light, no more than mid afternoon. The day seemed to be dragging unmercifully. The air was unsettled, they sky overcast, and a few flakes of snow blew across the great courtyard of the castle. He walked along the western wall toward the lady's house, alone and miserable. The walkway took him past Barncuddy's Ale House, and as he neared the door a group of apprentices heading toward their favorite retreat noticed the master.

'Why good Master Craycroft, it is you, indeed! You look like a bit of cheer might be just what you'd be needing. Come, join us in a bit of refreshment."

"Aye," spoke up another, "come, regale us with your tales. Weather such as this calls for some warm company and easy talk."

"Nay, lads, I mustn't, though your invitation is certainly a temptation."

It took little effort for the apprentices to change his mind, and soon they all entered the warm, musty cavern of the ale house. As they found a table and benches, Barncuddy came over quickly with the obvious intent of laying down the law for this group of rabble. The Brewster stopped short when he noticed Craycroft among them.

"My good master, what brings you in on a day such as this, and in such company as these louts?"

"Fie on you, you old bag-o-wind! This is our guest. He has most graciously agreed to join us in your esteemed establishment for some good brew and great talk."

"Humph! Indeed, Johnnie, it would do you good to show more than a token respect for your elders."

"That I shall, good Brewster, as I do become one."

The hearty laughter that greeted this exchange seemed to signal that all were ready, and, after another feeble attempt at establishing his authority, the portly Barncuddy turned and went to pour the flagons of ale.

As the ale flowed, and warmth returned to numbed fingers and toes, conversation at the table loosened. At first the talk was of work and the good fortune of an unexpected early release from labors. Eventually, the young men's eyes turned toward the master, and requests for a tale came from all corners. Even patrons at other tables, at the prospect of a story from the master healer and teacher turned their attention toward Craycroft.

"Very well, then, lads, I shall tell you a tale, a true one, mind you, one of woe and magic, and one from which we may all learn and perhaps profit."

"Aye, master, a tale of magic. Hear, hear! Now, mates be silent, and let the master speak."

Craycroft looked about at the rapt faces and cherished the moment. Teaching and telling stories (which he considered one and the same) had always given him profound pleasure, and his reputation for doing so was unmatched for miles around.

"Well, then," he began, "let me tell you of Brother Philip's journey. Now, mind you, this is a true tale, and one told me by a great lady, now gone (may she rest with the saints)."

"There is, or at least there was, a town in southern Spain called Navarrito, a prosperous town on a hillside, not far from the sea. Within the walls of the town there was a priory with perhaps a dozen monks, whose purpose in life, besides prayer and meditation, seemed to be the accrual of ancient books of knowledge, and the translation of these texts into Latin for their preservation within the Church."

"As it happened, the prior received word that in a seacoast town about two days' journey away, a cloth merchant had traded for a book from a seaman in port that he had brought with him from northern Africa. This book, it was said, had escaped the ravages of the destruction of the mighty library of Alexandria, hundreds of years before, and had been kept safe by a shepherd family in a cave in the hills. The nature and purpose of this book were unknown both to the seaman and the merchant, but both felt certain of its age and origin."

"The prior, naturally, was suspicious, but nevertheless did not wish to let an opportunity for such an acquisition go by. He chose, then, to send an emissary to search out and perhaps purchase this book. Of all his monks, Brother Philip was the only one the prior felt safe sending on such a mission. Now Philip, though young in years, was the most knowledgeable with respect to ancient texts (and did, in fact, serve the priory as librarian), and was also shrewd in matters of money and property."

"So it was that he sent brother Philip, alone, with a pony and provisions, as well as a small sack of the prior's silver money, in search of this book."

Craycroft paused, took a long draught of his ale, noticed that all eyes, including the brewster's, were on him. Encouraged by the attention, he continued his story.

"Well, the first day's journey took young Philip over hillsides and farms to a small village named Salamandro del Fuego, a place with a reputation as dubious as its name. By now, however, night was falling, and our good monk deemed it necessary to find a place of rest for the night. Finding that the old parish church had been burned down and not yet rebuilt, he found himself begging charity of the local innkeeper, a man most indisposed to offer such to a young monk who had taken vows of poverty, chastity and obedience."

'If it's a room you want,' he told brother Philip, 'you'll have to pay for it, same as everyone else.'

"Not wishing to spend any of the small sum in his purse on lodging, brother Philip chose instead to sleep the night out in the stables with his pony. Having eaten of his humble provisions, he spoke his evening prayers, then settled himself in a dry corner of the stable with some fresh straw, then fell quickly asleep."

"Whether he then woke or dreamt, he could never say, but in a most faint and peculiar light in the corner of his stable he saw a young child, a girl no more than six or seven years of age, sitting by his sack of provisions. As he sat and looked in her direction, she stood, looked at him fearlessly, then made a most peculiar gesture, in which she seemed to kiss the tip of her finger, then point to the heavens, smile, then without word or sound, vanish into the night."

"Disturbed greatly by what he had seen, brother Philip rose and quickly went over to his sack. He found that nothing had been disturbed, save for the presence of a small loaf of flat bread, still warm and fragrant from baking, left lying upon his satchel. He looked, but could not see the girl, so he sat down once more with the bread in his hands. The warmth and aroma were more than he could resist, so he began eating, noting that the flavor and texture of the bread were, in his words, like a taste of heaven."

"He did not finish the bread, however, as sleep once again overcame him. As he was falling asleep, though, he seemed to hear a voice, real or imagined he could not say, but quiet, like the breathing of the beasts of the stable. The words were clear, and brother Philip did remember them to his dying day. The voice said, 'that which you seek is great, but your search even greater.'"

"When he did awaken in the morning there was no sign that anyone but he had been in the stables, and no vestige of the wonderful bread. With a feeling of gladness touched with foreboding, he saddled his mount and continued on his journey."

Craycroft paused to clear his throat, then took another drink from his flagon. No one spoke, and all attention remained on the master. He put down his drink with a solid *thunk*, then resumed his tale.

"When he arrived that eve at the coastal village of San Ramon, he was received cordially by the old parish priest, given a plain but decent meal and a clean cot for the night. He told the priest of his mission, but did not tell him of the strange visitation he had seen the night before, for fear of alarming the good father with tales of the supernatural. The priest was able to tell brother Philip the name of the cloth merchant, and gave promise to escort him on the morrow."

"After morning mass the next day the priest and monk walked through the village toward the merchant's house. When they arrived at his home, they were surprised to see a crowd had gathered by the merchant's door, where there was much tumult. When one in the crowd noticed the father arriving, he ran out to meet him, exclaiming that he must come quickly, that the senor was hurt and dying."

"They found the man's worry to be true, as the merchant had been badly injured about the head and belly, had lost much blood, and was obviously dying. The father gave a hasty sacrament to the injured merchant, then allowed brother Philip to speak with him as his life ebbed away."

"Brother Philip found out from the dying merchant, to his dismay, that that very morning a large, powerful armed man had come to the house, demanding to know the whereabouts of a book obtained from a sailor, and when the merchant did not quickly tell him of its place, the man-at-arms beat the poor fellow to the point of death. The merchant then told them, with his dying words, that the intruder proceeded to crash through his house in search of the book, but whether he found it he could not say, as awareness was slipping away with the blood on the straw. When brother Philip asked where the book might have been, the merchant drew his last breath and died."

"Anger and dread arose from the gathered neighbors, and it was fortunate for brother Philip that he had been in the company of the priest, else they would likely have turned on him in suspicion. 'Justice must be sought,' they said, and turned to their priest for help."

"When brother Philip and the priest asked of the villagers, none knew of the armed man, save one boy, who said that while he was tending his goats, he had seen such a man, alone, riding quickly toward the forest, not one hour ago. He might not have noticed the rider, but for the fine horse he was riding, unusual in that part of Spain."

"The monk and priest observed as the servants tended to the care of the dead merchant and put his house back in order. Nowhere in all the belongings did they find any unusual books, nor did they find any books at all, for though he was a skilled merchant, he could neither read nor write."

Craycroft paused to drain the last of his ale, then, looking about, noticed the puzzled expression on the face of one of the youth.

"Felix, what is it? You seem perplexed."

"Only, Master, that I hope that is not the end of your tale, for I can make little sense of its meaning thus far."

"Ah, and well you should not, Felix, for no, my tale is not yet done."

"Go on, then, Master," Johnnie interjected. "Let not this young fool detract from your story. We are listening."

Felix shot him a glance that could curdle milk, but held his tongue.

"Very well, then, I shall continue. You must imagine now how young Philip felt. He had been sent on a mission which his prior felt likely to be of little significance, yet en route our good brother receives what he believes in his heart to be a divine message to the contrary—that his mission is of the utmost importance. But now, upon arriving at his destination, he has lost all chance of finding that which he should be seeking. As he was pondering all this, the words he heard in the night came back to him. 'That which you seek is great, but your search even greater'

"Now, under the weight of such a pronouncement, our monk did decide that he must obey. That which appeared to be a dream on a restless night was given added might and depth through the partaking of what brother Philip would later describe as Manna. How could he disobey such a direct order? His earthly vow of obedience, though, required him to seek his prior's guidance and blessing, which, he understood, might cause difficulties in a small priory. He resolved, then, to return to his priory and make a full accounting of his actions and encounters along the way."

"Before brother Philip left San Ramon, though, he did gather as many facts as he could concerning the merchant, the ship from which the sailor with the book had come, and also about his terrible assailant. About the merchant, there was much knowledge in the village, but little that would be of any value in a search for the book he possessed so short a time. About the ship, he found only that it had come from the Greek Isles, had traded in northern Africa, and had sailed on to parts unknown. About the man who attacked and killed the merchant, he was only able to find that he was a large man, dressed in fine armor, with pale yellow hair, who rode a magnificent gray war horse. He learned of the direction the man had ridden, but not his destination. The merchant's household, as well as his servants, provided no further help in this matter, becoming increasingly vexed with this meddlesome monk."

"After a sleepless night in the priest's house, brother Philip set out early the next morning on his way back to Navarrito. He stayed again that night at the stables in Salamandro del Fuego, but this night was quiet, with neither visitations nor dreams disturbing his rest."

"Upon his return to the priory, he told his prior all he had seen and done, fully expecting the prior to make light of his story of dreams and voices, and to send him back to his cell duly penitent and obedient."

"The prior did not such thing. 'My son,' he told Philip, 'many persons have sought all their earthly lives for such a clear statement of purpose and mission and never found it. To me it would seem as foolish for you to deny such a call by hiding here in the priory as it was for Jonah to seek escape aboard his fateful ship. No, son, I would tell you rather to go and make your search, and if you should find the object of your search, only then return here and bring with you whatever newfound wisdom you have gained. Come, then, we must prepare you for your journey, for you shall be going with the blessing of this priory and of God.'"

"Before brother Philip left that week, his prior had told him more that he himself had learned about the book, facts that had seemed unimportant at the time he had learned them, but which now took on greater meaning in light of the merchant's murder and the apparent theft, by a man-at-arms, of the object of Philip's journey to San Ramon. The prior told him that the book was alleged to contain writings from the fourth and fifth centuries, written on the Isle of Patmos, by late followers of Saint John, which espoused ideas felt possibly dangerous to the church, apparently gleaned from their contact with visitors from distant lands. He also let brother Philip know that word of the book's existence had surely reached the ears of Count Juan del Castillo, a powerful and dangerous man, from whom the church had purchased a number of rare books and relics, some of which were now housed in the priory's library and reliquary. It would be likely that any information about the book's whereabouts would be with the count, but the prior did not feel that the count would be one to commit murder for the sake of a rare book."

"Whether the prior truly believed this, or was saying so to ease brother Philip's heart, he could not say, but nevertheless, our good monk set out again from Navarrito, this time bound for Castillo del Sur. His provisions were little more than he had taken on his first journey, and he carried with him the same quantity of silver in hope of buying the book should he find it. In fact, after what his prior had told him, brother Philip felt little hope at being able to purchase the book with the pitiful bag of silver he had in his possession. He knew of Juan del Castillo, knew of his wealth and power, and knew that if he had in his possession a book which he considered worth murdering for, he would not likely part with it for such a small sum (you see, brother Philip did not share his prior's conviction that the count would not kill for the sake of an important possession)."

"You may well imagine that Philip had some misgivings as he approached the castle gate at Castillo del Sur, noticing the grim manner of the guards and the general appearance of readiness for war. When asked his business, he replied humbly that he wished to see the count regarding the possible purchase of a book for his priory. The guard, sensing no threat from the little monk, let him in with the admonition that he might enter, but that an audience with the count was something he should not consider likely, as the count was busy with more important matters. Sensing that the guard considered him a nuisance, brother Philip asked him no questions, but quietly entered the castle."

"The parish church was not difficult to find within the castle walls, and Philip knew that the priest should by obligation at least be willing and able to provide him shelter and sustenance for the night. He did not expect any more than that, but it might be enough to discover whether the count at least knew of the book's existence."

"When Philip found the priest, it was not the reception he had hoped for. Rather, the gruff old man was barely civil when the young monk came to state his business and request a meal and place to stay the night. He told brother Philip, in fact, that he could in no way offer him room within the church, nor could he grant him an audience with the count. If he required shelter, there might be some space on the floor of the hostel, where he might also beg scraps from the kitchen."

"As you may well imagine, brother Philip was startled and grieved by this response from a fellow cleric. When the priest turned to go back to his house, though, Philip realized that there was nothing further he could do but to go seek out the hostel that the priest had mentioned. He took small comfort in the thought that perhaps in the hostel there might be a person with some knowledge of the castle enough to gain audience with the count. He quickly offered a prayer for the priest's forgiveness, gritted his teeth, then turned to find a place of respite."

"When he did find the hostel, our good brother's hunger and weariness were beyond measure. The place was crowded with the poorest of the poor, and whatever food there might have been earlier had long since been given up to those already waiting. Philip found a small open area near the far corner of the building, then set down his satchel and prepared to try to sleep away his misery. 'Perhaps,' he thought, 'I shall find someone or something in the morning to help me.' But as he was drifting off to fitful sleep in the musty darkness he was awakened by a gentle touch on the leg. He sat up to look at the small form beside him. There, in the dimness, he could just perceive the form of a young child. As he sat, she bent and placed an object in his lap; then as she stood back up, there appeared a faint light about her face, enough to see that she was smiling. She then touched the tip of her finger to her lips, pointed heavenward, and was gone into the still night."

"Brother Philip's heart leaped and he thought to pursue the waif, but then noticed that the object she had placed in his lap was warm. He picked up the bread and ate his fill, unmolested by the poor and hungry all about him. As a thankful tear ran down his cheek, he knew in his heart that this was the same angel of mercy, and knew as well that his prior's conviction was true—that this was his task, his journey."

Craycroft paused again to look about him at the attentive faces in the alehouse. All waited on his next words eagerly. As he looked about, he saw that young Willie Minstrel had been listening to his tale, his stringed clarsach at his side on the floor.

"Before I continue my tale," he said, "I would ask that Willie play for us a tune on his harp, a tune befitting our story of mystery, joy and sadness. Will you play for us, Willie? A tune if you please? I would much enjoy some music as benefits our story and our company."

"Ah, well, Master Craycroft, as ye know it to be true, I am perchance the only other in this room to have heard your tale, and told me I'm sure by the same great lady as ye spoke of. For her I'll play ye such a tune, but only on condition as ye then finish your story, for it is worth the hearing."

"Very well, I shall, but now my throat does need a rest, and it has been such a long while since I have heard you play. My heart has ached to hear your sounds again. Do us the honor, good minstrel."

There was a sparkle in the eye of the minstrel as he placed the brass strung harp between his legs, readying himself to play. Before plucking the strings, he bent his head, closed his eyes, and paused with his hands on either side of the strings. The room was silent as he began to play, first a gentle rolling strumming of the lower strings, then the melody, plucked on the higher strings, each note ringing out like a bell.

All in the room were entranced. None had ever heard such playing, and never had they heard a melody so captivating in its simplicity, so moving. The ethereal sounds filled the dank alehouse, making it for those brief minutes a place of greater beauty than the most majestic cathedral. As the last note sounded silence returned, each person in the room barely daring to breathe, lest he break the magic spell Willie had woven with his fingers.

The minstrel himself broke the silence, returning the clarsach to the floor.

"Now, Master Craycroft, I return attention to you. If ye wish, I shall play again after your tale, but not before it is done."

"Ah, Willie, your sounds have torn at my heart. The lady should be most pleased, as I am certain your music did go straight to heaven."

"Your words do me too great an honor, Master. Please, continue your tale of brother Philip."

"Very well," Craycroft cleared his throat, paused a moment to gather his thoughts, then resumed his story.

"When Philip had eaten, he found that he was satisfied and sleepy, so, despite his inhospitable arrival and uncomfortable surroundings, he fell fast asleep. Upon arising the next morn, he began to consider if there be any way to find audience with the count. As it happened, he was found inside the hostel by an old man who had lived his life within the castle walls, and knew it intimately. Because of his infirmity, though, he was no longer able to work as mason, and was all alone in the world. He had come to rely on the charity of others for his very life, and when he had seen brother Philip's angelic visitation that night (and he seems to have been the only other person who did see), he resolved to talk with the monk and inquire as to the nature of such a man who receives charity from angels."

"That morning Philip told the old man of his search for the book which had been the cause of his first journey and of the merchant's murder. The old man nodded knowingly, saying that yes, indeed, it was possible that the count would value an object enough to kill to acquire it, but that the count valued money and fame more than any book of knowledge, and that Philip might use that information wisely. As to how to gain an audience with the count, the man said that might be difficult, but not impossible, certainly not for any man whose search had been sanctified by the angels."

"In fact, the old man was able, through friends with some influence in the court, to arrange for an audience with Juan del Castillo, who was every bit the imperious tyrant brother Philip had feared him to be. When the timid monk was allowed to tell the count of his mission and of the book in question, he was reminded of the wonderful artifacts the count had already sold to the monastery in previous years, and that the priory would certainly be given opportunity to purchase it. With that, the poor brother was dismissed from the count's chambers and told to return to his village, assured of the court's favor.

"Brother Philip, of course, did no such thing, for as the count was speaking, he noticed two things that troubled him deeply. The first was that the count's face displayed alarm at the mention of the book, indicating to brother Philip at least some familiarity with the object. Secondly, while Philip was telling of his journey, he noticed the count to glance knowingly at one of his knights, a large, well suited man with a striking head of yellow hair."

"Philip felt certain, then, that the count did have the book, and that it was that very knight who had beaten the poor merchant senseless to obtain it for his liege. As a poor and humble monk, though, Philip was powerless to compel the truth from the great nobleman. Again, as when he witnessed the death of the merchant, he felt a helpless rage well up within him, but resolved not to give in to despair or self pity. Instead, he left the count's chambers quietly, and with all dignity befitting his work and character."

"Philip then returned to the hostel and found the old man from the night before. The sight of the old mason, however, was not what brother Philip had expected. In a far corner of the building the old man lay dying, bleeding from wounds to the chest and belly. A small girl was stooping over him, giving him comfort as she was able. Philip rushed to the man's side and knelt at his right."

"'Old man' he said, 'who has done this to you? I must know. Has the priest been summoned?' The old man looked into Philip's eyes and with his last effort told brother Philip that it was Esteban, one of the count's men-at-arms, and to get out of the castle if he valued his life, and further, not to summon the priest, for the priest himself had told the count of brother Philip's arrival and search for the book. Philip cradled the old man's head as he breathed his last and went limp in the monk's arms."

"As he eased the old man's body to the floor, Philip looked up and noticed that the little girl was gone, again without a trace. In her place a small crowd had gathered, keeping a step back from the monk and the murdered man. Philip looked at a youth in the crowd and told him to quickly summon the priest, that this old man deserved a proper anointing and burial. When he felt certain that the youth was doing as he asked, brother Philip rose and left the hostel, the crowd parting respectfully as he walked out."

"Outside he found his tethered pony, placed his satchel on the pony's back, then proceeded toward the castle gate. His heart ached at the thought that his search for an ancient book had already cost the lives of two innocent people, but a search, nonetheless, that had received the blessings of his prior and, brother

Philip felt certain, of the angels. How could he now return empty-handed? He did not fear for himself, but did dread failure. He could not, for the life of him, conceive a way to search further for the book while in these castle walls, yet he knew with all certainty that the book was there, within the count's possession."

Craycroft paused once again to take another swallow of ale. As he had been speaking the Brewster had quietly and discreetly kept the ale flowing in everyone's tumblers. A story and music were very good for business on winter afternoons, and preferable to rowdy games and altercations.

"Tell us, master, what did brother Philip do?" Felix spoke again. "Surely his search did not end there."

"Right, Felix, it did not. For as Philip left the gate of the castle, he was joined by two urchins from within, children who had seen much of what had transpired, but were not noticed by the adults occupied with their own doings. The two boys asked brother Philip about the cause of the old man's slaying and of his role in the events. They explained that they could see that a good man had been killed, and another was being run out of the castle. They were orphans who had been befriended and cared for by the old mason, and had nowhere to turn, and further would do anything to avenge his murder.

"Brother Philip was alarmed at the anger and courage of the young boys, and explained to them that, as a man of the cloister, he was in no position to be seeking or promoting vengeance. He also had nothing in the way of wealth or possessions. He could offer them nothing but his friendship and advice.

"'Then advise us,' they said, 'what it is that you were seeking within the castle, and we will give you our solemn vow to obtain it or to die in the attempt.'"

"He did, however, tell them of the book, and of his journey thus far in its pursuit. After hearing Philip's tale, they told him that, upon their word, and upon the memory of old Paulo, they would find brother Philip his book, for he now gave them purpose in life and a means to recompense the loss of their adopted father. They told him to go on to the village not a half day's journey away, to wait there at the church where the priest was a decent man, who would surely allow him to stay."

"The village of Sangre de Bautista was, as the boys had said, only a few hours away, and the young priest readily took in brother Philip, after hearing of his most unusual journey."

"Philip stayed within the village for at least two months, becoming fast friends with the priest, and assisting him with his daily tasks while providing excellent companionship. He had almost forgotten about his original purpose for staying at the village until that night when he was awakened from sleep by a loud knocking at the door. There, in the dark, was one of the castle urchins, breathless and weary, holding a small sack."

"'Here, father, is your book,' the boy said. 'Alas, Jose perished by the guard's sword, but I have escaped and brought you what we promised.'"

"Philip took the boy in, brought him food and drink, while he listed to the boy's tale of how they had discovered the count's keep where precious objects were kept, how they found from the drunken guards where the book was hidden. The boy told him how they hid within the keep under straw and blankets, then after dark crept out and took the book, but also how the guard had been roused by their footsteps in the hall and gave pursuit, catching Jose's cloak as he ran. Jose had just enough time to toss the book to Leonardo before the sword felled him. Leonardo did not stop running until he came to the village."

"Brother Philip listened with a mixture of awe, thankfulness and shame, that his journey was deemed worth the cost of yet one more life, that of a young boy."

"Leonardo asked Philip what he would do now that he had his book. When he explained that he would take it back to his priory, for study and translation, Leonardo asked that he be allowed to accompany brother Philip on his journey back, as he had no one left here, and he felt some share in the safe passage of this book for which his brother and adopted father had given up their lives."

"Philip could hardly refuse such a request, and agreed to take the boy with him. They further decided that it would be best to set out at once, while still under cover of darkness. Philip quickly wrote a letter thanking the priest for his hospitality and explaining the urgency of his need to leave, quickly gathered his few belongings, then left with Leonardo riding and himself leading the pony."

"As they left the village, they heard the sound of horses' hooves riding hard, coming down the road toward them. They quietly hid in a small copse of trees until the riders had passed, then resumed their journey on the road to Navarrito."

"Brother Philip's worst surprise awaited him when he and Leonardo arrived at Navarrito. There they found the priory in ruins, burned out and destroyed. Nothing, they discovered, was saved, and four of the brothers had died, six were dying of burns. Philip's heart ached with agony and guilt, for he knew that this was the count's doing, and that he was in part responsible for this misery. When they found from the villagers that it was a band of riders that had come in the night with torches, they knew as well that it was the same band from which they had hid on the road."

"Philip's agony was beyond words. He looked into the small sack that held the book. There, in the bag, was the object of his search. Could this possibly be worth all the death and misery? He sat and wept, inconsolable in his grief."

"After a time, as the pain of grieving finally eased, brother Philip resolved that he would, somehow, make his search worthy of the lives lost in his behalf. He and his companion, Leonardo, resolved that they would take upon themselves the task of deciphering and translating this book they had come to possess. In the process, they became known throughout the region for their knowledge and wisdom, and translated many other important works that have come down to us through the years."

"And the book," Felix couldn't help but ask, "what came of this book, and what have we learned from it?"

"Aye, Felix, it is well you should ask, for that is yet a mystery. No one to this day knows with certainty where the book resides, or what it contains in sum, but I will tell you this—there is one on this very isle who has actually seen and read from the book."

"Here, on this isle!? Who would that be, Master?"

"That, Felix, should not be a surprise to you, for it is Drachma himself who has seen the book."

"Drachma! Of course."

Johnnie spoke up. "Here, now, Master Craycroft, that was indeed a tale worthy of the telling! We thank you, Master, and raise our toast to you."

"Here, here!" the rest joined in, drinking their ale, Willie's mixed with the tears on his cheeks.

"My thanks, lads," Craycroft said, raising his own tumbler, "and to you, men and lads worthy of the tale."

"Here, here!" and another swallow of ale all around.

"Now, Willie," Craycroft spoke again, "can you give us another song? Another as fitting as the last."

"Aye, for ye, Master Craycroft, I will, for your tale most worthy, and better in the telling than I recalled."

Willie took his clarsach back up between his legs, waited just a moment for quiet, then began. As before, he began with strumming in the lower strings, then from the middle strings there rose a melody captivating and unforgettable, swelling from his instrument and filling the room with sonorous magic.

Craycroft leaned back against the wall and closed his eyes, letting the music transport him. Feelings and images of warmth came to him, taking him beyond the castle in winter. It was springtime, with the smell of newly turned earth. Sunlight filtered through the new leaves, falling on the path below his feet as he felt himself taking the path into the forest. A longing so powerful that he could not resist overcame him; a feeling of inevitability so overwhelming that for Craycroft there was nothing more to do but follow.

# Epilogue

Her shift was mercifully quiet right now, as if to allow her some recovery. Judy had not gotten much sleep, and was still running on reserves. So she kept herself busy with mundane things, such as stocking and inventory.

"Hey, Theresa, I've got to go to pharmacy to get some more meds. We're running low on some of our cardiac stuff. I won't be gone but a few minutes. I'm sure that you can hold the fort down for a few."

"Sure, Judy, we'll call if we need you."

As she wandered the old hallways of the building, going toward pharmacy, Judy's mind was still on Dr. Gilsen, and on Josh. She had given up on the idea of paging him, but she still could not comprehend what could have happened to him. *Where could he be?* It was now a day since anyone had seen him. And Josh. Was this truly his last battle? Had he given up at last? Was there no one out there anymore to step in, and perform some sort of heroics?

As Judy turned toward the elevators, she saw her. She looked frantic, stressed, and lost.

"Janie, what's the matter? Is it Josh?"

"Oh, Judy, I'm so glad to see you. The nurse from ICU called, and said to come right away. She said that Josh is not looking good at all."

"Well, I'll just come on up with you, if that's OK. There's nothing much happening in the ER anyway."

Janie looked somewhere beyond tired, to the point where she looked as if nothing mattered anymore, to that point of utter physical numbness. Judy recognized it. She had seen it so often in the ER, and knew, deep down that this was it. So she did what came naturally, and just hugged Janie.

When the two of them got up to the Thoracic Surgery ICU, Judy quickly found out who was taking care of Josh. It was Brenda, an old-timer, and Judy sighed with relief. Janie was at Josh's bedside, while Judy quickly called down to the ER, and told them it would be a few minutes longer than expected, and to just page her if the ER got crazy. She asked Brenda if it would be all right if they had some time to be with Josh alone, and got Brenda's OK.

Judy walked on over to bed five, looked at the monitors, the readings from his blood pressure monitor, his heart rhythm, his ventilator settings, then she looked down at Josh. And she knew. Josh was not there. His body was there, but he was gone. There was the ventilator breathing for him. There were the IV lines and chest tube. There was the Foley catheter, draining his urine, though it was just about empty. His heart was still beating, though his heart rate was dropping. He still had a blood pressure, but barely.

After about ten minutes, Judy walked back to the nurses' station. She asked Brenda if they had gotten hold of Dr. Gilsen, and was told that they had been trying since yesterday, but that he wouldn't answer his pages. That was not like the Dr. Gilsen they all knew and loved—not at all.

Earl walked in right then, and looked every bit as sleep-deprived as his wife, and he looked shell-shocked to boot. Judy took him by the arm, and brought him over to bed five. He said nothing, just looked, and as he looked, Josh's heart rate suddenly plummeted, then his heart stopped altogether.

Janie looked at Judy, terror in her eyes. As alarms were going off, Judy managed to ask quickly if they wanted him to be resuscitated. Janie shook her head from side to side, and, with effort got out the words, "No. No more. Enough."

Brenda quickly silenced the alarms. Then gestured to Judy, indicating that she would call one of the residents to pronounce him. Judy just stayed where she was, at Josh's bedside, with Janie and Earl. She could do nothing more than hug them both, and cry with them.

Brenda found Dr. Peterson to come and pronounce Josh, officially listing time of death as 3:20 AM. The trio stayed with Josh for the next 20 minutes, while Brenda and another nurse removed the ventilator, turned off the monitoring devices, and stopped the IV fluids. Janie kissed his forehead, and said goodbye.

As Judy was helping them with the paperwork, the page operator called overhead for Judy Morrison to return to the ER. Every bit of her wanted to stay, but Judy turned to go, but before she left, she told Janie that she would be at Josh's funeral, and to just let her know where and when it was. She scribbled her phone number on a piece of paper, which Janie then put in her purse.

Judy went through the paces of finishing her shift, and when Lonie came back to work that morning, she found her colleague sitting down, red-eyed, and exhausted.

"Josh?" was all Lonie had to say, and Judy was reaching for another tissue. "Man, I'm so sorry. When?"

"Around three this morning. Oh, Lonie, it hurts so much, and I'm not even his family."

"Oh, but Judy, you are, and you know it."

With an effort, Judy got through her report to Lonie, telling her of the patients left in the ER. Who had lacerated what. Who took too much alcohol, and fell down, cracking his head. And who couldn't breathe, and was in bed six. Then she gathered up her coat, gloves and hat, and headed toward the door of the ER. Before she got out, an ambulance came screaming up to the entrance. The very sight of it made her nauseated. They got the back door of the ambulance open, pulled out the gurney with the victim, with the ER crew waiting. And as the automatic door hissed open, letting in the cold air, she just ran out to her car.

She was fighting tears again, as she let her car warm up enough to drive. She turned on the radio, to the NPR station, which, by now should be playing Morning Edition. She listened, with special intensity because that voice sounded so familiar, so erudite, so powerful.

"That which you seek is great, but your search even greater."

The words seemed to come directly from the forest, from the ancient conifers and hardwoods, and from somewhere deep within her own soul. She turned off her radio, and sat for a minute, as she felt the warm breeze of springtime, and the smell of the old trees envelop her. Somehow, somewhere, someone was listening to her cries.

"And to what do I owe this honor, my friend?"

The voice of Angelica was soothing to his ears and to his heart. It had been something of a struggle these last few days and weeks. And now, some repose, at last. He walked in, and sat down in the familiar chair, in the room where so much had happened over the years.

"Angelica, to your good graces and your excellent cooking. That is what I have missed."

"So say ye, m'lord, Drachma. It would be most foolish of me to ask, but have ye discovered that ye're hungry and tired?"

"Indeed, I am, very tired and very hungry for some of your most wonderful bread. And, if it would not be too much trouble . . ."

" . . . I know, some of the wine from the cellar."

"Good woman. I know they have reserved a place for you in Heaven . . ."

"Aye, right next to your own daughter, and my own dear Maggie, I know."

When she brought a glass of the wine, and set it down next to Drachma, Angelica noticed that, for the first time in a very long time, he looked tired, tired to the core. She became concerned. So she sat down in the chair next to him, sat and studied this man of shadows.

Drachma said nothing for a time, just sat and sipped his wine.

"What is it, m'lord? What is troubling ye so much that I feel left out of yer world?"

"Well, let me tell you, my dear Angelica, that we have now done it. We have let loose upon our world the powers of those forces that we cannot in any way control. You have heard me speak of them, and have heard me speak of the books that tell of these awful powers."

"Oh, aye, m'lord, that I have, indeed."

"Well, then, let me tell you that there shall come ancient forces, from the forest, from the hills, from the mountains. And that these forces shall now control our very lives in new, and dangerous ways. As well, there shall come visitors from another time, a time in the far distant future, who shall bring craft and knowledge with them. And let me tell you that my own time on this earth shall be short.

"So, for that reason, I have brought to bear new and perhaps even dangerous persons, to take over my own doings. They do include my own grandson, and namesake. And to assist him, I have assigned Kerlin to the tasks for which he was not yet ready, but soon shall be. And Craycroft, the healer, Rust of the Council, and someone new to take the reigns from Falma, a certain Melchior."

"Oh, my, it be no wonder that ye look tired, m'lord. And hungry, too. Now I shall have some warm yeast rolls fer ye, and some venison stew as well."

While Angelica puttered about in her kitchen, Drachma got up and went to his library, where he sought out some paper, an envelope, some ink, and began his short epistle, for he knew that there was one more cog in this chain of events that he still needed to set in motion, and he knew that there really was not much time.

After he had written it, he sat back in his comfortable chair, and he began the process of chanting and connecting, with the one yet to come. And he spoke the words that he learned so many years ago.

"That which you seek is great, but your search even greater."

And he could see the fruits of his efforts, for he could again see the lady healer, and he could sense that she heard, and knew. And he knew that his plans were now almost complete.

# Cast of Characters in the Book of Drachma

**Aaron:** Page of the castle
**Allen of Burridge:** An old carpenter
**Alonza Chavez:** ER nurse
**Angelica:** Long term companion/caretaker of Drachma
**Antoine LeGace:** Generally evil individual
**Barbara Greshin:** Cardiovascular surgeon
**Barncuddy:** Proprietor of Barncuddy's Ale House
**Bernard:** One of the Forest Guard
**Blodwen:** One of the Castle Guard
**Brother Philip:** The monk who found (and translated) The Book of Drachma
**Cairn:** One of the Forest Guard
**Carol:** ICU nurse
**Carruthers:** Servant to Reordan
**Cayman:** One of the Castle Guard
**Cartho:** The original Healer of Shepperton
**Carlo Vincente:** Felicia's adoptive father, and master of the guild
**Charlie McFerris:** Musician, and recluse
**Charlie Stephens:** Investigative TV reporter ,

**Chris Lewinsky:** Police detective

**Clarice:** Maid of the Castle

**Councilor Rust:** Member of the Council of Lords

**Craycroft:** Fifteenth century healer, locally trained by Cartho

**Diane:** Waitress/cook at Barncuddy's

**Donovan:** One of the councilors

**Dowdell:** One of the Castle Guard

**Drachma the Elder:** Enigmatic character—part intellectual, part teacher, part wizard

**Earl Crabtree:** Josh's adoptive father

**Earl of Derrymoor:** Earl with previous ties to Shepperton

**Earl of Shepperton:** The reigning earl, and liege lord of Shepperton

**Edgar Bryant:** Police detective

**Ervin:** One of the Forest Guard

**Eustace:** Son to Diane

**Falma:** Alchemist, Loremaster, but much more

**Felicia Vincente:** Grand lady of Shepperton, and grandmother to Tom

**Finch:** Mercenary, hired by Reordan

**Fitzgibbon:** One of the councilors

**Frankie:** Butcher

**Frieda:** Housekeeper to Felicia

**Genet:** One of the councilors

**Hermes:** Page of the castle

**Herschel:** Caretaker of the castle pigeons

**Jeremy:** Street urchin

**Jerry Beasley:** ER doctor

**Janie Crabtree:** Josh's adoptive mother

**Jeanne:** Lady-in-waiting, and confidante of Felicia

**Josh Crabtree:** Longstanding patient of Robert's

**Judy Morrison:** Nurse, and friend to Robert

**Kerlin:** One of the Forest Guard, who becomes Craycroft's Chief of Security

**Kevin:** One of the Forest Guard

**Leonardo:** Urchin, who became Philip's apprentice

**Maggie o' Killiburn:** Tom's mother (and more)
**Marcus:** Page of the castle
**Marilyn Gilsen:** Robert's wife
**Mark Hurwitz:** Cardiovascular surgery fellow
**Martin:** One of the Forest Guard
**McGill:** One of the Castle Guard
**Melchior:** Apprentice of Falma
**Michel:** Forest Guard
**Old Leroy:** Old beggar, and more
**Proust:** Leader of the Castle Guard
**Robert Gilsen:** Overworked late twentieth-century Cardiologist
**Reordan:** Leader of the Council
**Rowan:** Street urchin
**Sean:** Forest Guard
**Silvo:** One of the councilors
**Stoneheft:** One of the Forest Guard
**Tom (Drachma the younger):** Page in the castle (to begin with),
   yet much more
**Wheezer:** Street urchin
**Willie Minstrel:** Musician

Made in the USA
Columbia, SC
24 June 2020

12270162R00143

*Dorothy A Winsor*

# Glass Girl

## Dorothy A. Winsor

Inspired
Quill

Published by Inspired Quill: May 2023

First Edition

Content Warning: This title contains written references to murder, physical assault, kidnapping and miscarriage.

Chief Editor: Sara-Jayne Slack
Proofreader: Fiona Thomas
Cover Design: Marco Pennaccietti
Additional thanks to: Sannah Rabbani
Typeset in Minion Pro

Paperback ISBN: 978-1-913117-21-4
eBook ISBN: 978-1-913117-22-1
Print Edition

Printed in the United Kingdom
1 2 3 4 5 6 7 8 9 10

**Inspired Quill Publishing, UK**
**Business Reg. No. 7592847**
https://www.inspired-quill.com